TEN P(

C.H.B. (CLIFFORD HENRY BE
He attended Exeter College, Oxford, and published his first book, a collection of poems, in 1919. His first novel, *Streamers Waving*, appeared in
1925, and he scored his first success with the mystery novel *Death of My
Aunt* (1929), which has been frequently reprinted and translated into a
number of foreign languages.

Kitchin was a man of many interests and talents, being called to the
bar in 1924 and later amassing a small fortune in the stock market. He was
also, at various times, a farmer and a schoolmaster, and his many talents
included playing the piano, chess, and bridge. He was also an avid collec-
tor of antiques and *objets d'art*.

Kitchin was a lifelong friend of L.P. Hartley, with whose works his
were often compared, and was also a friend and mentor to Francis King,
who later acted as Kitchin's literary executor. In his introduction to the
Valancourt edition of Kitchin's *The Book of Life*, King recalls meeting
Kitchin after the two wrote fan letters to one another in 1958 that crossed
in the mail: King had written in praise of *Ten Pollitt Place*, while Kitchin's
letter had expressed admiration for the younger novelist's *The Man on the
Rock* (1957). King wrote, '[B]y the time that I met him, his fate was that of
many elderly, once famous writers in England. Instead of lead reviews,
he now got two or three paragraphs at the bottom of a page. Increas-
ingly critics would apply the dread word "veteran" to him, much to his
annoyance.' This frustration is echoed in his novel *Ten Pollitt Place*, where
Kitchin portrays himself in the character of the aging novelist Justin Bray.

Kitchin, who was gay, lived with his partner Clive Preen, an account-
ant, from 1930 until Preen's death in 1944. C.H.B. Kitchin died in 1967.

SIMON STERN received his Ph.D. in English literature from Berkeley
and his J.D. from Yale and is an associate professor at the University of
Toronto, where he is a member of the Faculty of Law and the Department of English.

Cover: The cover is a reproduction of the original 1957 jacket art by Val
Biro (b. 1921). In the 1950s and 1960s, Biro designed as many as 3000 book
jackets for first editions by many prominent authors, including J.B.
Priestley, Nevil Shute, and C.S. Forester. He now lives with his wife in
Sussex. The publisher gratefully acknowledges Mr Biro's permission to
reproduce the illustration.

By C. H. B. Kitchin

Curtains (1919) (poetry)

Winged Victory (1921) (poetry)

Streamers Waving (1925)

Mr. Balcony (1927)

Death of My Aunt (1929)

The Sensitive One (1931)*

Crime at Christmas (1934)

Olive E. (1937)

Birthday Party (1938)*

Death of His Uncle (1939)

The Cornish Fox: A Detective Story (1949)

The Auction Sale (1949)

Jumping Joan, and Other Stories (1954)

The Secret River (1956)

Ten Pollitt Place (1957)*

The Book of Life (1960)*

A Short Walk in Williams Park (1971)*

* Available or forthcoming from Valancourt Books

C. H. B. KITCHIN

TEN POLLITT PLACE

With a new introduction by
SIMON STERN

VALANCOURT BOOKS

Ten Pollitt Place by C.H.B. Kitchin
First published London: Secker and Warburg, 1957
First Valancourt Books edition 2013

Published by Valancourt Books, Kansas City, Missouri
Publisher & Editor: JAMES D. JENKINS
20th Century Series Editor: SIMON STERN, University of Toronto
http://www.valancourtbooks.com

Library of Congress Cataloging-in-Publication Data

Kitchin, C. H. B. (Clifford Henry Benn), 1895-1967.
  Ten Pollitt Place / by C.H.B. Kitchin ; with a new introduction
by Simon Stern. – First Valancourt Books edition.
    pages cm
"First published London: Secker and Warburg, 1957"–T.p. verso.
ISBN 978-1-939140-25-8 (alk. paper)
  1. Novelists–Fiction. 2. Boardinghouses–Fiction. 3. Precognition–Fiction.
4. Premature death–Fiction. 5. London (England)–Fiction. I. Title.
PR6021.I7T46 2013
823'.912–dc23
                    2013007050

All Valancourt Books publications are printed on acid free paper
that meets all ANSI standards for archival quality paper.

Cover art by Val Biro
Set in Dante MT 11/13.5

INTRODUCTION

B Y the time C. H. B. Kitchin published *Ten Pollitt Place*, in 1957, he
had already published fourteen books, including the detective
novels that account for most of the attention he still receives today.
He had first established a name for himself in the 1920s as a writer
of evanescent, witty prose in novels such as *Streamers Waving* and
Mr. Balcony, which were published by the Hogarth Press and which
earned him comparisons to Ronald Firbank. L. P. Hartley observed
of these novels that they 'display an element of fantasy sometimes so strong as to overpower actuality, and a glitter of surface
and brilliancy of technique that dazzle while they enchant'. The
Hogarth Press also published *Death of My Aunt* (1929), Kitchin's first
detective novel and probably the book for which he now remains
best known. It was widely praised by the reviewers, one of whom
observed that Kitchin had 'adapted his style' to the mystery genre,
suffusing the story with an air of quiet realism and imbuing the
narrative with 'quick touches of description and . . . minute psy-
chological "pointers"' that, taken together, were reminiscent of
'the technique of Stendhal'.

Over the following decades, Kitchin abandoned the extravagant
mode that had characterized his earlier fiction, instead writing
more contemplative, even nostalgic novels about the state of England. This trend was forecast in *Olive E.* (1937), which surveys a variety of English personalities as they react to the harbingers of the
oncoming war, some by preparing for crisis and others by ignoring
it. *The Auction Sale* (1949), often seen as one of Kitchin's best novels,
centres on a three-day sale of the effects of a great country estate,
which provides the springboard for a set of meditative reflections
by Miss Elton, the novel's main character, about the history of
the estate and the uncertain outlook facing the country. The book
ends, however, on an optimistic note, as Miss Elton looks toward
the future with the aid of two mementoes that she has acquired at
the sale: a painting called *The Pleasures of Love and Retirement* and a

bowl inscribed with the motto 'He knoweth thy walking through this great wilderness'. To some extent, *Ten Pollitt Place* continues this inquiry into England's past and its prospects for the future, now focusing closely on a group of characters living together in a London boarding house.

In situating 'the Pollitts' in the book's first chapter, Kitchin evidently had his own London neighbourhood in mind. Like the house described at the outset, his three-story terrace house at 23 Montpelier St. (where Thomas Hardy lived briefly in 1870) was in a 'roughly triangular area' just south of Kensington Road and east of Exhibition Road, in a tangle of streets including Montpelier Walk, Montpelier Square, and Montpelier Mews, a dead-end street like the 'obscure cul-de-sac called Pollitt Mews'. Garrows, the large store where Dorothy Fawley goes shopping and eats lunch, apparently refers to Harrods, near the Montpeliers and just on the other side of Brompton Road (called Parkwell Road in the novel).

Similarly, Kitchin seems to intend the novelist Justin Bray as a self-portrait. Once regarded as 'dangerously advanced, a highbrow-ish *enfant terrible*', Bray is now sniffily disdained by one reviewer as 'only fit to be read by elderly ladies wearing lavender-scented gloves', while another reviewer condemns him as offering 'a mixture of stale platitudes unhealthily sweetened with a pinch of saccharine'. Kitchin himself did not receive such negative reviews; if anything, his novels were more likely to be criticized for being too enigmatic than for being syrupy. Nevertheless, while his most recent books—*The Auction Sale, The Secret River* (1956), and his short story collection *Jumping Joan* (1954)—had been highly praised when they came out, they were not widely reviewed, nor apparently did they sell many copies. When Justin Bray observes that his new book, *Seven Silent Sinners*, cannot be found in the shop-windows, he echoes a remark of Kitchin's about *Jumping Joan* in a letter to Nevill Coghill: 'The book is a flop. It doesn't seem to exist in the shop-windows. My amour propre resents the thought that I am becoming known throughout the trade as a "worst seller".' Kitchin's sense of amour propre was hardly improved by a typographical error on the dust jacket of *Ten Pollitt Place*, which added a decade to his age by listing his year of birth as 1885 instead of

1895. In the copy that he inscribed to Coghill, Kitchin crossly annotated the date with the observation that if only the printer had put 1855, he would 'truly be the grand old man of English literature'.

It is tempting to speculate that in choosing the street's name—and in referring to the locality as 'the Pollitts'—Kitchin was inspired by the Pollitts of Tennessee Williams's play *Cat on a Hot Tin Roof*, which won the Pulitzer Prize for drama in 1955. The play explores a complex web of sexual deceit and emotional manipulation through a set of conflicts involving two generations of the Pollitt family, centring in particular on the inheritance of the family fortune. What Williams presents in a high-octane emotional register, Kitchin presents in a more muted register, although the novel does have occasional moments of melodrama. One of the primary features contributing to this effect is Hugo Muller's prediction, in late October, that someone in the house will die before the end of the year. In a novel that often proceeds at a slow and measured pace, Kitchin builds suspense by placing the date in the title of each chapter, making us wonder when Hugo's prediction will come true. The structure is one that Kitchin had used twenty years earlier in *Olive E.*, which also includes a prediction of death and a series of chapters captioned according to their slow march towards the announced date.

As we await this outcome, the house's residents pursue various activities ranging from the mundane to the erratic. Miss Tredennick spies on her neighbour and keeps a journal full of salacious details that she imagines submitting, one day, to 'the authorities' as 'evidence'—until the object of her obsession suddenly vanishes. Justin Bray, working desultorily on his twenty-fifth novel, entertains aristocratic acquaintances whom he appears to despise. Robert Fawley carries on an affair with Mrs Muller's daughter Magda, and seems to be on the verge of breaking up with his wife Dorothy. Fifteen-year-old Hugo Muller is the house's oddest resident, and the one who seems to manage the others' fates through a combination of chance and preternatural instinct. In love with the dustman (who is twice his age), Hugo not only understands the erotic challenges that he faces, but even tells his mother that he never wants to grow up because 'nobody loves a grown man—at least, not the kind of person I want to love me—and not in the way I want to be loved.' Suspicious about his sister Magda's affair and intent on trailing her, Hugo proves intuitively capable of selecting just the right kind of cab driver to help him out—one with 'three or four children, whom he had spoilt for the sake of peace and quiet, but by now . . . [were] grown up', and a nagging wife whom he 'was always relieved to get away from'. Significantly, even though his own moral judgments chime almost perfectly with Miss Tredennick's, Hugo is also familiar with the 'vulgar and barbaric tune' favoured by their scandalous neighbour across the street—so familiar that when this maddeningly repetitive song awakens Miss Tredennick in the middle of the night and sends her into a temporary blindness, Hugo is able to tell the doctor its name: 'Will you do the doodle 'em with me?'

Hugo, one of the queerest characters Kitchin created, seems to be the one who connects—and disrupts—the lives of everyone else at Ten Pollitt Place. While it appears that Miss Tredennick is slowly losing in her struggle to preserve the dignity of the neighbourhood, the novel ends on a far more ambiguous note than *The Auction Sale*. Hugo's own interventions serve directly to resolve the uncertainties about the Fawleys' faltering marriage and indirectly to precipitate the death that he has predicted. Yet even as he constitutes the linchpin of the novel's wayward plot, Hugo himself stands as an inscrutable figure whose own fate is impossible to discern. Dorothy Fawley's assessment of Hugo, when she begins to grasp his understanding of her marital situation, might well apply to his role in the plot as a whole: 'That little flaxen-haired boy with his angel-face, on which the bitter experience of a thousand years seemed suddenly to have left an imprint—what an envoy to choose!'

Simon Stern
Toronto

April 20, 2013

TEN POLLITT PLACE

To
NEVILL COGHILL

CONTENTS

I

THE POLLITTS

THE surname of William Pollitt, a speculative builder of the eighteen-thirties, still provides Londoners with a sevenfold chance of confusion. Even postmen have been known to go astray in 'The Pollitts',—such being the generic name for a roughly triangular area which has one of its vertices almost in Parkwell Road, another within a stone's-throw of Kensington Gardens and the third jutting out towards Exhibition Road. A letter directed to a house in Pollitt Square may find its way to a similar number in Pollitt Crescent, Pollitt Place, Pollitt Terrace, Pollitt Row, Pollitt Rise, and, if the number is below eight, in an obscure cul-de-sac called Pollitt Mews. The list is arranged in a descending order of social significance, which, however, might in these days be almost reversed, since the fine houses of Pollitt Square have all been split up into flats or tenements. Much the same is true of Pollitt Crescent, though in its gracious curve there are still one or two lucky families who manage to keep a whole house to themselves. The charms of the Terrace, the Row and the Rise were first recognised in the early twenties of this century, when those who preferred a home, however small and with however limited a view, to the largest and most luxurious of flats, began to buy the freeholds as they came into the market, or bribe away residents of the type for which those narrow streets were originally designed.

Pollitt Place, which is more or less in the middle of the Pollitts, now lies, as it has always lain, more or less in the middle of the social scale. The houses, which were once far too small to attract those who boasted of living in the Square or the Crescent, are now too large for the housewife of middle-class resources. The south side of the street shamelessly takes in lodgers, but the north side (even numbers from two to forty-two inclusive), though *sub rosa* it may do much the same, still makes a parade of being privately residential, with one family—or shall we say, one group of friends?—to each house. The real difference is that on the north side, the freeholders for the most part live on the premises, while on the south side they are nearly all absentees, and indeed never could be present in the flesh, since they are corporate bodies, such as insurance companies and Garrows, the big store in Parkwell Road, and have an eye only to the lucrative day when they will be able to get rid of the occupants and rebuild. At all events, on the north side of the street, brass, paint-work, door-steps and net curtains are apt to make a braver show than they do across the way.

One of the pleasantest features of the Pollitts is that its unity does not exclude diversity. Not a single house is precisely like its neighbours,—as house-agents learn to their cost when they assume that the description of a house they have just sold will suit the one next door. Number Ten, for example, has an extension at the back which one would never suspect from a frontal view. It is a house of four storeys,—basement, ground-floor and two floors above, with the hint of another in embryo in the roof. It is faced with white stucco up to the level of a balcony on the first floor, and thereafter with well pointed red brick, which has evidently been cleaned since the end of the Second World War. Three broad steps lead up to the front door, and the railed-in area between the house and the pavement is so big that it not only lets ample sunshine into the basement but gives those who live there a generous view of the far side of the street. The balcony, though too narrow to use with any comfort, is a pleasure to look at, with its balustrade of intricate iron scroll-work, its curved lead canopy and wide french windows.

'How pleasant,' one might be tempted to exclaim, 'it is to see a real Regency house in such good trim.' This description may be a little too flattering, but in the middle nineteen-fifties Number Ten does suggest a more elegant age,—till one notices three bells by the front door, and a brass plate adjoining them:

MISS TREDENNICK

FAWLEY

JUSTIN R. BRAY

and underneath, is a name with no corresponding bell:

MULLER (Basement-entrance)

Then, if one is an old-fashioned reactionary, one will add, 'What a shame! They've had to turn it into flats after all.'

II

THE FIFTEENTH OF SEPTEMBER

THE summer that year had been unusually fine and persisted to the middle of September with hardly a break. After a day of continuous, windless sunshine, the night air was heavy and hot, but without any hint of thunder.

Two o'clock had just struck in the Neo-Gothic tower of St Ethelred's Church and Miss Tredennick, dozing fitfully in her bedroom on the top floor of Number Ten Pollitt Place, lurched awkwardly on to her left side and faced the windows. She had just dreamt that she was back in Cornwall, in sole possession of Polvannion, now that her father was dead. But she was still plagued by his stuffed birds. They were everywhere,—on the stairs and in the bathroom and even in the cupboard where she kept her hats. She had offered them to museums in Truro, Falmouth, Camborne and Penzance, but nowhere could the collection find a home. There was no escape from those beaks, those glassy eyes, those moulting feathers, unless she ran away and lived in London. She could take Gwen and Magda with her and open up her father's townhouse, left derelict during the war. Miraculously the bombs hadn't damaged it, and still more miraculously the local Council hadn't yet filled it with unwanted guests, who would carve their names on the pinewood panelling of the dining-room, let cigarette-ends burn on the chimney-pieces, wrench the ormolu handles from the doors, keep coal in the bath and steal the lead from the roof.

But she must be quick. There were horrid stories of the havoc which the new Labour Government was making or planned to make of the best residential areas in London. She must decide at once. She *had* decided. (At this point her musings became less of a dream and more of a retrospect.) Gwen pushing and Magda pulling, she had climbed the stairs to the top floor and said imperiously, '*I* shall live here—and I hope to die here. You can do what you like with the lower part of the house—within reason, of course,—but if you look after me, you won't fare too badly.'

And there she had gone, with Gwen, Magda and Hugo,—the Muller family who lived in the basement and ran the house for her. Not that they were at all uncomfortable in the basement. There were still obliging builders to be found, who didn't set much store by the silly limits which the Government, regardless of rateable values or the surtax one paid, imposed on house-decoration. At all events, the conversion was most handsomely carried out, and the house soon comprised an agreeable 'lower ground-floor' (with four rooms, a kitchen and bathroom), a self-contained flat of two big rooms, kitchen and bathroom on the entrance-floor, another somewhat similar flat above it, and above that, on the top floor, Miss Tredennick's quarters,—her bedroom, facing the street, her sitting-room, bathroom and kitchen behind it, and a box-room that was half-way up in the roof.

She was now fully awake, but prolonged deliberately the train of thought which had taken shape in her sleep. She and Mrs Muller had chosen their tenants well. Mr Bray was an ideal occupant of the ground-floor, where, she had been told, special caution was needed in the selection of lodgers. Nor could one say anything against the Fawleys, if one was content to take them as they were. They were both exceedingly respectable. The husband was a worthy, if dull, youngish man with a smile that could sometimes break through his boorishness, while his wife would have been of no account at all, had it not been for an introspective nerviness that redeemed her from nullity. Poor thing, she seemed unable to realise that we are living in a cold revolution and must grin and bear it—and kick back when we can.

Miss Tredennick herself had no illusions, or thought she had none. The whole world had changed for the worse and would soon be changing to something still more hideous and hateful.

Meanwhile, the old survivors of a derided and dying civilisation—like Romans who had read Horace and Martial and had been left behind in ancient Britain among the Celts, awaiting the Saxon onslaught—had somehow to live. 'And we *do* live,' she thought. 'Here am I at seventy-six, arthritic and dyspeptic, but with keen ears and eyes that are still keener.'

But she admitted to having made one mistake. She had assumed that though the Square and the Crescent might have lost every trace of their old dignity, the Place would remain comparatively unchanged. She had vaguely heard of the tussle between the Periwinkle Insurance Company and Garrows for the ownership of the south side, but thought it was of little consequence as long as a few freeholders held out. She had been assured by her old friend Mrs Molyneux-Green that nothing should induce her to stir from Number Seven. The Bastions were once more settled in Number Fifteen, as were the Laxtons in Number Twenty-one. Number Nine, that most important of all the houses on the south side, since it was immediately opposite Number Ten, was still owned by the wealthy Miss Webster, though the unfortunate woman seemed destined to spend more time in a clinic than in her own home. Miss Tredennick valued these neighbours far less for their friendship or their company—Lady Bastion was an insufferable woman—than for the stability they gave to the tone of the street.

Then came the first blow. Mrs Molyneux-Green, hard pressed by a falling income, increased taxation and difficulties with her staff, sold her house to Garrows. 'My dear Theresa, I simply hate doing it, but they offered such a good price. In any case, I can't afford the repairs.'

She went, and the Bastions and the Laxtons soon followed her example. It was true that there was no immediate threat of wholesale demolition. Garrows' plans, like those of the Periwinkle, looked to the distant future, and it was said that even the newest leases had ten years to run. But how different were the new lessees from the old landlords. Number Seven, of which Miss Tredennick had an excellent though side-long view from her bedroom windows, was the most sadly changed of all. Instead of the graceful Mrs Molyneux-Green, a slatternly Irish woman now possessed it and treated it frankly as a rooming-house. And what people she took in as lodgers,—seedy middle-aged men with attaché-cases, bedraggled matrons in moth-eaten furs, dim, shabby spinsters— succeeding one another, while taxis arrived and left, with baskets and bundles, canvas bags, tin boxes and hampers tied up with string! But these were not the worst. Since the turn of the year, Pollitt Place had been invaded by a type that was very much more deplorable. . . .

At that very moment, as if to justify the sourness of Miss Tredennick's reflections, a car roared into the street from the fur- ther end,—a cheap, would-be sports-model that emulated the real thing in noisiness, even if it could do so in no other respect. It came in jerks, emitting waves of sound each more deafening than the last, till with a screech it stopped outside Number Seven. There was a moment of peace, then two doors slammed, feet pattered on the pavement and a man's voice said, 'Now can't I come and tuck you up in your little bed?' The thick, tipsy voice of a young woman replied, 'Really, Archie, what would the old cats opposite think?' Miss Tredennick's skin quivered as if pricked by hot pins. It was *she*—the horror, doing it yet again, with the same utter lack of regard for other people, the same effrontery,—but was it with the same man? Miss Tredennick, who had a good memory for voices, waited eagerly for him to speak again. But the car-radio was the next to speak, and it suddenly blared out something that sounded like:

> *Doodle 'em, me doodle 'em, me doodle 'em, me doodle 'em,*
> *Yip, yip! me doodle 'em: Hiya! me doodle 'em,*
> *Doodle 'em, me doodle 'em, me doodle 'em, me doodle 'em . . .*

and repeated itself in a *moto perpetuo* suggestive of a lunatic obsession.

The rhythm was evidently of the order known as 'infecti- ous'; for Miss Tredennick, with all the speed her arthritic knees allowed, was out of bed and standing by the window, where she drew the curtain aside and peeped. It was as she had suspected, the *horror* and the man were locked in one another's arms. Their feet hardly moved, but their bodies swayed to the music, in the

light of a street-lamp. The woman's dark ringlets were in disarray and her ample olive-skinned shoulders were almost bursting
out of her dress. It was harder to see her face, but amid its turn-
ings and twistings, one had an impression of thick, blood-stained
lips, black eyelashes, over-long, and thick black eyebrows arched
above a pair of enormous black eyes. As her body wriggled and
writhed, it seemed to exude a rank, animal vitality, that might well
(thought Miss Tredennick) evoke a thousand odious obscenities in
the mind of the average male. In every way that woman typified
the enemy,—a breaker of homes, a seducer of virtuous husbands,
a mocker of modesty, chastity and decorum,—the last of the three
being far the most important.

> *Doodle 'em, me doodle 'em, me doodle 'em, me doodle 'em,*
> *Nein, nein, me doodle 'em: Ja, ja, me doodle 'em . . .*

Would the debauch never end? Shivering with heat rather than
cold, Miss Tredennick stood watching and participating, as it
were, in a Witches' Sabbath. Surely the police would come and do
something about it? And what of the other residents in the street?
Were they so hardened to such practices that they didn't bother
to protest? Or were they too timid? Miss Tredennick wished she
had a revolver so that she could send a couple of bullets whizzing
through the window. The killing of creatures like that couldn't be
murder.

Then suddenly the music came to a stop. The man and the
woman held one another still tighter and the man's ugly hands
pawed round her shoulders, till, after a long slobbering kiss, the
farewells began.

'*Good* night, darling. . . . Gorgeous evening. . . . Simply divine.'
The woman walked unsteadily up the two steps to the front
door, fumbled with her bag, dropped it, screamed, 'Oh, damn!'
picked it up, took out a latch-key and dropped the bag again. 'Hell!
There goes all my money down the drain!' They grovelled about
together in the gutter and kissed once more, as they hunted for the
pennies. Then they straightened themselves and the woman stood
still for a moment, as if she were minded to strip in the light of
the street-lamp, and summon all the males in the district to covet

her body in its nudity. Such, at least, was the impression she gave Miss Tredennick, who shut her eyes to blot out the visible so that she might dwell the better on unseen enormities. She looked again when the key clinked against the lock. The front door opened. 'Night, night, you lovely man!' 'Night, night, girlie darling. See you again on Thursday,—no, that's to-day, I mean Saturday—do I or don't I?' 'No, darling, Sunday!' 'All right, all right.' (Was the drink making him quarrelsome?) 'I'll give you a tinkle in the morning.' A light flashed on in the narrow entrance-hall. Another moment of possible strip-tease. Then the front door shut with a crash. A few seconds later, a light shone in the bedroom on the top floor. Without drawing the curtains the *horror* tore off her clothes, letting them fall on the floor and, as the car below made its noisy start, ran naked towards the window, the lower sash of which was wide open. Covering her firm but fat breasts inadequately with her podgy left hand, she knelt down and waved through the window with her right. Toot-toot-toot went the car and turned into the Crescent. The woman got up from her knees and, presenting a view of her arched back and generous buttocks, went to the far end of the room. Then the light was turned out.

Feeling extremely unwell and rather sick, Miss Tredennick forced her stiff legs to carry her back to bed.

[2]

'How is she, Doctor?'

Mrs Muller and Dr Jamieson, who hadn't spoken on their way downstairs, were standing in the front hall. There was no one to overhear them. Mr Bray had gone to luncheon at his club, Mrs Fawley was looking at the shops in Parkwell Road and Robert Fawley always lunched at the works, except at week-ends. Hugo wasn't yet back from Mr Middleton's, and Magda was busy in the kitchen,—not that it would have mattered what she heard.

Dr Jamieson smiled teasingly. He was a fat little man with pink cheeks, blue eyes and a moustache that was even whiter than his white hair. It was rumoured in the Pollitts that he bleached his moustache.

'Well,—she's seventy-six.'

'Oh, Doctor, don't always say that! Magda told me she'd never found her quite like this before. Did she have an attack of some kind?'

'No,—I shouldn't say so. That car that came round between two and three in the morning,—did you hear it?'

'No. But it was quite real. I mean, she didn't invent it, because it woke Hugo up. As you know, he's the only one, except Miss Tredennick, who sleeps in the front of the house.'

'Wouldn't this be a good opportunity of persuading her to change her rooms round and sleep at the back?'

'She'll never do that. She says there's a smell from the little delicatessen shop at the end of the Mews. I can't say I've noticed it, but she's always smelling and hearing and seeing things other people can't. Did you—I must ask you, because it's only right I should know—did you find anything wrong with her heart? Magda said she looked really blue.'

'Her heart is in splendid condition,—all things considered.'

As he made this ambiguous statement, he gave Mrs Muller a sidelong but searching glance. Did she want Miss Tredennick to die? It wasn't impossible. Could she stand the strain of another ten years,—for, in the normal course, it might well be that? Mrs Muller's appearance was in all ways reassuring,—a straight, almost virginal figure in a clean grey house-coat, her mouse-coloured hair gathered neatly round her long head. Her eyes were a watery blue, her nose was thin and rather long and her colourless lips framed a row of good-natured white teeth which took one's attention from too receding a chin. She had a look of Nordic honesty about her,— as if she had suffered, but was none the worse for it and bore no malice,—a creature of dulled sensibilities, but kind and efficient,— the incarnation of a domestic treasure. Yet one never knew. A time might come when he'd have to be on the look-out for arsenic in puddings and powdered glass mixed with tea. He hoped not. He was an easy-going old man and hated any kind of melodrama.

'Then what was it?' she asked,—as if she had been patiently considering his last words, while he was taking stock of her. 'Magda said she could hardly speak this morning. And vomiting her breakfast! I scarcely remember her being sick before. Besides, she ate so little.'

'It was merely a reflex, brought on by an excessive secretion of adrenalin. That car must have annoyed her very seriously. Do you remember when you called me in to see Mr Bray? About a year ago, wasn't it?'

Mrs Muller remembered very well indeed. She had enjoyed the episode enormously, till Mr Bray seemed really taken ill. It was a fine Sunday morning of the previous November. A cheaply smart, youngish woman was walking down the Place with a white poodle, expensively dolled up, on a silvered leash. It smelt at all the doorsteps till it came to Number Ten, where it paused to deposit its worm-ridden excreta on the newly-scrubbed threshold. The woman paused too, and waited with a smirk of contentment on her face. Mrs Muller, who had a view from the basement window, would have rushed into the area and protested, if the front door hadn't burst open to disclose Mr Bray (who hated all dogs and all women resembling the owner of that particular poodle), white with rage and very ready to give tongue. 'You filthy bitch!'—yes, those were his very words,—'You ought to be made to lick up that mess from our doorstep. I've a good mind to rub your bloody nose in it.' Then the woman broke into irrational volubility. 'He's got to do his business *somewhere*, hasn't he?—same as you do—and call yourself a gentleman——' She continued, but Mr Bray was not outdone by feminine logic and continued also. For a while, Mrs Muller was content to be the umpire, though her sympathies lay strongly with Mr Bray—for was it not Magda who had to wash that doorstep?—till, realising that Mr Bray was losing ground, she darted through the area door and up the steps. The offender, seeing herself outflanked and outnumbered, beat a hasty retreat towards the Crescent. Mr Bray gave chase, talking of the bye-laws and the police, but he soon came back looking so very ill that Mrs Muller said, 'Oh, Mr Bray, how good of you—but it hasn't done *you* any good. Do go and sit down. These things take it out of one. Magda will soon have everything clean again.' And he went to his sitting-room and sat down, while Mrs Muller, knowing all wasn't well, watched him round the edge of the open door. Then he put his hand to where he thought his heart was and said, 'I wonder if you could get me the doctor.' And Dr Jamieson had come and reassured them, and Mr Bray soon seemed all right again.

Mrs Muller nodded, and the doctor went on, 'Well, this is much the same kind of thing. It doesn't do, when you're in the seventies or even the sixties, to get into tantrums. Miss Tredennick's a tough old bird and no harm's done. There's no point in my coming to see her again, unless she sends for me or you think she's worse. But that's the last thing I anticipate.'

He took his hat and his gloves from a Regency chair and a neatly rolled umbrella from a big crackle-ware vase which served as a stand, and went through the door which Mrs Muller had opened, into the street, where he raised a finger to his hat and turned to the left. Mrs Muller watched his jaunty little back, till a shuffling footstep from the other direction made her look round. It was Hugo coming home, half an hour before the usual time. His mother's face blanched with sudden apprehension.

'Why, Hugo, what's the matter?'

'Nothing,' he answered in a voice that was strangely deep for such a small body. Although he was over fifteen, he might have been an under-sized eleven. His back was humped and his right arm and leg were longer than the left. Seen from behind, he looked like a malevolent gnome and aroused a feeling of acute repulsion that vanished completely when he turned round and you saw his sweet little baby-face. He had deep blue eyes, which were quite unlike his mother's, while those who remembered the late Friedrich Müller said his were dark brown, matching his almost black hair. Hugo's hair was several shades lighter than his mother's and verged upon flaxen. His nose was broad and snub, and his mouth, when he smiled, was as traditionally cherubic as a choir boy's.

'Come downstairs, dear, and tell Mutti all about it.' *Mutti* was the only German word Mrs Muller ever used, though it was said that she had learnt to speak the language quite well.

Hugo looked at her thoughtfully, with his mouth half open. Then, as if he realised that she was anxious about him and that he must allay her fears, he said, 'There's nothing to tell. I felt rather tired. And Mr Middleton has a very bad cold. I thought I might catch it if I stayed any longer. Besides, it's such a beautiful day.'

Mrs Muller as a rule took little heed of the weather. She knew when it rained—for that affected the washing hung up in the back-yard, and she knew when it was too hot—for heat made her ill and fretful—but she was almost indifferent to the colour of the sky. She looked up at it now and saw that Hugo was right. It was a lovely day, with a hint of autumn to temper the strong sunshine. The poor boy was pale and ought to have more fresh air. Had she been at fault in not making sure he got it? But she was too tied to the house to take him for walks and he didn't seem very fond of taking them by himself. Next year she must see to it at whatever cost that he had a real long holiday by the sea.

She patted his arm and said, 'Yes, indeed it is a very beautiful day—and you must enjoy it. Why not go and watch the birds by the Serpentine? I'll give you something to feed them with, if you like. There's still an hour before dinner-time.'

Hugo wriggled away from her touch and said, 'I went to the Serpentine on Tuesday. I should like to go and sit quietly by myself. I want to think about something important.'

He walked down the basement stairs to his little bed-sitting-room, which was a narrow slit cut off the Mullers' communal sitting-room and opened out of it. Already he had somehow con-trived to invest it with such an air of privacy that his mother and Magda knocked before coming in.

At twenty to one, the dust-van stopped outside Number Ten, and Bert, the burly red-headed dustman, came down the area steps that partly hid the window of Hugo's room. The lower sash was wide open and the boy gave a cry of welcome.

'Hello, sonny!' The dustman smiled and braced his shoulders to take the weight of the bin.

Then Hugo said, 'Aren't you rather late to-day?'

'No, we're not late, but we're working the street from the other end.'

'Will you always do that?'

'I think so. At least for a time. Why?'

Hugo didn't answer, but put his hand in his pocket and pulled out a flat tin box labelled 'cough lozenges', though when he opened it, it contained seven cigarettes. 'Do have one,' he said, as shyly as a young girl, who for the first time offers a rose to her lover. The dustman hesitated.

'You know, it isn't right for lads of your age to smoke.'

'I don't smoke. I got these for you. I thought I'd give you one every time you came.'

His face lost its smile and seemed on the verge of tears.

'All right—all right—and it's very nice of you.' Bert put his enormous bare arm through the window and brushed it lightly against Hugo's cheek, so that the boy felt the tickle of red hair and smelt the mingled odour of sweat and garbage. Then, after Bert had patted the little round head and given an affectionate tug to the flaxen hair, he took one cigarette from the proffered box, withdrew his arm and put the cigarette in his pocket.

'Bye-bye for now. But mind you don't start smoking. I'll bring you a few sweets when I'm next this way. That'll be Monday—so you watch out for me.'

He gave a grin of farewell and carried his burdens to pavement-level.

When the dust-van moved on, beyond any possible glimpse, Hugo went to the back of his room, took off his coat and rolled up the right sleeve of his shirt as far as the elbow. Then he drew his white, skinny, hairless forearm across his cheek time and time again. But there was nothing either to feel or smell.

[3]

'Oh, Magda, if Hugo isn't doing anything, would you ask him to come up and see me? I've kept two little cakes I think he might like.'

Miss Tredennick was still in bed, where she had just finished her afternoon tea.

'Certainly, Madam. I expect he is in his room.' The words were obsequious enough, but there was a touch of disapproval about the tone in which Magda spoke them.

Miss Tredennick thought, 'Surely she can't be so silly as to suppose that it's improper for Hugo to come into my bedroom. Besides, she's getting too pretty to be a prude. It must be jealousy, because she knows I prefer Hugo to her. She does the work and he gets the little plums.'

Miss Tredennick was under no illusions about Hugo's parentage. Though she had never been told the story directly, she was convinced she had gathered the gist of it, if only because Mrs Muller had shown such clumsiness in evading her more searching questions.

Ingrid Gwendolen Muller, whom Miss Tredennick called Gwen, was the daughter of Amos Ambler, who had been coachman and afterwards chauffeur (though as such he was no great success), to Miss Tredennick's father. Gwen's mother had been a Swede. It was whispered that she was a girl of good family and that Amos had seduced her before marriage. But this was going back to a distant past which was vague even in Miss Tredennick's memory. Still, when she thought of that signal lapse from virtue in one who was in latter days so stiff and prim, she felt she had a clue to Gwen's inner life. Like mother, like daughter. Beneath that dull marble there was a latent fire, which could blaze up once, though probably once only. It had never really blazed for Friedrich Müller, who had entered her life a year or two after the Tredennicks had moved from Warwickshire to Cornwall, bringing Amos Ambler and his daughter with them. Mrs Ambler had been dead for a number of years.

Friedrich Müller was an agent in Camborne for a German firm that dealt in Cornish china-clay. Later, of course, people said he was there to spy. He was a dull-looking man, though not unhandsome, with formal manners and always well turned out. He spoke excellent English, if rather too precisely, and was said to have some university degree. One couldn't imagine him falling in love, but he courted Gwen, whom he met at a local dance, with an assiduous correctness that flattered both her and her father. The marriage took place in 1934, and Gwen ceased to belong to the staff of Polvannion and became a lady—or very nearly one. Her father remained a chauffeur, though by now it was an act of charity to keep him on. Magda was born in 1935. The next year, Friedrich

Müller was suddenly recalled to Germany. He went there alone, but three months later he wrote to say that he was settled in a very good post and wanted his wife and baby daughter to join him. All those who saw the shape of things to come did their best to dissuade her, but Gwen's Scandinavian sense of duty triumphed, and after a tearful farewell to her ailing father, and another, hardly less tearful to the Tredennicks, she obeyed the call.

What happened next was more conjectural. Amos Ambler died in 1937, and contact with the Mullers was almost lost, except for a few short letters written by Gwen to Miss Tredennick. 'She was very happy, but a little worried.' As time passed, the worries loomed larger than the happiness. Well, what could the foolish woman expect? She had been well warned. Then in the autumn of 1939 war came and the letters ceased, and Miss Tredennick, whose father died in 1942 aged eighty-eight, almost forgot her old maid, till in the autumn of 1945 she had the surprise of another letter from her. 'We are still alive, I, Magda and Hugo, my poor crippled boy who was born four years ago. Just before he was born, my husband disappeared. They say he is dead. He was suspected of being a Communist, but I know nothing of that. He treated me badly after the war began and I am not sorry to be rid of him. Now all I long for is to come home again. Please help us, oh, please do help us, dear Miss Tredennick. . . .'

So she came back, with her two children,—a colourless creature, yet more capable than ever of earning her keep. Those accustomed to the lamentations of refugees and their exciting or horrifying tales found Gwen a great disappointment; for she never spoke of her experiences save in the most general terms. 'Yes, bread was short. . . . At that time, one worked three hours to buy a cabbage. . . . We slept in the air-raid shelter every night.' Once, Miss Tredennick caught her off her guard and gathered that she laid Hugo's deformity at her husband's door. From this it was an easy step to imagine a kick in the belly, such as Nero is said to have given the pregnant Poppaea, and in the background a handsome and blond storm-trooper, who was Hugo's real father and loved Gwen sufficiently to find Friedrich Müller very much in the way. Magda must have been six when Hugo was born and ten when the

Mullers—dropping the two dots over the *u* in their name—came back from Germany. Did she know that Hugo was only her half-brother? Once or twice Miss Tredennick had been tempted to try to find out, but a feeling of loyalty towards Gwen deterred her.

Magda was still going in and out of the bedroom, industriously busy with little elegances,—changing the water in a vase of flowers, folding the newspapers, washing the tea-things in the kitchen and putting them away. In fact, she put away the two iced cakes Miss Tredennick had destined for Hugo.

'No, leave those here—on this table. They're the ones I shall give to Hugo. I'm quite ready for him now. Will you send him up, please?'

Again the same glance, submissive but resentful.

'Certainly, Madam.'

She put the two cakes by the bed and went downstairs. Three minutes later Hugo's shuffling steps sounded on the stairs, despite the thickness of the carpet. Then he came in, looking sweet and meek and clean and gave a little bow.

'Good evening, Madam. I do hope you are much better.'

'Thank you, Hugo, I am. I had a very bad night,—a kind of nightmare. Do you know what nightmares are, Hugo?'

(One spoke to him always as if he were under ten.)

'Oh yes, I have nightmares,—very dreadful nightmares. I had one last night too.'

'Last night? You must tell me about it.'

'It was very late, and there was a terrible noise in the street and someone shouted, "That's the house—Number Ten." I didn't know what they meant,—and yet I did, and was very frightened. Then someone I know'—he couldn't resist bringing the dustman into his story—'bent down to my window and said, "*You* needn't worry. It isn't coming for you," and I felt much better. Then I woke up and got up and went to the window, but there was nothing there except a nasty, cheap car, playing awful music, and a man and woman dancing on the pavement. She was one of the women who live opposite. I don't think I'd ever seen the man before, but I didn't like the look of him.'

Miss Tredennick, who had been reluctant to confess to Gwen,

Magda and even Dr Jamieson into what a paroxysm of rage the episode had plunged her, found it a relief to confide up to a point in Hugo.

'Yes, there was a car. I heard it too—and saw it. It distressed me very much. The others aren't as sensitive as we are. Besides, it's only you and I who sleep facing the street.'

Hugo nodded gravely, as if he appreciated the compliment of such an intimacy, and Miss Tredennick went on, 'Now, Hugo, will you do something for me? I want you to put this letter in the box of Number Seven. But I'd rather nobody knew except you. So don't let yourself be seen, if you can help it.'

The boy nodded again. 'That's all right. I may have to wait a little, till Magda comes up to get your dinner ready and Mother starts preparing our supper. But you can rely on me.'

'I know I can. Now, Hugo, here's the letter, and here are two cakes. They're quite fresh, but I don't feel like eating them myself.'

With some affection she watched his brightening eyes and his smile of pleasure. He put the letter carefully in his pocket and was about to take the two cakes in his fingers, when Miss Tredennick said, 'No, carry them down on the plate. I'm sure you won't drop it. Magda can bring it up when she comes to cook my dinner. It's quite all right. I told her I was going to give you the cakes.'

She smiled at him and he smiled back at her like a fellow-conspirator and said, 'Oh, Miss Tredennick, thank you so very much.' Then as her silence seemed a signal for him to go, he gave her another formal little bow and wished her good night.

'Good night, Hugo dear.'

When he got downstairs, he found his mother and Magda in the sitting-room, the former knitting and the latter mending some linen. His mother looked with approval at the cakes but said, 'I shouldn't eat them now, Hugo. Keep them for supper.'

'But that won't be for two hours. I'm going to make myself a cup of tea in my room, to drink while I eat them.'

Magda raised her eyes from her work and said severely, 'You had some tea only an hour ago.' This made his mother come at once to his defence.

'Another cup of tea can't do him any harm, Magda. Would you like me to make it for you, Hugo?'

'No, Mutti, I should like to make it myself.'

He went into his room, brought out an electric kettle, filled it at the sink in the kitchen, laid a tray with cup, saucer, spoon, a jug of milk and a sugar-bowl and carried it, with Miss Tredennick's plate of cakes, carefully into his room and shut the door.

As soon as he had switched on the kettle, he looked at the envelope Miss Tredennick had given him. It was addressed to 'The Occupier, 7, Pollitt Place, S.W.'

When the kettle boiled he steamed the envelope open and read the letter inside.

'MADAM,—Last night between two and three in the small hours, I was roused by a motor-car which noisily deposited a young woman at your front door. Not content with thus disturbing the sleep of the whole neighbourhood, she and her male companion (both of whom I fear were the worse for drink), turned on the wireless in the car and danced together on the pavement to a vulgar and barbaric tune. When at last they tired of these activities, the woman went upstairs, only to reappear a few moments later at what, I presume, is her bedroom window, where she exhibited herself in a state of nudity to her friend below—and incidentally to all those who might have been drawn by the unseemly commotion to their own windows.

Before the war, this street was inhabited by gentlepeople, and it still retains a little of its former good repute. But it will soon degenerate into a slum, if antics such as I witnessed last night are permitted to continue.

As a lessee, you are morally and up to a point legally responsible for the conduct of your lodgers. I trust therefore that you will take all possible steps to ensure that there shall be no repetition of this disgusting incident.

Yours faithfully,
THERESA TREDENNICK (Miss)'

[4]

The reply was delivered by hand three days later. It was flamboyantly written in green ink on pink paper with an elaborate Y embossed in the left-hand corner.

'MADAM,—Mrs O'Blahoney has shown me your note. I'm frightfully sorry we disturbed your *beauty*-sleep! All the same, times have changed and the sooner old people get used to that the better. As a matter of fact though, I hadn't any idea it was so late. But as for the car being noisy, we can't all have Rolls-Royces.

As for what you say about me making an exhibition of myself at the window, all I can say is I've never had much respect for Peeping Toms—or peeping *she-cats* either. They're always either filthy-minded or jealous.

Yours faithfully,
YVONNE VARIOLI (*Miss*)'

III

THE TWENTY-EIGHTH OF SEPTEMBER

JUSTIN BRAY was entertaining three ladies of title to tea. It gave him a very faint glow of snobbish satisfaction, such as he himself had ridiculed in one or two of his novels. But can anyone satirise a foible without in some degree sharing it? One can denounce, one can express indignation or contempt, but one cannot parody without a fellow-feeling.

The Lady Victoria, the oldest of his three guests, was gazing meditatively round the room, while the other two women talked together and their host busied himself with preparations for tea. Her eyes passed over the thick, crimson velvet curtains, their pelmets fringed with gold tassels, the ivory panelled walls broken by oil-paintings of the Italian school—a Marieschi, a Tiepolo, a Magnasco—a big break-front secretaire-bookcase the shelves of which were filled with beautiful bindings, a flat-topped knee-hole desk

covered in red leather and littered, but not untidily, with books
and papers, an exquisite little cabinet lit up to display a few china
figures,—Bow, Chelsea, Longton Hall—some fine Persian rugs
almost hiding the parquet, a pair of damask-covered wing-chairs,
a sofa covered with chintz, a pembroke table supporting a silver-
gilt tray—Paul Storr, perhaps?—a Chamberlain-Worcester tea-set,
and last of all, her host stooping over the hearth for a dish of hot
currant tea-cakes,—tall, rather stout, round-shouldered and grey-
haired. His thick neck seemed hardly strong enough to support his
large oblong face, with its bushy grey eye-brows and moustache,
wide-set liverish eyes, full nose and fleshy jaw. He had long legs,
long arms and long nervy fingers with very white nails.

'Oh, Justin, I can't say how I envy you! It carries me back,—it's
really almost painful. All the same, it's nice to think that in a few
privileged spots the flag of *our* civilisation is still flying.'

Justin gave a deprecating smile of embarrassment; for he found
the implied comparison between his own affluence and Lady Victoria's extreme poverty a little painful. He said, 'You mustn't judge my
life by the few bits and pieces I've managed to save from the wreck.'

Lady Beatrice shook her head provocatively and said, 'Come,
come, Mr Bray, you can't deny it. You really are disgracefully comfortable. I know bachelors, although they're so helpless, always
seem to get along better than spinsters, but I don't know anyone
nowadays who lives in quite such a luxurious lap as you do.'

She tittered, as though she had said something not only clever
but a little naughty.

Lady Farless on her right exclaimed, 'The *cleaning*! How is it
done?'

Lady Beatrice nodded vigorously. 'Yes, Mr Bray, the cleaning.
I don't believe you even know how to use a Hoover. Do you ever
do any dusting? Do you wash those adorable pieces of china? Do
you polish your furniture? Do you clean the grate? (By the way,
what a glorious chimney-piece. Your Miss Tredennick certainly
had good taste, if she put it in.) Do you ever furbish up those handsome books of yours? Even in the good old days, my brother used
to polish the leather bindings himself, and he had an enormous
library. Who does it all for you?'

'The daughter of the house. Her name is Magda.'

'What—Miss Tredennick's daughter?' Lady Beatrice gave a little scream. Justin thought, 'What a very silly woman she is.' (Phrase for a novel,—*one of those women whom only a fool would know, if they hadn't a title.*)

Lady Farless, though her acquaintance with Justin was slighter than that of the other two women, was better informed and enlightened her. 'Miss Tredennick isn't Mr Bray's landlady,—at least not ostensibly. She's let the whole house, or made it over, to an old servant of hers who married a German called Müller. The invaluable Magda is her daughter.'

Lady Beatrice, who did not relish being corrected by Lady Farless, sought another subject for conversation. As soon as tea was well under way, she said, 'Now, Mr Bray, we want to know all about your last book. *Seven Silent Sinners.* Such a wonderful title. However did you come to think of it?'

Justin smiled mysteriously. 'Well, you see—there are seven people living in this house.'

'That gives you the number,' said Lady Victoria, rousing herself from her memories of the past. 'But are you sure you all sin?'

Justin answered, 'I think we do, you know.'

Lady Farless, who, unlike the other two, had read the book, said, 'But, Mr Bray, there's no——' Before she reached the word *similarity*, Lady Beatrice gave another of her shrill cries and asked, 'Do you all sin in the same way, or have you allotted a different sin to each character? I've got your book, of course, but I've so very little time for reading nowadays. However, I promise I'll make a start on it to-night. I'm dying to find out what your particular sin is.'

Lady Victoria said, 'I think you'll find it a very innocent one. Being a little too fond of pretty things, perhaps, instead of practising self-denial and doing what we used to call *good works.*'

'But the Welfare State has abolished charity, like so many other old virtues. No, it must be something else. Still, perhaps it isn't very tactful to cross-examine poor Mr Bray about it. I hear the book is selling very well. I do hope it is.'

'No, not very well,' said Justin. 'In fact, you'll hardly find it in a shop-window.'

Lady Farless announced, 'I saw a pile of five in Garrows yester-day. Not the main table,—the small one on the left as you go in from the lift. I think the jacket might have been a little brighter, don't you?'

Before Justin could agree or disagree, Lady Beatrice said, 'At any rate, the notices have been wonderful.'

'Do you think they have?' Justin asked rather acidly. He was always irritated when he heard people call reviews *notices*, a word which, however aptly it described the criticism of trivial productions, such as ballets and musical comedies, struck a jarring note when used with reference to anything really sacred like a book. Besides, he was convinced that Lady Beatrice had never read a book review in her life and wouldn't know one if she saw it.

He went on, with a deliberate touch of pomposity, 'Perhaps I've reached the age when one is more hurt by an unkind review than pleased by a kind one. Did you see what Fanny France wrote about me in *The Striking Hour*? She began by saying how incredible it was that in the twenties I was considered to be dangerously advanced, a highbrowish *enfant terrible*, whereas now I am only fit to be read by elderly ladies wearing lavender-scented gloves. She did at least allow me the merit of a cultivated style, but James Lorry, in *The Sunday Beholder*, ripped even that to shreds. I think I know the nastier passages by heart. Let me see if I can recite them to you. "Still fettered by the rusty chains of an obsolete educational system, Mr Bray gives us the mixture as before. It is a mixture of stale platitudes unhealthily sweetened with a pinch of saccharine, that to our taste is almost nauseous. His inspiration seems to come exclusively from writers of his own calibre, who were discredited thirty years ago. His style is as laboured as theirs, but thirty years staler. His values are also theirs, but even less vital, since they hark back to a past which, for those writers, still had a kind of dim, ego-centric life, but now appeals only to antiquaries. Beneath a thin show of objectivity, we discern the festering ulcer of self-pity, and at times the petulance of a tiresome child that sulks because it isn't *understood*."'

Justin paused, as though he anticipated cries of 'Shame!' But when these were not forthcoming, he continued, 'After this fine preamble, Mr Lorry quoted one of my less inspired sentences—a clumsy one, I admit—I see now that I phrased it as I did to avoid ambiguity over a personal pronoun, but I ought to have taken more pains—well, he took this wretched sentence and browbeat me with it for half a paragraph. But this bores you. Please do have a cigarette. Lady Victoria? Oh, of course, like me you don't smoke.'

As he spoke, he went to a side-table, picked up a mahogany tea-caddy case, opened it and looked a little puzzled. 'Oh dear, there are only two Virginians left. I thought I emptied a packet of twenty into it a few days ago.'

Lady Beatrice said, 'Do you think perhaps the invaluable Magda——?'

Justin shook his head. 'Oh no, I'm quite sure she wouldn't. I must be mistaken. Please don't be deterred. As I said, I never smoke now.'

Lady Beatrice took a Virginian, and Lady Farless, after taking one from the compartment reserved for Turkish, which contained a great many, reverted to the subject of Justin's reviews and said, '*The Sunday Beholder* is so dreadfully left-wing, I never take any notice what it says.'

Nobody contradicted her, and Lady Victoria, who had been busy with thoughts of her own, murmured, 'You'd hardly think it, Justin, but I was once considered an *enfant terrible*.' (Indeed, no one could think so, who saw her small, starved-looking body, her bluish skin and her trembling little hands. Yet she had a graciousness and a sweetness of which the other two women were devoid.)

Justin, ignoring both the last remarks, said introspectively, 'The worst of it is, I'm not sure that James Lorry isn't right.'

Then Lady Beatrice, feeling that it was high time that the conversation should be pulled together, asked, 'Mr Bray, how many books have you published?'

'*Seven Silent Sinners* was my twenty-fourth.'

'Oh, but you should have a silver jubilee. You *must* write one more, to make up the twenty-five.'

The advice was meant to be encouraging, but even Lady Beatrice realised that she had put it rather tactlessly. It implied a number of unpleasant things,—not only that Justin's twenty-fifth book would certainly be his last, but that he would be hard put to write it, and that even if he did succeed in doing so, the book's only merit would lie in ending a series,—the merit of the hundred thousandth purchaser at Garrows' sale, who received a free gift for having the luck to complete such a spanking total.

Lady Farless thought the whole subject should be dropped.

She said, 'Oh, Mr Bray, I've a piece of news for you. I spent a fortnight in Cornwall this summer with some friends and they remember your Miss Tredennick quite well. Do you know, they said she wasn't Cornish at all? Her grandfather—or it may have been her great-grandfather—who was more or less a self-made man, took the name simply because he liked the sound of it. Later, Miss Tredennick's father sold the family business, left the Midlands and bought Polvannion, where he passed as the genuine article. He sailed and fished and shot birds and had them stuffed and sat over his port after dinner reading Horace. Has Miss Tredennick ever told you her father read Horace?'

'Oh yes, she has. She can even quote one of the Odes—

Aequam memento rebus in arduis
Servare mentem. . . .

I forget it now. I've never discovered if she can translate it.'

Lady Farless, who had once gone to tea with Miss Tredennick, tried to patronise her and was snubbed for her pains, continued, 'I can't think she was ever an attractive woman. She suffers too much from *acidity* to have any charm. Do you like her, Mr Bray?'

'Yes, I quite like her.'

'That means you don't, of course. I wonder if anyone does. Do you think her ex-maid, your treasure's mother, really cares for her, or is she hanging on for a legacy?'

'I think Mrs Muller is a very *good* woman.'

'So she's hardly one of your seven silent sinners,' said Lady Beatrice.

'She may *have* sinned, but be repenting for it.'

'And the perfect Magda,' Lady Farless went on, 'what a time that girl has. Of course it must be a pleasure to look after *you*, but if she has to spend all the rest of her time dancing attendance on that old woman, I'm really sorry for her.'

Then Lady Victoria, who, if she was following the conversation at all, was doing so at a distance of ten minutes, said, 'Justin, do you remember the day I came to tea with your dear mother in your beautiful home at Haresley, and you came in and recited a very long piece from some Greek play you were going to act at school the next term? I can't have been much more than twenty-eight, but I suppose I looked just as old to you then as I do now. Oh dear, how quickly this delightful afternoon has gone. Thank you so much for it. Let me see, the girl put my coat on a table in the hall, I think.'

Justin said, 'I ordered a car to take you back. It should be here in about five minutes.'

'But that was most wrong of you. No, I'm not even going to thank you. I can still get on buses and I want to do it as long as I possibly can. I love them.'

It was a chance for Lady Farless to let it be known that she never used such a means of conveyance.

'But don't you find the conductors terribly rude? I'm told they simply show no respect at all.'

'Why should they? They help me on and off and see to my parcels if I'm carrying one, and call me "Mum" or "Ducks", which I adore. And nobody ever gives them the smallest tip. Try that on a taxi-driver and see what happens!'

Lady Beatrice said, 'I agree to that,' and Lady Farless, making it quite clear that she never used taxis either, added, 'Yes, I'm told they're just as bad. What are your views, Mr Bray?'

'Like Lady Victoria I take buses whenever I can—and make it a point of honour to climb the stairs to the upper deck. I devoutly hope I shall die before that simple pleasure is taken from me.'

Lady Victoria shuddered and said, 'Oh, Justin, don't talk of *your* dying,' while the other two women made deprecating noises. The front-door bell rang and Justin went into the hall. When he was out of earshot, Lady Beatrice said, 'I'm afraid he *is* looking older than when I saw him in the early summer.' Lady Farless agreed. 'It must be that book of his. Between ourselves, I did manage to finish it, but found it heavy going. Well, I think it's time we heavily went ourselves. Can I give you a lift? My car's in the Crescent. My chauffeur said he thought he'd better park there, as this street was so full of cars when we arrived. Oh, Lady Victoria,—if only I'd known you hadn't a car, I should have been delighted to take you home.'

Lady Victoria smiled and said, 'That's very kind—but even so, I should have preferred to go home by bus.'

Justin came back. 'Yes, Lady Victoria, your car is here. But really there's no hurry. Won't you have a little sip of brandy before you go? After tea is an excellent time for it. Are you quite sure? What about you, Lady Beatrice,—and you, Lady Farless?'

Lady Victoria and Lady Beatrice shook their heads and smiled. Lady Farless also shook hers, but she didn't smile, as she felt that Lady Victoria's rejection of her car had been meant as an affront. (Thank goodness she still had a lot more money than these two daughters of impoverished earls.)

Half in and half out of the room, the farewells began. When the hired car had left with Lady Victoria, and the backs of Lady Beatrice and Lady Farless could be seen crossing the end of the road into the Crescent, Justin turned round and saw an angel-face beaming up at him from the area. He quite liked Hugo,—more sincerely than he 'quite liked' Miss Tredennick.

'Oh, it's you! Have you been spying on my guests?'

'No, Mr Bray, I didn't come out for that. I'm not a spy, though they said my father was one.'

'Who said that, Hugo?'

'Oh, the boys in Cornwall, when Mother brought me back there after the war. But I think they got it quite wrong.'

'What do you mean?' As Hugo didn't answer, he added, 'You'll catch a cold in that thin pullover.' Hugo looked at him intently for a moment, as if summing him up, then said, 'Good night, Mr Bray,' and went through the area door.

Justin looked at the sky, now dark with clouds and the coming of dusk, and then up and down the street which was empty except for a young woman who strode along it from the further end with a jaunty swinging of her hips. She wore a thin bright dress which

fluttered about her knees in the rising breeze. When she came
nearer, Justin recognised her as one of the lodgers who went in
and out of Number Seven. Her body seemed alive with enterprise
and appetites which gratification would only serve to renew. She
was on the south side of the street, but as she passed, she turned
her head and gave him a bold, interrogative stare. Justin turned
his eyes again towards the sky, affecting to study it, and thought,
'What a difference between her and those three women who have
just had tea with me! If it comes to that, what a difference there is
between her and me! And yet, she's probably had more happiness
already than any of us. Well, it isn't my fault that I wasn't born like
her.'

He sighed with a stab of envy, went indoors to his room and sat
down at his desk, alone.

IV

THE TENTH OF OCTOBER

THE mists dissolved, the gauzy vapours obscuring the critical brain
quivered and shrank into smoky wreaths, while a ring of light,
both perilous and precious beyond all imagining, seemed to swim
round inside Robert Fawley's head.

He sat up in bed, and looking deliberately at his wife's empty
bed by the opposite wall, admitted to himself, for the first time and
without any kind of reservation, that he had no longer an atom of
love for her. Not an *atom*! The word made him almost laugh. His
job was to deal with atoms, and he knew very well that in spite
of their smallness they were far from contemptible. Words were
funny things. Poets like Swinburne and novelists like Justin Bray
strung them together to make jingling noises all about nothing.
Figures and facts were the only gateways to reality. Yet were they?
A delicious confusion muddled his mind, though two vital anti-
theses stood out clearly enough,—he was out of love with his wife
and in love with Magda.

He yawned, stretched himself, jumped out of bed and stood up.

His body was well-proportioned and showed few signs of middle-aged fat. He had fairish hair and small, rather closely packed features that could relax into amiability. He stretched again, inflating his chest and extending his arms, as if preparing for physical exercises. There was a time when he'd done them regularly—it was a fellow's duty to keep fit—but Dorothy had caught him in the act and tittered, and somehow, like so many things since his marriage, even bodily fitness had seemed to lose its importance.

Then he looked out of the window. The sky was grey and clouds of a deeper grey were coming up from the west, and a few raindrops spattered the panes. Summer was over,—but how lucky they had been that it had lasted just long enough, by one day, to give him and Magda their first glorious afternoon together. How lucky they had been in so many ways, with so many almost insurmountable obstacles miraculously removed. First of all, there was Dorothy's decision to spend a few days with her sister in Cambridgeshire, and to come back, not on the Saturday, as was her habit, but on the following Monday. The second blessing was Magda's being free on that particular Sunday. In theory she and her mother took it in turn to go out on Sundays, but in practice they were both often tied to the house. And finally,—a real stroke of genius on the part of the god of good luck—Robert had sole right of entrance to a cosy little flat in Twickenham. A bachelor colleague of his, who had been sent on a mission to the United States, had given him the key for domestic reasons. 'If you'd just look in once a week or so, to see if my letters are being forwarded,—and so on. . . . And if you'd like to give your wife—or a lady-friend!—a meal there, after going on the river, it's O.K. by me.' That was six weeks ago, and the bit of facetiousness about the lady-friend had then seemed dismally irrelevant to Robert.

Of course, he had told Dorothy about the flat, and with her usual curiosity about houses and how people lived, she insisted on making the expedition with him. So they went on the river and had a kind of high tea at 25, Underbourne Mansions. It wasn't a great success, and when it was over, Dorothy had said, 'Another time, we'll go on to Hampton Court and dine properly at the Mitre.' And Robert had thought, how different, how very different, the afternoon might have been with a different companion,—say with that fine girl he'd noticed going in and out of Number Seven. How often the sight of her strong thighs, as she strutted down the street, had tempted him to an ocular adultery!

For at that time,—only a month ago, though it seemed much longer—Magda was no more than a sweet unapproachable vision, a phantom of delight, but not flesh and blood to be kissed and cuddled and fondled and made love to. Robert had never been one to waste much time over visions, however alluring, and though he spoke to Magda every day, and had never spoken (nor intended to speak) to the girl over the road, the latter had seemed far less unattainable. Nor was he looking for illicit diversion. Free love? Well, that was a very difficult question. The old religious taboos had gone by the board, of course, but there was the *state* to be considered.

Robert believed very strongly in the state. He wasn't a Communist, though he met a good many in the course of his work—some of them very pleasant and intelligent fellows—and could see their point of view, and like them didn't hold with an unrestricted individualism. It might be that absolute equality would make nonsense of life, just as zero values made nonsense of certain otherwise reliable mathematical formulae, but some approximation to equality was a desirable social experiment. At least, it would sweep away a good many unwanted cobwebs,—not only the prestige of rank and wealth, but the more odious and insidious prestige that still attached to the old classical tradition, abstract philosophy, the airs and graces of a 'culture', which paradoxically throve only because it was not universally diffused.

He himself had suffered from the superciliousness of its exponents,—people who sniffed at you if you stressed the *o* in Pythagoras or pronounced Archimedes as three syllables. He had met them even at the technical school and at the newish provincial university where he had won a scholarship, and there were one or two at the research institute where he had his job. Dorothy's father had paid lip-service to these shibboleths, though they played little part in his make-up, and lamented that he hadn't been given an education such as he'd done his best to give his daughter. Dorothy was hardly a blue-stocking, but her smattering of what she called 'the arts' was quite enough to humiliate her husband. At that very moment, Swinburne's *Atalanta* was on the table by her bed.

The sight of it carried Robert's thoughts back to his expedition with Dorothy to Twickenham. They had gone there circuitously by Putney Heath and Kingston, and while they were in the bus on their outward journey, Dorothy had noticed the blue L.C.C. plaque on a house on Putney Hill. She exclaimed, 'So that's the famous *Pines*! To think I've never been to see it before!' And when he asked her what the Pines was famous for, she said, 'Don't you know that Swinburne lived there many years with his friend Watts-Dunton? I really must read some Swinburne again. I used to love his poetry.' And she had bought the book the very next day, though she didn't seem to look at it very often.

Yet Robert was not altogether a doctrinaire. His nature was easy going and lazily kind. He liked simple pleasures,—good, plain food, light music, an occasional film and a glass of beer drunk matily in a pub. These were solaces to which everyone had a right. They bolstered no ego, fed no class-consciousness and roused no unhealthy or antisocial impulses.

The only time, hitherto, he had been thrown off his unambitious balance, was when he met Dorothy. She was twenty-nine and he twenty-three, still young enough emotionally for calf-love. She was unlike all the women he had met—not that they were numerous—and when she fell for him, as she did with a neurotic possessiveness, he was more than flattered,—he was overwhelmed and thought himself on the threshold of a new life. And so he was, though it didn't take the form that his transient mood of romance had pictured for it. Romance apart, it wasn't a foolish marriage on his side. Dorothy had a bit of money of her own and the expectation of more when her father died. He was a sick man at the time of their courtship and only kept them waiting a couple of years.

Robert's instincts were conventional enough to make him unwilling to live on his wife's income. Let her spend what she cared to on clothes and that sort of thing, but their establishment must be his affair. The small, semi-detached villa they found at Hackfield, a new suburb in the Hendon-Edgware direction, was very much to his taste. It was within easy reach of his work, the garden was big enough to give him exercise during the week-end and surely there was all the society Dorothy needed,—a tennis club, a bridge club, a drama league and so on. But Dorothy never cared for the neighbourhood, and as the years went by, her dislike of it grew. She loved a pretty home, but theirs, to her way of thinking, wasn't pretty. Besides, there was far too much house-work to be done, and domestic help, however much one was prepared to pay for it, was at Hackfield almost non-existent.

One day she came back from a trip to the West End of London (which she visited as often as she could), with the news that she had found the perfect flat,—a whole, self-contained first floor in Pollitt Place,—a beautiful sitting-room with a balcony, a fair-sized bedroom behind, a tiny modern kitchen and a sweet little bathroom. And there was another small room, tucked away in a projection at the back, which Robert could turn into whatever he liked,—a study or even a carpenter's shop. (He was one of those people who can't sit and read or meditate or even listen long to the radio or watch TV, but must always be doing some sort of manual work,—taking things to pieces to clean them or repair them or merely to see how they are made. No wonder in his scale of values the artisan ranked higher than the artist.)

His opposition was useless. She said she could afford to pay all the rent herself and would gladly do so. She had always had a longing to live in The Pollitts,—and when he said he had never heard of them, she looked sick with disgust and would hardly speak to him for the rest of the evening. But she spoke a lot the next day,—to such effect that he gave up his free Saturday morning and went with her to inspect the property. He had to admit, that as such places went, it was not at all bad. At least, it was better than a flat in a big block, which he knew to be the alternative in his wife's mind. He liked Mrs Muller, though when she said that it would be as well for them to make up their minds at once, as two other people were interested, he whispered to Dorothy, 'That's an old wheeze. They always say that.' He didn't know then that Mrs Muller never told lies.

However, Dorothy whispered back at once, 'I simply can't bear the thought of not getting it. I shall settle things now, if you don't.' And he gave way, rather than have a scene. A short interview with Miss Tredennick followed, though it wasn't clear to either of them why they had to submit to it. 'Was it really Miss Tredennick's house?' No, but Mrs Muller didn't care to take any tenants of whom Miss Tredennick didn't approve. Robert cursed a social system which put such power in the hands of useless old women, but gave way, and the meeting was an unexpected success. Miss Tredennick, who happened to be at her best, said with a smile, 'You've guessed that I'm a tedious, tyrannical old woman, but as long as Mrs Muller is good enough to give me a kind of Russian veto, I intend to exercise it when I think fit. But in your case, I'm sure I shan't need to.' No dogs? No young children? Splendid! Well, Mrs Muller would take up the usual references, and if they satisfied her, as no doubt they would, the Fawleys were welcome to move in when they wished.

They did so a month later, and there, for nearly four years they had lived their humdrum, steady-going life,—while Magda developed from an awkward, shy, over-grown girl into a pretty, if rather tame, young woman. At least, she had seemed tame to Robert, who, seeking perhaps a contrast to his wife, had acquired an abstract taste for flamboyant beauty,—till, one day, as he was passing through the hall, so strange a look flashed from Magda's eyes to his, that he saw her suddenly in a different guise, and half alarmed, half tickled by such a freak of fancy, found himself first desiring, then almost adoring her.

This cerebral passion might soon have died, if chance had not given it a physical basis. One night when Robert had come home from work, his hand and Magda's met on the stair-rail. Neither of them knew how or with what excuse it had happened. Their hands might have been two magnets drawn together by an irresistible force. She was the first to recover from the shock, withdraw her hand and say quietly, 'I'm so sorry.' 'I'm not,' he answered, almost brutally, 'this had got to happen.' And he took her hand again and gripped it, regardless of the landing above, where his wife might emerge, or of the door in the hall, through which Justin Bray might pass at any moment in quest of the evening paper. Then, as if ashamed of his boldness, he said, 'I love you, Magda. Do you think you care at all for me in that way?' She nodded her head, drew her hand gently away and went down the basement stairs.

And now, on this wet Monday,—this start of the workaday week,—the dream had become a reality with consequences that would somehow have to be faced. He didn't fear them, primed as he was with a virility doubled by the sweet adventure of the previous day. Ways and means could be found,—should be found. He was too elated to worry very much how he would find them,— although that very night he would once more be boxed up with his unwanted wife, and there was no knowing into what indiscretions her natterings, naggings and moanings might not goad him. Sufficient unto the morning was its joy.

[2]

Dorothy Fawley was treating herself to lunch at Garrows. It wasn't cheap, but she loved having it there, and found an excuse to do so nearly every week. That morning's excuse was the end of her little holiday in Cambridgeshire. She was half glad and half sorry to be back. The country as such didn't interest her at all, but her sister, Louise, who was married to a fairly well-to-do gentleman-farmer, had a comfortable, well-staffed house and plenty of friends. It is true they mostly talked about agriculture and horse-racing and local politics, but they were all 'nice and substantial' people with a real background and had a soothing effect on the nerves. Despite the odious aftermath of the war, their little world seemed so securely established that you felt a hydrogen-bomb would just bounce off it and explode far away in a more suitable setting. Louise had always been a lucky one. She had good looks and good health and a cheerful, energetic and practical nature. She had made a perfect marriage and had three children who presented no problems. They never appeared to be ill, their manners were good, if rather free and easy, and they had all their parents' common sense. A happy family! And yet, while Dorothy envied them, she felt towards them that touch of superiority which those who have suffered (or think they have, which is much the same thing), always tend to feel towards those who haven't suffered.

The people at the tables round Dorothy had the same air of enterprise and well-being as her sister's friends, but they were much nearer Dorothy's own way of life, or her ideal of it. These lively women, these kind, indulgent men, all with money to spend and intent on spending it, exuded a collective consciousness in which Dorothy's small ego could shelter and bask and expand, till it tasted an abundance of house-proud joys that filled her with a vicarious contentment. She loved the snippets of their conversation she overheard. Even a phrase like, 'My children *never* need a laxative' (which Aldous Huxley satirically recorded in an early novel of his), would evoke a delighted response in Dorothy's mind. After all, though it may sound rather grotesque, especially if said loudly while others are silent, how gratifying its import should be, not only to the mother and her child, but to anyone privileged to hear of their good fortune.

'We're putting central heating in the hall, *as well as* the dining-room. . . . Tommy has grown so big, I shall have to buy him another overcoat. . . . Another time, dear, ask for Zephyr Bob; it makes perfect bathroom curtains and the patterns are so much prettier than the *ordinary* ginghams. . . . Small coloured fairy-lights all down the drive. . . .' It reassured her to think that so many people, in these deadening days of perpetual levelling-down, still had halls and dining-rooms and drives, and that she and her class—or the class she would like to belong to—hadn't yet been altogether liquidated.

Dorothy's life was overshadowed by three great fears,—of death, of painful illness and of the poverty into which a thorough-going Labour Government would surely plunge her. And Robert gave her little sympathy. Death and illness? Well, we've just got to face them, so what was the use of worrying beforehand? As for a Labour Government, his job would be safe whatever government came into power and should keep the two of them in very fair comfort. That was all *he* asked for, and all *she* should ask for, too. Such was the gist of his replies to her, though they may not have been so callously worded. In earlier days he had seemed really concerned when she was distressed, but she cried 'Wolf!' so often, that when she mentioned her symptoms or drew his attention to some threat from the Left, he was apt to shrug his shoulders and change the subject.

That evening she would be seeing him again. He would give her a kiss and ask her how she'd got on and how Louise was and, more perfunctorily, how Charles was. (He never got on with Charles, whom he called an old Die-hard.) Then she'd tell him that she'd brought back a duck for dinner, and he'd cook it while she sat in the drawing-room, reading or listening to the radio, turned very low, so as not to disturb Miss Tredennick overhead. Then they'd have dinner,—some powdered soup, the duck (which might make her bilious, though Robert loved it), and perhaps a simple mushroom savoury—Louise's children had picked some that morning—and then she'd say, 'Now, I'm going to do the washing-up to-night; you've done all the cooking.' But he'd laugh and say, 'No, you know I like it,' and she'd sit alone again, with a book or the radio or perhaps writing a letter. Then he'd come in and chat with her for a few minutes, then make some excuse to slink off to his work-room with a broken watch that he'd picked up somewhere for sixpence and stay there till she called through the door that she was going to bed. And he'd come out rubbing his oily hands on a rag and say, 'Very well, dear, I shan't be long,' and give her a kiss, and she'd go through to the bedroom and—yes, she would have to take one of her sleeping tablets, she felt so restless.

The earlier part of the evening went very much as Dorothy had pictured it, but when she made her offer to wash up, Robert amazed her by saying, 'Well, if you really wouldn't mind—I've got a nasty headache this evening, and I feel like going for a long walk.' There was something unusually shy and pleading in his voice. Dorothy thought that its strangeness must be due to the nature of his admission. He was one of those men who hate to confess to any kind of illness. For a moment she wondered if there was any need for her to be alarmed. Then he added, 'Oh, it's nothing. They had the new heating on in the office to-day for the first time. The place was unbearably stuffy. They'll have to regulate it better or we shall all be crocks.' It was almost pathetic how he seemed to be waiting

for her consent, like a school child asking a master for permission
to go to the village and buy some sweets.

She didn't know what time it was when he came in, as her sleeping tablets were having their fullest effect.

[3]

Mrs Muller and Magda were having a cup of cocoa in the kitchen,
before going to bed. The day's work was over at last, and Mrs Muller
felt tired. Magda looked pale, and, if not exactly tired, strained and
preoccupied. She had been like that for some days, mechanical in
her work and once or twice a little absent-minded, which was most
unusual. When she was darning Mr Bray's socks, she would look
up and listen if she heard a noise in the upper part of the house,
though it might only be Mr Fawley coming downstairs. Was she
finding the routine of Ten Pollitt Place too much of a strain? Did
she need a change? But with Miss Tredennick immobile on the top
floor, that was out of the question. Mrs Muller didn't mind it for
herself. She had made her bed and she must lie on it,—a phrase that
came very often into her thoughts. But it was hardly fair that Magda
should have to share the same bed, through no fault of her own,
and without those secret hopes that her mother cherished. Miss
Tredennick had never taken to Magda, however much she might
depend on her. The old lady was just, according to her lights, and
no doubt had mentioned Magda in her will,—but it wouldn't be
much, a hundred or two at the most. For that matter, Mrs Muller
had no great expectations for herself. The freehold of the house
was hers already, though leased back to Miss Tredennick for her
life. The reversion of course should be quite valuable, though the
prices of such houses were coming down, as they needed so much
repair and were not suitable for conversion into those agglomera-
tions of tiny gilded cages which nowadays fetched the money. But
Miss Tredennick probably wouldn't know that, and might think the
house a generous reward for the service of most of a life-time.

Yet it was by no means enough for Mrs Muller. She was prepared to work hard day and night till she died, provided that when
that day came she could feel assured about Hugo's future. He

must be rich,—so rich that his bodily disabilities wouldn't count in his life. He must not be despised or pitied; he must be sought after, flattered, entreated, admired. Only thus could amends be made to him. As she thought of his poor little body lying asleep in his slit of a bedroom, and pictured the pale gold patch made by his hair just emerging above the sheet, a smile of affection formed on her pale lips. Well, for the time being, there was no need to worry. Miss Tredennick, who had been kind to him even as a baby, now seemed to be really fond of him. Almost every day she sent for him to come to her room to have a chat with her, or so that she might give him a little present. There was every hope——

At that moment Magda, who had been sitting motionless in her chair, stood up and, by doing so, roused her mother from her wandering thoughts. Yes, of course, it was Magda, not Hugo, who was the problem. Mrs Muller turned to her daughter anxiously,— the smile of affection fading rapidly—and said, 'Are you feeling all right?'

'What do you mean, Mother?'

Magda's voice held nothing but a slightly indignant surprise, but there was a wariness in her expression.

'I mean,' her mother answered patiently, 'are you feeling quite well? I don't say you look ill,—but there's something about you that isn't quite right. I've noticed it for some days.'

'I'm feeling perfectly well. I can't think what makes you imagine I'm not.'

'Well, it's your manner. When you were getting the cocoa just now, you looked so bored with what you were doing—which you never used to look like—and as if you were interested in some- thing else. And then when a door opened upstairs—the Fawleys' I think it was, because I could hear somebody coming down from the first floor—you gave quite a start. I thought you'd drop the jug. What *is* it, Magda? You know I want to help you.'

Magda looked at her mother with a kind of detachment, as if she were trying to solve an abstract problem. (Sooner or later the truth would have to be told. But not yet,—not just yet.) Mean- while, attack was the best form of defence. She lowered her gaze and said rather sullenly, 'Well, if it's anything, it's about Hugo.'

Her mother started. 'Hugo? What about *him*?'

'I know you don't like to hear him criticised or found fault with, and I don't want to make you uneasy, but——'

'But what? Don't keep me on tenterhooks.'

'Well, I've got an idea he goes upstairs. I don't mean when Miss Tredennick sends for him, but at other times, when he'd rather we didn't know.'

'But, poor boy, I should hear him, with his dragging leg.'

'I'm not sure you would. He can walk very much more quietly than you think, when he wants to.'

'You're making him out to be deceitful, Magda. That's a quality that isn't in any of us,—not in me, at least—and it wasn't in your father, nor in——'

'Nor in whom?'

'Nothing. I mean, it isn't in Hugo, either. And if he does go upstairs, is any harm done?'

'I don't know about that. What I do know is that you told him he must never go upstairs without permission, and he promised he never would.'

'Oh, that was a very long time ago,—when we first came here. Besides, I don't think he does.'

Magda went on reflectively, 'I don't say I blame him. I know his life can't be like other boys', but I don't agree that he'll never be able to take up any career. I'm sure he could get some sort of clerical work. At least, why not let him try? He isn't stupid, and there are plenty of commercial colleges. Send him to one of them for a term and see how he gets on. This Mr Middleton may be a nice old man—he must be, as he was recommended by Mr Bray—and he may be very clever, but he can't manage Hugo, or doesn't bother. Besides, what's the use of Hugo learning Latin and poetry? The trouble is, he hasn't enough to do. I know he reads a good deal and he does his drawings. I don't like them myself; they give me a nasty feeling—those people without arms and legs and faces or with too many of them. And I'm nearly sure——'

She hesitated. She had been going to say she was nearly sure Hugo did other drawings which he didn't show but kept locked up in his play-box,—vile, morbid things no doubt. But this would needlessly upset her mother and antagonise her still further. After all, though her concern over Hugo's welfare wasn't altogether hypocritical, she had shifted the conversation to him so as to escape her mother's awkward questions.

'What were you going to say?'

'Well, only that the kind of life he's leading isn't doing him any good. Why don't you set about getting him some work, or at least let him learn how to make a living? Not just for the sake of the money,—for Hugo's own sake?'

Mrs Muller's indignation boiled over.

'One thing I *do* know, and that's that you're jealous of Hugo. You always have been. I suppose it was natural when you were a girl, as I had to give so much more time to him than to you. But you should have grown out of all that by now. As a matter of fact, I *have* suggested he should take up something,—go to a college or have some postal course—though I'm told they're not very much good—but he doesn't want to at present, and till he does, I'm not going to press him. He says he's perfectly happy living here as he is, and that's all *I* worry about. No, I don't want to talk about it any more. I'm too tired, for one thing. I'm going to bed. You won't forget to take in an extra pint of milk for the Fawleys, now Mrs Fawley's back again? Good night!'

With hardly a glance at her daughter she went out of the kitchen and into her bedroom. After she had undressed, she knelt down by her bed and prayed:

'O most merciful Father, I pray Thee forgive me my sins. Visit not, I implore Thee, the sins of the fathers on the children. Grant me long life and good health so that I may tend my dear son and give him happiness and comfort. O take him not from me, I beg Thee, I beg Thee, I beg Thee. Let me die before him, but not till I see him really settled in life and able to enjoy it in his own way. And bless my daughter too, and may she learn to think more kindly of her brother. Amen.'

V

THE TWENTY-SEVENTH OF OCTOBER

IT seemed, these days, as if Miss Tredennick had almost given up using her sitting-room, into which the dwindling sun could no longer twist a single ray, and had made permanent winter quarters of her bedroom. Here it was always bright, if there was brightness anywhere in the sky. She had a big arm-chair put near the window, with a table at its side on which she wrote, and ate such meals as she didn't eat in bed.

All the time she had lived at Ten Pollitt Place she had made a point of never gossiping with her staff about the neighbours. Let them bring her up what tit-bits of news they liked—she would swallow them and digest them at leisure—but she would never ask for information or lend herself to any form of espionage other than that undertaken by her own sharp eyes. This explains, in part, why she had been so 'cagey'—as Mrs Muller put it—about the night when she had her little attack,—that September night when Miss Varioli and her boy-friend with the car disgraced themselves outside the door of Number Seven.

But Miss Tredennick had been very far from dismissing Miss Varioli from her mind, and could now give you a number of precise facts about her which would have earned a private detective a handsome fee. It is true that most of these facts were very dull.

'*Wednesday, 12th October, 9.30 a.m. Y.V. left the house wearing . . .* (Full details followed.) *Carried a small grey plastic bag. Turned to the left when she came to the Crescent.*'
5.35 p.m. Turned in from the Crescent, carrying a large parcel done up in mauve paper.
6.47 p.m. A small green Morris car parked outside Number 11,—no room opposite Number 7—and a youngish man not the man—got out and went to No. 7. Admitted by Mrs O'Blahoney.

44

*7.50 p.m. Y. V. and the man came out together. Y. V. had changed into
. . . Walked down Pollitt Place towards Lampstone Lane.*

Some of the entries, however, had more meat about them and
were underlined in red pencil. One of these, for example, came
under the heading *Saturday the 15th October*:

*3.25 p.m. A taxi dropped Y. V. and a good-looking young man in Ameri-
can Air Force uniform at No. 7. Y. V. and the man went in together.
5.18 p.m. The American came out alone and stood on the doorstep,
counting the notes in his note-case. Then he walked towards the Crescent. Y. V. stood at her window watching him.*

And there were other entries, even more striking by reason of
peculiar interpolations, which added nothing to their factual basis,
but might have shed light on the compiler's state of mind. Take
Tuesday, the 18th October:

*9.22 a.m. Y. V. came out, wearing a very small bright red felt hat. Red
hat and no drawers! She walked more slowly than usual down the
Place towards Lampstone Lane.*

Red hat and no drawers! The phrase startled Miss Tredennick
when she re-read her Journal. How on earth had she ever come
to learn it? If she had heard it from someone—and she must have
done—it was probably from the Cockney charwoman who came
to Polvannion during the war. But what had induced her to put it
in writing? Her first impulse was to scratch it out, but on second
thoughts she decided to let it stand. If ever she submitted her 'evidence'—and she was confident that some day she would—to the
authorities, the sensational passage should be suppressed. Till then
it might as well remain to stimulate her zeal for further research.
Much the same could be said for an outburst of poetry which followed the entry for Friday, the 21st October:

*4.13 p.m. Y.V. turned in from the Crescent. She carried a bouquet that
looked like the cheaper kind of orchid—cypripediums?*

> *Swing the buttocks, heave the hips,
> Brace the bubs and pout the lips.*

That remarkable couplet, Miss Tredennick knew, was a legacy from her father, who, in his declining years, when—to put it politely—his mind was clouded, had developed a gift, hitherto unsuspected, for such improvisations. (Alas, that they should always have turned upon the same theme!) Filial piety was hardly a justification for quoting the lines. None the less, she didn't expunge them; for she now enjoyed being reminded of the white hot anger and disgust which the sight of that self-advertising body aroused in her.

She was savouring it yet again, when there was a tap on her door. She covered the Journal with a piece of blotting-paper and said, 'Come in.' It was Mrs Muller, looking slightly excited, though she did her best to appear unconcerned, and made one or two routine domestic inquiries before coming to the point. Then she said, 'I don't suppose you see the local paper, Madam, but there's something in it that might interest you, as it's about this neighbourhood—Number Fifteen in the Rise, to be exact. What times we live in!' As she spoke, she produced the paper from the pocket of her house-coat, and laid it on Miss Tredennick's table.

'There's the article, Madam. *Husband and wife in Court*. It really makes you ashamed, doesn't it? You expect that kind of thing *north* of the Park, but this side, it's too bad. Still, I'm not altogether surprised. I've seen some very odd-looking characters even in *this* street. I'll leave it with you, Madam.'

Miss Tredennick said quietly, 'Thank you, Gwen. I shall be interested to read it,' and began to do so as soon as Mrs Muller had gone out. It was a story such as those who read a certain type of Sunday newspaper would find commonplace. A Mr and Mrs Thucydides had been convicted of knowingly letting rooms to six habitual prostitutes. The police, acting on information received, had kept watch from the windows of a house opposite. One of the girls was seen going in with a different man seven times in three hours. The defence was very thin, and the fine—according to Miss Tredennick's ideas—disgracefully inadequate. (If she had her way, the strumpets should be whipped at the cart's tail, and those who organised these filthy practices should be branded and pilloried. On the other hand, she regarded the clients merely as innocent victims, who should be saved from their weakness by the removal of temptation.)

The police kept watch at a house opposite. Most important. So far as Miss Tredennick remembered, from the days when she used to struggle out for little walks, Number Fifteen was a house with an ugly blue door containing two panes of frosted glass. The opposite house would be Number Four, which had been turned into two maisonettes. The lower one was used as offices, and two maiden ladies—yes, their name was Brett—lived in the upper one. Well done, the Misses Brett! She would have liked to send them a note of congratulation on their public spirit, but feared it might give her own game away. Meanwhile, the first thing to do was to copy the article into her Journal,—a task which kept her happily occupied for half an hour, since her arthritic hands found writing laborious.

When Mrs Muller next came in, Miss Tredennick gave her back the paper with an air of indifference, and said, 'What very unpleasant reading, isn't it? I think you'll have to warn Hugo—at any rate when he's a little older. I should hate to think of him getting into the clutches of such awful creatures.'

Mrs Muller smiled confidently. 'Oh, I'm not worried about him on that score. He doesn't like that kind of woman at all. He says the sight of them makes him want to spit.' Miss Tredennick did her best to restrain her applause and said, 'Really, Gwen!', to signify that the conversation was closed.

Mrs Muller went out and Miss Tredennick resumed her observation of Number Seven. It had been a dull morning, except for Mrs Muller's news, and so far the enemy hadn't made her sortie, or Miss Tredennick had somehow failed to spot it. Still, one never knew. There had been days when Y.V. hadn't stirred out till quite late, though she had never been so late as this before.

It was a quarter past twelve. The street was full of cars, parked there for the day, while their suburban owners did their shopping at Garrows or the cheaper stores near by. Miss Tredennick hated these cars, which reminded her of her own immobility. At times she had thought of buying an old Rolls-Royce and having it permanently stationed outside her front door to keep intruders at bay. No doubt she could get a man to clean the coach-work. The car might be old—it needn't even have an engine inside it—but it must be spotless.

Ah, there was Hugo, coming back from Mr Middleton's. Wasn't he early—or was her clock slow? He seemed to be hurrying. It was wonderful how he managed with his poor leg. She heard the click of the area-gate as he climbed down the iron steps leading to the basement. Sometimes she had qualms about forcing him to make such a perilous descent and thought of allowing him to use the front door and the easier flight of stairs leading down from the hall. But it wouldn't be wise. If she gave him this privilege, she would have to extend it to Gwen and Magda and destroy all distinction between her staff and her tenants. The Fawleys might not mind, but Mr Bray would—and he'd be quite right.

The dust-van turned into the far end of the street, manoeuvring with difficulty among the closely packed cars, while the two dustmen—if one was still allowed to give them such a familiar name—dived through the spaces between them, fetching and replacing dust-bins and sacks and bags of waste-paper. What a fine strapping fellow the red-headed one was, and he seemed so cheerful. What would it be like to spend your day hauling other people's refuse up and down steps, your clothes and your body impregnated with filth and vile smells? But no doubt, if one was trained young enough to such an employment, it might seem quite agreeable. There was no sense in wasting pity there. Besides, how would *they* like to be seventy-six and shut up in one room, hardly able to move and very rarely quite free from pain? Old people were often reproached for being selfish. Perhaps they were selfish, but hadn't they every excuse, leading monotonous lives that every day became more like mere bodily processes,—teeth, eyes, ears, muscles, digestion all slowly crumbling into a decay that nothing could arrest? The selfishness of the young was much uglier.

Then all at once she ceased to philosophise; for the shabby yellow door of Number Seven swung open, and Y.V. came out, stood on the cracked threshold and looked to her left towards Lampstone Lane, tapping the tiles impatiently with her toes. (What common shoes she wore, and how oilily her black hair shone in the late October sunshine!) Then she stepped back inside and shut the door with a bang. The vision had only lasted for thirty seconds, but every detail of it was safely recorded in Miss Tredennick's brain and was soon to be recorded in her Journal. But while she was jerkily busy with her pencil, she was presented with yet more material. The front door of Number Seven opened again, and Y.V. appeared, this time wearing her red hat and carrying her small grey plastic bag. She didn't hesitate, but crossed straight over the road, behind the dust-van, which had now drawn up as near Number Ten as it could, and walked westward along the north side of the street.

[2]

Hugo was talking in the area to Bert, the red-headed dustman, as Miss Varioli passed. He saw his friend raise his head at the whiff of scent that she exhaled, and noticed that his eyes gazed up her skirt. The dustman said, 'My word, she's a nice bit of goods. Friend of yours, eh?' Hugo's face became quite bloodless as he answered, 'No, she isn't. And I don't like the smell she leaves behind.' The dustman laughed and said, 'Maybe you'll like it better when you're older. At present, I dare say you'd rather have one of these.' He took a small bag of caramels from his pocket and offered it to Hugo, who replied angrily, 'No, I don't want one.' Bert drew back in surprise and Hugo instantly changed his mind and said, 'Oh, but I do! How very kind of you! Please, may I have one?' The dustman laughed again and said, 'Well, you are a funny kid. Here—take the lot. I haven't any kids of my own to give them to.' Hugo said, 'I wish you were my father,' then blushed and offered his gift of a cigarette. Then the other dustman, who was only too glad to let Bert do most of the carrying, leant over the area railings and shouted, 'Come on, Bert, or we shan't get the street finished to-day.' 'Coming, Joe. So long, sonny! See you on Monday, I hope.' And the peculiar little idyll was over.

[3]

It was the morning for turning out the hall. In the normal

course the work would have been finished long before, but Magda prolonged it deliberately so that she might be on hand to catch Justin when he came out of his sitting-room to go to his luncheon. He did so a good deal later than usual and in her impatience she almost barred his way to the front door.

'Would it be convenient for me to speak to you, Sir?'

'Of course, Magda. Would you like to come in for a moment?'

'If you don't mind, Sir.'

As they went into his sitting-room, he thought, 'Oh dear, what can it be? Do I need fresh net curtains in the windows? Have the covers got to be cleaned? Or is she going to ask for higher wages?' She had had a rise in April, but he supposed that if she asked for another, he'd have to give it to her.

He shut the door and tried to look sympathetic.

'Well, Magda, what is it?'

She seemed to find it difficult to begin—always a bad sign. Then, after swallowing nervously, she said, 'It's about your cigarettes, Sir.'

'My cigarettes?' (Did she think he'd burnt a hole in one of the rugs?) 'But I don't smoke. I only keep them for visitors.'

'That's the point, Sir. I don't want you to think I've been spying or that I'm what they call "nosey", but when I polish that lovely cigarette-box of yours, I have to lift the lid to do it properly. During the last few weeks I couldn't help noticing that the fat cigarettes in one compartment remained more or less the same, but the smaller ones, in the other compartment, if you understand me——'

'Yes, the Virginians. The fat ones are Turkish. It's rather old-fashioned to smoke them nowadays, but I keep them in case they're needed.'

'Yes, Sir,—but who smokes the Virginian ones?'

'Let me see. I think the very last time anyone smoked a cigarette in this room was when I had Lady Beatrice Lurcher to tea. Yes, I remember. There were only two Virginian cigarettes in the box when I offered it to her. She smoked one, and I believe Lady Farless took one of the Turkish. I refilled the Virginian compartment the next day with two packets of twenty.'

'So there should now be forty-one of them, Sir.'

'Really, Magda, I hope you don't think I count them!'

'I'm sure you don't, Sir. But—I don't like telling you this—*I* have been counting them lately. When I began there were thirty-eight. Now there are twenty-six,—or there were this morning, when I did the room. And I haven't seen a single cigarette-stub in the ash-trays. Now, Sir, apart from my mother and myself, there's only one person who could have taken them.'

'You must mean Bath.' (Bath was the ex-naval man who came in at eight for two hours every morning, to call Justin, get him his breakfast, clean his shoes and look after his clothes.) 'But Bath only smokes a pipe. Besides, I've known him so many years, I'm quite certain he——'

'Oh no, Sir. I wasn't thinking of Mr Bath. I'm sure he wouldn't dream of taking anything. It's—it's Hugo I'm worried about. I know he prowls about the house sometimes, though he's been told not to.'

Justin's mind moved with a sudden speed, as a scene from Victor Hugo's *Les Misérables* flashed into it,—though it was forty years since he had read the book. He remembered how, when the police found the stolen candlesticks in Jean Valjean's bag, the priest, to whom they belonged, declared he had made a present of them to the culprit. (Was it a trick of verbal association? Victor Hugo— Hugo Muller?) At all events, as a literary man is apt to do, when he finds himself in a literary situation, he felt impelled to live up to his prototype, and said, 'Oh, I'd quite forgotten. He has at times asked me for one or two—I don't think he smokes—they were probably for a friend—and I've given him just a few.'

'He had no right whatever to do that!'

'No, I suppose he hadn't, but don't be hard on him. Don't tell him anything about our talk, or he'd be bound to think you suspected him—and your mother might blame me for giving him cigarettes at his age. I would much rather you let the whole matter drop. I'm sorry for Hugo.'

She answered bitterly, 'Yes, everybody is. It makes me rather jealous of him sometimes.'

Justin smiled and said, 'Well, *you* don't look as if you need much sympathy.'

She blushed deeply, feeling ashamed of having let herself go
and reading an unintentional irony into Justin's remark. So she
didn't look as if she needed sympathy? And what of the hopeless,
irresistible, guilty passion to which she had yielded, and to which
she would yield again, if occasion offered? Wasn't it branded indel-
ibly on her face? Didn't her movements and her voice betray it to
the whole world?

Without saying any more, or even thanking Justin for his for-
bearance, she went into the hall and down the basement stairs.

[4]

Hugo had been for a lonely walk in Kensington Gardens. He
had wandered slowly along the Serpentine to the fountains at the
end of it, and then, circuitously to the Round Pond, and through
the trees beyond it to the Albert Memorial. Then he crossed the
road into Hyde Park and continued eastwards along Rotten Row.
Both his legs were very tired, and the left one ached, but he hardly
noticed it. He had noticed nothing during his long walk—neither
the waterfowl on the Serpentine, nor the thinning trees, nor the
drifts of fallen leaves on the grass, nor the dull red clouds hanging
over Kensington Palace, nor the boys by the pond, nor the riders
cantering along the Row, nor the dusk, nor the time. He was com-
posing a poem, and thought the first three lines above all praise.

> Love, like a healing wave,
> My twisted form doth lave
> Making it strong and brave.

He was less satisfied with the continuation and found it difficult
to sustain the threefold rhyme, but he was resolved upon doing
so, and there is no knowing how long he might have stayed in the
park, if he hadn't run into Justin near Albert Gate.

Justin was on his way home from an exhibition of modern pictures in Bond Street, and was not in one of his happiest moods.
The pictures, most of which had already been sold for enormous
prices, seemed to him to be the daubs of an unintelligent child,—
overlapping rectangles and circles (none drawn with any accuracy),

in crudely contrasting colours, with here and there a diseased travesty of a human eye surrounded by eyelashes like small wriggling snakes. And yet, not one of his friends would agree that the whole thing was a tiresome imposture. On the contrary they vied with one another in producing new epithets of admiration. Was the whole world mad, or was he alone in his madness? Or was he simply hopelessly out of touch,—hopelessly old?

On his way, he had looked into three bookshops, none of which displayed a single copy of *Seven Silent Sinners*, though it was little more than three months since it had first appeared. Was it worth while trying to write another book and achieve what Lady Beatrice had called his silver jubilee? He wasn't even sure that his new title, *The Righteous Heart*, hadn't been used before,—indeed, he now thought it had, or something very like it.

Apart from all this, he wasn't feeling too well. It might be that the steak and kidney pudding he'd had for lunch at his club had upset him a little, or he might have done too much walking that afternoon. At all events, in the left side of his chest he had a suspicion of the same pain that had attacked him the day he lost his temper with the woman whose poodle had fouled the doorstep of Number Ten.

He was on the point of looking for a taxi, when he saw Hugo and was reminded of what Magda had told him that morning. It was clear that he'd got to come to an understanding with Hugo, if only to protect himself from having his white lies exposed. Besides, a few words of caution and reprimand were certainly due—for the boy's own sake—and no time could be more convenient that the present for delivering them.

He called, 'Hugo, Hugo!'

Hugo looked up with big, startled, tired eyes, like a sleepwalker suddenly aroused from a dream.

'Yes, Mr Bray? I—I was just taking a walk, before going home for tea. I think I'm late—yes, very late, but I've walked too far and can't hurry.'

'Very well, Hugo. I'm tired too. We'll have a taxi together. I've got something rather important to say to you.'

They found a taxi quickly and got in. For some reason Justin couldn't bring himself to feel any real anger with the little thief, though he did his best to speak in a schoolmasterish way.

'I'm going to ask you a question, Hugo, and I want you to tell me the truth. Have you ever taken any of my cigarettes?'

Hugo pondered a moment, realising in an obscure way that a great deal depended on whether he said 'Yes' or 'No'.

Then he said, 'Yes, Sir. Six times,—but I've only taken a very few each time. I'm very sorry. I know it was very wicked of me indeed—but the shops wouldn't sell me any. They said I was too young.'

'Does your mother know you smoke?'

'I don't smoke, Sir.'

'Then why did you take them? Not to sell them, surely?'

'No, Sir. I took them to give to a friend.'

The memory of Justin's own half-forgotten romantic school-boy friendships came back to him and made him feel almost sentimental.

'You realise that what you did was very wrong?'

'Yes, Sir. I promise I'll never do it again.'

'You see,' Justin went on, 'what you did might so easily have thrown suspicion on an innocent person. I don't smoke myself, and I don't often have guests who do. Who, do you think, was the most natural person for me to suspect? No, I don't mean Bath. He only smokes a pipe, and I've known him far longer than I've known you—or your mother or sister. Who was the obvious person?'

Hugo looked at him with an expression of horror—though Justin misinterpreted its origin—as he whispered, 'Magda!'

'Exactly. Was it fair to her?'

'No, Sir.'

'Now, Hugo,—this is a secret between us, and I rely on you to keep it. I told your sister that I'd given you the cigarettes,—so, if anything's said, though I urged her to let the whole matter drop, you'll understand the position. Perhaps I may have done wrong—perhaps it might have been better to let you get a good scolding from your mother. It's hard to know, in these cases. If your mother really cross-examined me, I doubt if I should have the face to stick to my story. So, as I told your sister, don't refer to the subject again.

And if you want any more cigarettes, you might do me the favour of asking permission, before you take them. By the way, how old is the friend to whom you give them?'

Hugo blushed and said, 'He'll be thirty-four his next birthday—in February.'

Justin looked a little surprised and said, 'Really! I only asked, so as to be sure that he was of an age to smoke. I see he is.'

For two minutes they drove on in silence. Then Hugo asked suddenly, 'What started you counting the cigarettes, Sir?'

Justin replied with a touch of indignation, 'I've never counted my cigarettes in my life. I explained to you how——' Then he broke off, realising that he hadn't meant to tell Hugo outright that it was Magda who raised the alarm, even though he might have implied it.

Hugo said softly, 'So it was Magda who counted them. She told you about me.'

Justin gripped the boy's arm and gave it a warning squeeze. 'Now, Hugo, put all that right out of your thoughts and don't ever mention it to your sister or your mother. Your sister had to tell me, for her own sake. It was a very unpleasant position for her to be in. As I said, I'm not at all sure I ought to have shielded you. You've been very lucky this time, but if anything like this ever happens again, you won't get off so lightly. As it is, if anything else should disappear in this house, I shan't be able to stop myself wondering if it isn't you who have taken it.'

At these words, Hugo began to cry. Justin was greatly embarrassed and took Hugo's arm again, but more affectionately, and said, 'For goodness sake, pull yourself together. What will your mother think if you come home with tear-stains on your face? Let's forget the whole thing.'

They didn't speak again till the taxi drew up at Number Ten. Hugo got out first, held the door politely for Justin, and said, 'Mr Bray, I'm more grateful to you than I can tell you. Thank you very, very much.' Then he climbed down the iron steps to the area, as fast as he could, while Justin paid the fare.

[5]

In Cornwall, though only a child, Hugo had quite a reputation for possessing the gift of second sight. He had displayed it three times. When told that the household Corgi (which had contracted an irregular union), was going to have puppies, he said, 'Yes, she'll have six. Three will be brown and two will be black.' And when they laughed and said, 'That still leaves one. What colour will that one be?', he answered, 'I don't know. It'll be so small, it might be any colour.' And sure enough there were three brown puppies and two black ones and the sixth, the runt of the litter, was such a mixture of black, brown, grey and white, that it was hard to describe it.

The second instance was vaguer but more alarming. There was a billiards-room built out at the back of Polvannion. It hadn't been in use for over twenty years, and Miss Tredennick had said that Hugo might play there whenever he liked. But he said he hated the room, and seemed so frightened of even going into it, that they gave up trying to persuade him to play there. Then, one day, without any kind of warning at all—there had been neither cracks nor creaks—the heavy Victorian ceiling collapsed with a crash, and huge jagged chunks of plaster covered the billiards-table and one end of the floor. Most fortunately the room was empty at the time. Anyone who had been caught in that thunderous avalanche would have been badly injured, if not killed.

But the third manifestation was the most formidable. Hugo was devoted to an enormous tortoise-shell cat. One afternoon, the gardener found him clasping it in his arms and sobbing violently. When asked what the trouble was, Hugo said, 'Darling Timmie,— we're going to lose him soon, and I love him so much. I can't bear it. I can't.' For the next two days he refused to be comforted. In vain they assured him that Timmie's health was robust to the point of unruliness, that he had eaten three mackerel for breakfast and had caught a rat in the coal-cellar afterwards. Alas, the next news was that Timmie had been found in a rabbit-snare, strangled, with the cruel brass wire cutting deep into the flesh round the throat.

Of course, there were sceptics who qualified these stories and played them down. Magda was one of them. But Mrs Muller, who had a strong vein of superstition herself, inherited from her Swedish mother, was a firm believer, half proud of her son's clairvoyance and half terrified of what he might prophesy next. However, since that time, he had prophesied nothing, and people who had heard of his three lucky shots, began to think that, if they had been inspired, the inspiration had vanished with his childhood.

That evening, at supper, he hardly spoke and seemed to have little appetite. Mrs Muller kept saying, 'He's tired out, poor boy, that's what it is,' and she looked reproachfully at Magda who had a way of urging him to take more exercise than was good for him. When the meal was over, instead of getting up at once, as he usually did, he remained in his chair and put his hand to his head, half shutting his eyes.

'What is it, Hugo? Have you a headache, darling?'

Without looking up, he said in a low, flat voice, 'Before the end of this year someone in this house is going to die.' Mrs Muller uttered a cry of horror and said, 'Not us, not us! Oh Hugo, say it's not going to be any of us three!' Hugo opened his eyes, and gazing with an expression of hatred straight at Magda, who was standing aghast by the opposite side of the table, he said, 'I don't know. I don't know,' and went into his room.

VI

THE FOURTH OF NOVEMBER

DOROTHY was waiting for Robert to come home from his work. She felt no special eagerness to see him, but his return marked a stage in the day's routine, and was for that reason something to which she looked forward. The tiniest landmark in her aimless life was better than its unidentified emptiness.

Since Robert had left the flat that morning, she had done nothing of any consequence. One or two small household tasks, a few words with Mrs Pye (who came to oblige five mornings a week for two hours), a stroll down Parkwell Road with a visit to Garrows—

though she hadn't bought anything there—a cheap lunch at a café kept by two ladies, another short stroll towards Kensington Gardens—but it looked so like rain that she soon turned back—a few minutes' spiritless reading, a nap, her solitary tea at half-past four and the boredom of washing up afterwards—these were the sum of her physical activities.

Of course, her thoughts had been busy the whole time, in their uncontrollable way. She had vaguely pitied herself for leading the kind of life she had to lead, though she knew quite well that it was her own inner nature that fixed the pattern. She had thought about Robert, too,—and here she really had something to think about; for since she had come back from her visit to Cambridgeshire, he seemed oddly changed. He struck her as more alive and brighter than he had been, and yet on edge. He was also better looking, and there were times when she could almost understand how, during the spell of her infatuation for him, she had thought no other man in the world could be so handsome. At such moments she felt a physical attraction emanating from him, that almost tempted her to break down the barrier that she herself had erected between them four years before. But even if her pride would have allowed her to try, she hadn't the courage.

It was both novel and humiliating that his initiative should now exceed her own. For many years it was she who planned their diversions and devised little changes to vary their fixed way of life. 'If it's fine, we might spend the afternoon at Windsor. . . . Do you know, I've never been to the Prospect of Whitby. . . . How about the Zoo? . . . Don't you think you'd like to see the Radio Exhibition?' But now she seemed spiritually tethered to a mile radius round Ten Pollitt Place, and he was the restless one. 'I want some fresh air. Won't you come out for a stroll?' But what was the use of going for a walk after the shops had shut?

Any moment now she might hear the front door opening and his feet on the stairs. He trod more springily, and yet more aggressively, than any other resident in the house. Mrs Muller thumped, Magda hardly made a sound, and Hugo's shuffle was like a throaty whisper. Mr Bray moved like a delicate old woman, while poor Miss Tredennick hardly moved at all. Ten to six. It wasn't worth while settling down to anything, though it might be as well to change the water in that vase. What a pity it was that chrysanthemums made the water go such a poisonous colour and so smelly.

Instead of carrying the vase, as it was, to the bathroom, she lazily spread a newspaper on a table and laid the twelve flowers on it. Some leaves and a good many petals fell on the floor. She picked them up, resenting the effort, and threw them into the waste-paper basket. Then she emptied the water out of the vase, refilled it, brought it back to the sitting-room and arranged the flowers in it. They had a bleak look after losing so many of their leaves, and more of their petals fell. Really, the labour had hardly been worth while,—like so many of the tasks she set herself. Ignoring the second batch of fallen petals—they weren't very many, and Mrs Pye would sweep them up in the morning—she spent a couple of minutes saying 'Tweet, tweet' to Peter and Wendy, the two budgerigars. Even they were unresponsive, as were the four goldfish lurking amongst the weed in a small aquarium at the other end of the room.

Six o'clock struck. The clock kept perfect time, since Robert looked after it. He was now twenty minutes late. But it was silly to worry. It was true, he was very seldom kept late at his office. His department, in the tradition of the democratic civil servant of to-day, worked by the clock rather than by the needs of the job. But there might be fog out at Hackfield, the power might have been cut, or there might have been a slight mix-up on the line. Nothing alarming, of course, nothing like a real accident—O God, not that!—but even if there were, it would be most unlikely that anyone would be seriously hurt or killed. At the very worst it would be one or two people in the extreme front of the train or at the rear, say the engine-driver or the guard, who might be taken to hospital with slight shock. Meanwhile, how unfair, how inconsiderate it was of fate that she should be kept on tenterhooks like that,—especially as Robert had said he'd make the pastry for the stewed steak pie they were going to have that night. (He had a wonderfully light touch with pastry, and his, unlike other people's, rarely gave her indigestion.) Should she try to make some herself? In the early days of her married life she had taken one or two courses in cookery, and she wasn't too bad when she gave her mind to it. She went to the kitchen and took the tin of flour down from the shelf. What a pretty tin it was,—one of a cream-coloured set, each one with the name in gold on the side, a red top and a ring of red flowers round the bottom. If only one could regard them as ornaments and never have to fill them or use them or clean them!

She looked at the time, but the electric clock in the kitchen had stopped at a few minutes past eleven. Mrs Pye must have unplugged it for some reason. Better leave it for Robert. There were so many plugs and flexes—Robert was one who loved electric gadgets—she might very easily make a wrong connexion and burn something out. And Robert would be, not angry, but coldly severe. 'I do wish you wouldn't fiddle about with these things. You don't understand them and you don't really want to.' (That was more or less what he'd said when she'd burnt out the new refrigerator.)

Dispirited, she went back to the sitting-room, said, 'Tweet, tweet,' to the budgies and tapped the aquarium. When the half-hour struck, she was in a state of panic. What would she do if Robert never came home?

[2]

There had been no fog at Hackfield, no power-cut, no mix-up on the line. Robert had left his office two minutes before the usual time and found a train waiting for him in the station. His good luck held at Leicester Square, and he reached South Kensington having gained another four minutes. Magda was walking nervously up and down the little arcade. Regardless of who might see him, he took her in his arms and kissed her.

It was their first real meeting since the glorious Sunday, more than three weeks before, when they had been to his colleague's empty flat in Twickenham,—three weeks of suspense and frustration, while the physical side of his nature, newly awakened, almost goaded him into open defiance of all conventions, and his accustomed prudence, reinforced though it was by some odd scruples, was hard put to restrain him. But this equivocal and explosive situation couldn't be allowed to go on very long. The strain on the nerves was becoming too great. He was far from being a hypocrite, and playing a perpetual part in front of Dorothy was making his romance into a nightmare.

And there was Magda too to be considered. He had sense enough to realise that in her, as in her mother, there was a strong vein of what he called Puritanism. She was capable of sinning in the grandest of manners, but capable also, alas, of the most austere and uncompromising repentance, once temptation lost its keen edge. The very readiness with which she had surrendered to him had been a sign not of moral looseness, but of its opposite, true love, which if her conscience so decreed, wouldn't shrink from a life-time's aftermath of misery. For her sake as well as his, he must bring things to a head. After all, it was the certain happiness of two against the doubtful happiness of one. Dorothy didn't love him and didn't need him except in small, menial ways.

He took Magda's hand as they turned out of the arcade and held it while they walked down Thurloe Street into Thurloe Square. His face was rather grim and had a suggestion of nobility in its expression. He said, 'My darling, every moment is precious tonight, because we've got so few of them together. I've had plenty of time—too much time—to think things over, and so have you. The position is this. My colleague, who's now in America, is due back at the beginning of next month. This means, we may, with great luck, be able to pay two more visits to Twickenham, but not more than that. Now, I *could* take a small flat somewhere—a couple of rooms, or one room even would do, provided it didn't cause too much talk—where we could go. There'd still be the difficulty of fitting in your free time with the time I could slip off from Dorothy. I know you don't like this hole-in-corner business any more than I do. But there's nothing else for it, unless you and I get married.'

She gasped and said, 'What—*married*—you and I?'

'Yes. Surely the idea doesn't come as a shock to you. It's the obvious thing. I know I should be happy with you, even when——'
He paused for a moment, searching for words, then continued—

'even when this wonderful fire that seems to be burning me up, dies down a little. You see, I'm looking a very long way ahead. And I think I could make you happy.'

'But, Mr Fawley, I'm not good enough. I'm a servant.'

He squeezed her hand almost angrily, and said, 'Oh, Magda, you sound so dreadfully old-fashioned. *Mister* Fawley, indeed! I'm lucky enough to earn a moderate income, which should be pretty safe, as incomes go, with the prospect of a pension. As for my family, it's probably nothing like as good as yours. My father taught at a village council-school and my mother's people were small tobacconists. But even suppose I were the Duke of Whatnot, what difference would it make?'

Magda said reflectively, 'I think my grandmother—on my mother's side—came from quite a good Swedish family. My grandfather was old Mr Tredennick's coachman and then his chauffeur. You know what my mother is. I don't know very much about my father, who was a German. He was a kind of clerk or agent for some firm. But apart from all that—which, as you say, perhaps isn't important—think what would happen if we really did marry, to so many other people. First of all, Mrs Fawley.'

He said shortly, 'She's my affair. I told you, that day in Twickenham, that we're no longer lovers and haven't been for several years. My feeling for her is exactly the kind of feeling one might have for a rather tiresome elder sister, for whom in a way one is responsible, but who hasn't any right to direct one's life—still less spoil it. She'll have to have a good slice of my income. I don't grudge her that, and I don't think you will, either.'

'No, no indeed. But Mrs Fawley isn't the only person. There's my mother, and Hugo and Miss Tredennick to think of.'

He looked at her in surprise and said, 'Your mother is certainly a bit of a problem. I can understand she might be very shocked. But mind, don't think that when the divorce action comes on, *you'll* be named as the co-respondent. I'll go through the usual farce with some odd woman. These things can be managed, even though the law is a bit stickier than it used to be. When I ask Dorothy for a divorce, I shan't mention you, and she won't ever suspect you—till she finds out we're legally married. As for the other two you mentioned—Hugo and Miss Tredennick, I fail to see that they have the slightest claim to be considered.'

She replied, 'I'm afraid they have—at least, my mother will think so.'

'Why should she?'

'Well, apart from loyalty—and she's quite a loyal person—she'd be most unwilling to offend Miss Tredennick in any way. She's doing very well at Number Ten—far better than she could do anywhere else—and saves every penny she can for Hugo.'

'Do you mean to say Miss Tredennick could turn you all out? What a ghastly thing the capitalist system is! But darling, we won't waste time on politics. As a matter of fact, I had a kind of idea that the house was your mother's, not Miss Tredennick's at all, except for some understanding about the top floor.'

Magda said, 'I don't really understand the legal position. Mother's rather close in some ways. But she needs my help to look after Miss Tredennick, and it wouldn't be easy for her to find someone else to take my place—apart from the expense.'

He didn't answer, but put his arm round her and pressed her very closely to his side. They had walked round the square half a dozen times, and he suddenly looked up at the houses, all tightly sealed up for the night, except for the glow showing through the glass above the front doors. 'What a world,' he said, 'what a silly, muddled world! Here are you and I wanting to talk about things as important to us as our lives, and we have to walk, like squirrels in a cage, round and round this smug square. I hate this part of London. Magda, promise me that when we're married you won't make me live anywhere near The Pollitts. I'd rather live in a slum in Bethnal Green. My word, I'm more than half an hour late! Don't think I'm in any way frightened of Dorothy, but she might get into one of her states and ring up the police. Magda, tell me this with all your great honesty. Will you stick to me, whatever happens?'

She sighed, bent her head and said, 'Yes, I can't help myself.'

'And, secondly, will you leave things to my judgment?'

'Yes, I will. But have you made up your mind what you're going to do?'

He said, 'Very nearly,' took her in his arms and kissed her many

times. She half closed her eyes and murmured, 'A few nights ago
Hugo said that somebody in Number Ten is going to die before the
end of the year. Mother thinks he's clairvoyant. Well, if he is, I only
hope he meant me—if I can die, like this, in your arms.'

He gave her a little shake in mock indignation and said, 'That
would be most inconvenient of you! I can think of one or two
people at Number Ten we could spare far more easily. You dear,
dear, silly girl, you mustn't have these fancies. Now I've got to go
and face the music. Don't come any further with me. It wouldn't
be wise. Good night, my darling.'

'Good night, my darling Robert.'

He tore himself away from her almost brusquely, waved and
ran down the road.

                              [3]

As he neared The Pollitts, Robert slowed down his pace,
mopped his brow and said to himself, 'Phew! I'm damnably out
of training.' Then he tried to put his thoughts in order so that he
could anticipate the coming scene.

What would Dorothy say to him when he came in? 'So you're
back at last? What on earth have you been doing? Don't you think
it's a little inconsiderate of you not to give me warning you were
going to be late? There's the pie to make. I thought of getting it
ready myself, but I know you don't think very much of my pastry.'

If she took that line, she should have it straight from the shoulder. 'So you want to know what I've been doing? Very well. I've
been having a lovely time with the young woman I'm going to
marry, after you've divorced me. Oh yes, I understand all about
alimony. You shall have your stud-fees, or whatever they're called.
Our relationship henceforward is purely commercial.' He lashed
himself into a factitious frenzy, which subsided almost as soon as
it arose.

But what if she merely gave him a cold, 'classy' look, and said
with arched eyebrows, 'You're *very* late to-night!' Well, then he
would answer a good deal more quietly, but say much the same
thing. 'Look here, Dorothy, there's no sense in putting off an

unpleasantness which has got to come. I've something very serious to tell you.' Etc., etc.

When he reached the front door of Number Ten, he was
annoyed to find himself feeling those qualms which even the
toughest of men are apt to feel when they reach the front door of
their dentist. With what bravado he could, he went into the hall
and saw some letters lying on the table. Mrs Muller—for it was
probably she who had taken them out of the box—had arranged
them in two piles. One was for Justin Bray,—circulars, auction
catalogues, literary magazines. The other pile consisted of three
envelopes. The top one was Garrows' monthly bill, addressed to
Mrs Fawley, the second, also addressed to her, was a bright blue
envelope with a crest on the back, and the third was an airmail
letter addressed to him. He put the two for his wife in his coat
pocket and eagerly tore open his own. As he knew, it was from
his colleague in America. His hands were almost trembling as he
skimmed it through, searching for one key sentence.

'. . . *So unless there's another complete change of plans, I shall be here
till the end of January. I shall be awfully glad if you'll go on keeping an
eye on the flat and of course using it, if it's any use to you—though I don't
suppose it will be now that it's winter again. Last night, the temperature
here . . .'*

Robert didn't bother to read the rest, but gave a big sigh of relief.
An emergency-door had suddenly been revealed, and though he
had no intention of getting out that way, it was comforting to
know it was there.

He took the stairs in twos, then stood outside the flat door which
was also that of the sitting-room. If he believed in prayer, he would
have prayed—though it would hardly have been a prayer such as any
orthodox believer could have uttered. Then he opened the door.

His wife was sitting in a chair by the fire, hunched up, looking
shrunken,—more like a doll than a woman—her elbows on her
legs and her head in her hands. She said nothing, and remained
quite motionless, while he shut the door gently. He walked
towards her and said, 'Why, Dorothy, what's the matter? I know
I'm frightfully late. As a matter of fact, I took a bit of a walk and
didn't realise——'

He stopped. Did she understand what he was saying? Was she listening? Was she ill? Was she dead? No, that slight heave of the shoulders showed that she wasn't dead. He came close up to her. 'Dorothy, *please*—do say something. Don't just sit like that. Would you like me to ring up the doctor?'

Slowly she drew her hands away from her face and turned it towards him, making no effort to hide the tears streaming down from her swollen eyes. Not knowing what to say, he waited for her to speak. Her first articulate words were, 'I'm so sorry. . . . Quite absurd. . . .You see, I thought you'd had an accident. You've never been late—so late as this, before. And the steak-pie, too.' As she said the last words, she gave an hysterical giggle.

He put his hand on her shoulder protectively, and said, 'Don't worry, you'll soon feel much better, darling.'

To his extroverted mind, there was neither irony nor incongruity in his use of the word *darling*, even though only a quarter of an hour before he had been pouring it passionately into Magda's delicious ear. 'What can I do?' he went on, fumbling nervously with his right hand among the silver in his trousers-pocket. 'Shall I bring you a glass of sherry—or gin, if we've got any left? I'll go and see.' Delighted to have an excuse for doing something, he darted to the cupboard where they kept their small supply of drinks. 'No, damn it, there isn't any, and the sherry's almost finished too. I'll tell you what, I'll slip round the corner to the off-licence and get half a bottle of gin and some sweet Martini. You'd like that, wouldn't you?'

'Yes—I should.'

He hurried out, before she could change her mind or begin to reproach him.

He had to wait ten minutes in a queue before he was served, and became almost afraid that Dorothy would construe his long absence into another accident or, worse, into another attempt at desertion. He bought a whole bottle of gin, another of sweet Martini and another of medium sherry. What a lot of money they cost! He himself rarely drank anything but beer. It was all very well to talk of taking a couple of rooms as a love-nest for Magda

THE FOURTH OF NOVEMBER

and himself, but he'd have to consider his finances rather carefully. It seemed hardly fair to let Dorothy make a bigger contribution towards Ten Pollitt Place (which she was continually suggesting) so that he could spend the money thus saved on a project which would be so little to her taste! He had given up all idea of having things out with Dorothy that evening. Besides, thanks to that most comforting letter from America, the need was less urgent. He must somehow smooth over the immediate crisis and get things running normally again. Some day, with any luck, he'd find a solution.

When he got home, he was very much surprised to see Dorothy sitting calmly in her chair looking her usual self. She had bathed her eyes and tidied herself up, and even had the same expression on her face which he had noticed when they gave one of their infrequent small parties and she was preparing to welcome her guests. (If only she'd looked like that when he first came in!)

He said, 'I'm terribly sorry I've been so long. The whole of Kensington seemed to be buying drink.'

She acknowledged the witticism with the faintest of smiles and said, 'Oh, you really shouldn't have bothered. Now, Robert, before we resume our—er—our ordinary life, I just want to tell you how extremely sorry I am that I behaved like that. It was quite idiotic. There was no excuse for it, except, I suppose, my nerves,—and one's nerves always seem a very poor excuse to other people. For goodness sake don't blame yourself in any way. Now I want to forget the whole thing from this very moment.' She paused, then glancing at the bottles which he was still holding, she added, 'Still, now that I've put you to all that trouble, a gin *would* be nice.'

'I've got gin *and* sherry, ducks.'

'That *was* extravagant, but I won't complain, if you'll let me pay. No, I insist on that. I and my friends drink our drink. You hardly touch it. Yes, half and half, please. Thank you. Now you have one. You must need it.'

Her hand as a rule was apt to tremble a little, but this time she held the glass quite steadily while she waited for him to fill his own. He did so, raised it and said, 'Cheers', which she repeated, though she didn't care for that form of convivial greeting and thought it

common. Then she said, 'Now, what about dinner? I don't at all
mind waiting while you make the pastry for the pie, but if you're
hungry . . .'

The *détente* was complete.

It wasn't till dinner was over that Robert remembered that he
had two letters for his wife in his overcoat pocket. He apologised
for his forgetfulness and produced them. She read Garrows' bill
with a frown and tossed it into her bureau, murmuring, 'I'm quite
sure this is the second time they've charged me for those stockings.
I shall have to see them to-morrow.' Then with much more interest she turned to the second letter.

When Robert came into the sitting-room, after washing up, she
said with great animation, 'I've had such an exciting letter from
Susan. She's managed to find a small flat in Brighton and she's
moving in at the week-end. And she's bought what she calls a bric-
à-brac and decorating business, which caters for the rich old ladies
of Hove. She's longing for me to see it and the flat and says I could
help her enormously. In fact, she's asked me if I could go to her on
the tenth and stay with her for a fortnight.' Dorothy paused and
gave her husband a look that was almost pleading. His heart leapt,
but he did his best to show no trace of emotion.

She continued, 'I shall have to tell her it's not much more than
three weeks since I came back from Louise.'

Robert said as judicially as he could, 'I really don't see why you
shouldn't go, if you'd like to. You might get rid of that little cough
of yours in the sea air. You know I can manage here quite well for
myself and I can always find something to do. So it's up to you,
ducks.'

She thought for a moment and said, 'Well, she's such an old
friend and I've hardly seen her for the last two years. Besides, I
really do think I could be useful to her. I could tell her what kind
of things Garrows are stocking, and what's in the other shops. I
don't suppose she's seen anything for ages, living in the country.
She always used to think a lot of my taste.'

Robert thought to himself, 'A fat lot of use she'll find you, if
there's any real work to be done!' Aloud he said, 'Well, think it over

and let me know what you decide. It's about time the vacuum was overhauled. I'll go and see to it while you write to Susan.'

Oddly enough, Dorothy felt in no way unstrung or debilitated by the scene before dinner. On the contrary, it seemed to have done her good. And though every moment she was more ashamed of her breakdown and her dependence on Robert which it implied, his reaction to it could not have been more reassuring. When it came to the point it was she who wore the trousers—she winced as the ugly phrase came into her mind—and would always wear them. That being so, she had no need of his constant presence any more than,—as she had to admit—he had need of hers. Theirs surely was the only lasting form of married love,—a love based on very deep feeling, but full of give and take and allowances for all the many incompatibilities that exist between every man and every woman.

It was in this mood of feathers well smoothed down that she tapped on his door and said she was going to bed. She didn't take any sleeping-pills that night.

VII

THE FIFTH OF NOVEMBER

DOROTHY was surprised the next morning to find herself still happy. Far too many nights she had gone to bed feeling quite serene, only to wake with the same ghastly realisation of impending doom that a convict sentenced to death must have when he wakes up from sleep in his prison cell.

It was Saturday, the Fifth of November, and incidentally Miss Tredennick's birthday. Strange to say, it was Magda who reminded Dorothy of this,—Magda, who did no work for the Fawleys and thus had no reason to enter their flat unless sent there on some unusual errand. She tapped on the door about ten o'clock and said, when Dorothy in her dressing-gown opened it, 'I'm sorry to trouble you, Madam, but Miss Tredennick asked me to give you this.

She says there's no answer.' Her voice was curt and embarrassed and she knew it, and hoping to remove any bad impression she might have made, she added, with a nervous attempt at a smile, 'You may remember, it's her birthday to-day.' Dorothy took the letter with some surprise, but said graciously enough, 'Oh, thank you, Magda. And thank you for reminding me. I'm afraid I had forgotten.'

'Good morning, Madam.' And before Dorothy could say, 'Good morning, Magda,' the girl was half-way downstairs. Dorothy thought, 'She seems odd this morning,—so pale and tense. Surely it can't be shyness. I dare say it's some young man.'

Then she read the letter. It was short, but though not written in the third person, it had a touch of old-world formality which Dorothy found almost as charming as if it had begun, 'Lady Theresa Tredennick presents her compliments to the Duchess of Fawley and requests her Grace, etc.' (These were little emotional subtleties of which poor Robert would never have a glimmering.) Frills apart, the purport of the letter was simply to ask Dorothy if it would be convenient to her to call on Miss Tredennick at eleven. The tone of the letter was so exceedingly friendly that Dorothy, who was always on tenterhooks lest some noise from her flat—a door allowed to slam, her radio, Robert's occasional fits of hammering or even the chirping of the budgerigars—might provoke a complaint from above, felt no misgivings while she prepared for the visit.

She found Miss Tredennick in her arm-chair by the window, through which streamed a warm and misty sunshine. She looked formidably aristocratic, Dorothy thought, with her long fastidious nose, keen grey eyes and determined mouth. And what a lovely boudoir-gown she was wearing. People might laugh, but lace really suited old ladies. And those two rings, the sapphire and the diamond,—if anyone else was wearing them, you'd say they couldn't be real. Dorothy felt as if she had been admitted to a queen's levée and was enjoying a social elevation which was, if anything, enhanced by her dread that she might commit some breach of etiquette.

After a few compliments on both sides, which included Dorothy's birthday greetings, Miss Tredennick came to the point. 'As you know, Mrs Fawley, I can't get downstairs without causing such a commotion that I've given up trying. What I'm going to ask you, though I'm afraid it may put you to great trouble, is, will you be kind enough to do my Christmas shopping for me? Gwen Muller did it last year, but she bought such dull things. I think she has very little imagination and, of course, she has no experience. I hear you are so very clever at these things. . . . Now these are my lists.'

Dorothy looked through them with a professional air and did her best to hide her excitement. What a huge vista of pleasures had opened up,—hours and hours of exploration in Garrows, and perhaps in those exclusive shops in Mayfair, where her investigations had hitherto been limited to peering into the windows. She almost regretted that she had promised to spend a fortnight with Susan in Brighton. But, as Miss Tredennick was at that moment telling her, there was no hurry. She could prolong her mission to the middle of December, if she liked, except for the Christmas-cards and one or two presents that were going abroad. Miss Tredennick summed up by saying, 'If you're in any doubt, just send a message by Gwen or Magda,—or come and see me, if I'm well enough. This is one of my better days, Mrs Fawley.'

She smiled and Dorothy, while making her farewells, felt she ought to curtsey. When she had opened the door and was just going out, Miss Tredennick said, 'Oh, Mrs Fawley, I do hope you and your husband are happy and really settled. It is a great relief to me to think that Gwen has such charming tenants as you both and Mr Bray. I should hate her to have to replace any of you.'

Dorothy's voice vibrated with enthusiasm as she replied, 'We're absolutely enchanted to be here, dear Miss Tredennick. I do hope we shan't ever have to go.'

Perhaps Miss Tredennick didn't altogether relish the *dear* with which Dorothy had apostrophised her; for she made her final remark in a different voice.

'I'm afraid that some day we shall all of us have to go. But I trust not just yet awhile. Goodbye, Mrs Fawley.'

[2]

Miss Tredennick had always loved the fifth of November, not only because it was her birthday, but because of its associations with fireworks. A branch of the family business had made them and pyrotechnics had been almost a part of her education. In her younger days, whenever she saw a public display of fireworks, she judged the set-pieces, rockets, Roman candles and shells like a connoisseur, and could calculate how much the beano had cost the ratepayers. Even a simple bonfire gave her pleasure, and the burning of the guy symbolised to her not only the destruction of Popery, Guy Fawkes and Titus Oates (whom, incorrectly, she regarded as another Popish conspirator), but of more recent villains, who in their various ways and at various times had threatened to disturb her peace and prosperity,—President Kruger, Lloyd-George, the Kaiser, Lenin, Trotsky, Mussolini, Hitler, Stalin and others still living, who shall be nameless.

The Silver Jubilee of King George the Fifth stood out in her memory as the grandest social occasion in her life. Polvannion had been thrown open to three hundred guests, who had the entrée to the mansion, while a suitable part of the grounds was allocated to the general public so that they could watch the show while drinking the King's health in free beer. A special coach on the train had brought the fireworks—alas, no longer made by Tredennick's Explosives—and a band of experts to fix them and let them off. The night was warm and cloudless,—very different from the night of the party which the poor Penruddockes gave with misguided emulation two years later to celebrate the Coronation of King George the Sixth. (Talk about damp squibs!) There had been no accident, no kind of hitch, no tedious waiting. And if, as was later said locally, the fiesta had left a trail of illegitimate babies behind, what touch could have been more feudal?

But those were times which would never come again. Those fiery fountains, those wheels of molten silver, those showers of coloured stars, those smoky lights, pink, green, blue, crimson, amber, which had transformed the clumps of camellias and rhododendrons into a vision of paradise, had burnt out never to be rekindled. Their extinction had marked the end of an era. Within a few weeks of the party, old Mr Tredennick had a slight stroke. He rallied well, but his long and tedious dotage had set in. His habits became eccentric and often embarrassing. Those round him lived in a continual state of apprehension, and meanwhile the further horizon was darkened by the threat of impending war. Then all the lights went out for six years, and when at last they were switched on again, they glimmered feebly over an alien landscape.

Yet life still offered a few shy consolations, and on this fifth of November Miss Tredennick was resolved to make the most of them. Chief of these was her Journal which was now becoming more like a diary, though she never lost sight of the purpose she had in view when she began it. As soon as she had got rid of Mrs Fawley, she made the morning's entry:

> Saturday, 5th November. Slept well. Fine after early fog. Showed my Christmas-lists to Mrs F. who is delighted to do my shopping. Y. V. left No. 7 at 9.20, wearing her black hat and blue two-piece, and carried her large blue bag. She walked rather slowly towards the Crescent.
>
> Hurry up, girls, the men want their treat!
> Hurry up, girls, and get on to the beat!
>
> She seemed so much less jaunty than usual, I wonder if trade is bad.

Then once more Miss Tredennick read the Journal right through from the beginning. She had to admit that the essential part, which she intended some day to copy out and present to the authorities, was, as it stood, too meagre to be impressive, and not for the first time she was strongly tempted to embellish it with details such as the following:

> A buck-nigger called at 5.30, another one at 6.10, two American sailors at 6.48. A fat, blond elderly man drove up in a Mercedes at 7.15. When the two sailors came out, he banged the knocker on the door.

But if she gave way in the smallest degree to her imagination, gone were all her hopes of bringing respectability back to Pollitt Place. She must stick to facts. Already the line between fact and fancy was becoming a little blurred, and that way, as she knew from her experience of her father in Cornwall, lay lunacy.

In the street, a very small boy threw a very small firework into
the gutter, ran a few yards and waited for the bang. Miss Tredennick smiled indulgently from above. Mrs Muller had told her earlier
that the Americans who lived at Number Nineteen in the Terrace
were having a firework party that evening for their three children,
and Miss Tredennick had said that she would like to watch it from
her sitting-room, which had an oblique view of the little gardens
behind the Terrace. She would have been glad for Hugo to come
and watch with her, but she had already sent a line to Justin, suggesting that if he had nothing better to do, he might care to come
and take a glass of sherry with her at half-past six, and she couldn't
suppose he would welcome Hugo as his fellow-guest. At the same
time it really was a shame that the poor boy shouldn't see the show.
She had even thought of writing to the Americans, who she heard
were very nice people, telling them that she had a small crippled
protégé and would be most grateful if he could join them. Americans set no store by class-distinctions—or were said not to. Besides,
Hugo's manners were perfect. You'd never think his mother was
a servant. But Miss Tredennick hated asking favours, especially if
there was the chance of a rebuff.

She was still wondering what she could plan for Hugo, when
Magda came in with her lunch.

'By the way, Magda, have you or your mother made any
arrangements for Hugo to see some fireworks to-night?'

Magda answered shortly, 'No, Madam, none.' Then she added,
as if forced to disclose something she would rather have kept
hidden, 'He did ask Mother if he could go up to the haunted room,
as he calls it,—the box-room at the top of the little staircase—and
watch the Americans from there. But of course Mother told him
he mustn't. I keep reminding him he's not allowed above stairs
except when you send for him.'

Miss Tredennick smiled almost sweetly. 'Oh, you mustn't make
me out such a dragon as all that. It wouldn't do, of course, in a
general way, for him to have the run of the upper part. One has to
consider the tenants. But just for once, there couldn't be any harm

in it. Will you tell your mother this, when you have your midday meal? You won't forget, Magda, will you?'

'No, Madam. But I don't think it's very wise, if I may say so.'

'Why, what harm could it do?'

'Well, he might get into the habit of going up on his own.'

'Oh, nonsense. I'm sure he wouldn't. And by the way, why does he call the box-room "the haunted room"?'

'He says that when we were first moving in, one of the workmen told him it was haunted, and that somebody had committed suicide there by hanging himself. My own belief is he made it up himself. He's full of the silliest fancies.'

Miss Tredennick laughed and said, 'I sincerely hope it isn't haunted, because, as I expect you know, it's supposed to be my fire-escape. The Borough Surveyor made a tremendous to-do about the sky-light,—though I can't think how you'd get *me* through it. However, just this once, Hugo shall go to the haunted room, if he wants to. I'm sure he'll manage to exorcise the ghost.'

'Very well, Madam, I'll tell Mother what you say.'

[3]

By two o'clock the mist had a yellowish tinge and the sun was no more than a circle of dull luminous paint on a smoky wall. An hour later it had disappeared and the mist had quite definitely turned into a fog. The houses opposite became first smudgy then invisible. Traffic slowed down and almost ceased. The shoes of people walking on the pavement might have been bound round with cotton-wool and made vague vibrations rather than clear-cut sounds.

Miss Tredennick, who had moved laboriously from the armchair by her bedroom window to a similar chair in her sitting-room, was bitterly disappointed. She had hoped to see the Americans preparing for their party,—pinning Catherine-wheels on boards, erecting some sort of stand for the jack-in-the-box, planting the Roman candles in wine bottles and attaching sticks to the rockets. But their little garden was a well of blackness. Once or twice, it is true, she heard voices which made it clear that so far there had been no change of plan. 'No, Emerson, not quite so near the shed. . . . It shouldn't catch the cherry-tree from here. . . . How far does this one spurt? Surely you asked the salesman when you bought it? . . . Oh, he wouldn't know. . . . Just another couple of bangers for the guy's feet. . . . Gee, Pop, look at Otis! He's smuggling some indoors. . . . Now, sonny, if I catch you up to those tricks again . . . Emerson, come right down. . . .'

Then there was silence,—a very long and tedious silence, which lasted till Justin, panting slightly from the effort of two flights of stairs, tapped on the door.

'Oh, do come in, Mr Bray. You're looking well. It's such an age since I have seen you. And thank you so much for your very charming card of good wishes. . . . If you draw up that chair, you'll have a good view, if there's anything to see. This fog is too cruel. Now, tell me . . .'

They chatted together like two very old friends of the same sex. Justin glowed inwardly at the thought that his presence could still confer a pleasure, and Miss Tredennick glowed too, because she could, at the age of seventy-six—no, seventy-seven!—summon distinguished authors to her salon. (O loneliness, the nightmare of old age!)

'It's really wonderful what respect Americans have for our traditions. We have passed the torch of our civilisation to them, even though in our fog we can hardly see it.'

'Yes, we've been most misguided to underrate them. After all, if it weren't for them, you and I would be digging for uranium in Siberia.'

'True,—sadly true.'

(Why couldn't the show begin?)

'I suppose they're all having a kind of tea indoors.'

Justin said, 'I always hated fireworks when I was a boy. I suppose I was frightened of them. Now I regret I didn't enjoy them when I could.'

Miss Tredennick answered, 'How funny, I always used to love them—and still do. Ah, I think I hear something. Look, they've opened the french window leading into the garden.'

The fog seemed to have lifted just a little, and they could see

vague shapes trooping into the garden, and the darting beam of
a torch. There was a rising hubbub of young voices, which suddenly sank to that special sound which is only emitted by those
who watch fireworks,—a kind of 'Ooaaah!', like the backwash of a
wave which has broken on a sandy beach. The first Roman candle
had launched its first tiny star. Miss Tredennick thought, 'How
pitifully small,—but better than nothing, very much better than
nothing', while Justin sipped his sherry and regretted that he'd
never assembled his Seven Silent Sinners round a bonfire, each
guilty face shown up luridly by the blaze. (But even that wouldn't
have made the book a success.)

Next came a triangle-wheel, which seemed to have been inju-
diciously sited; for a shrill female voice was deploring the danger
to Mrs Anderson's trellis, and a man shouted, 'Dwight, Dwight—
Dwight! Keep away. Do you want all your hair singed off?' From
the top floor of Ten Pollitt Place the danger looked very slight.
Miss Tredennick murmured, 'Of course, they don't make them
now, as *we* used to make them.'

'I beg your pardon?'

'Nothing. I was dreaming of my girlhood.'

Their silence was broken by a very loud bang, followed at once
by the sound of children crying. 'Oh, Waldo, I said no really noisy
ones. You'll make our neighbours hate us. Now, Lorna, isn't that
pretty?' A silver fountain shot up near the post which on Tuesdays
held one end of the washing-line. 'Ooaaah!' Yes, that one was a
real success. Then more Roman candles, then three Catherine-
wheels let off simultaneously. A good touch, that. Miss Tredennick
nodded with professional approval. Then a couple of crackers
spat through the lower darkness, feet scuttled in a stampede, and
among the shrieks a male voice shouted, 'Otis, you wait! I'll give
you such a tanning when I catch you!' Something about the words
and the quality of the voice which had uttered them gave both
Miss Tredennick and Justin an obscure masochistic thrill. (What a
fine show it was!) Then came the jack-in-the-box, though when it
exploded, it didn't rival the crackers. More Roman candles, more
Catherine-wheels, and then three timid rockets which hardly rose
as high as the Fawleys' windows. Then the voice which had threat-

ened Otis with a tanning, said, 'Well, I guess it's time we had the bonfire.'

There were movements, counter-movements and in the background a slightly impatient shuffling of feet. Then, with a roar the whole scene was lit up, revealing two hot adult males, three adult women still full of their transatlantic poise, and a dozen children, dancing and clapping and nudging one another and giggling at the crude face of the guy, whose outer covering was already aflame. 'That's Hitler, that is. No, it's Stalin. No it isn't, he's dead. It's ——, it's —— or ——' (The blanks represent candidates for the position of America's Public Enemy Number One, and to fill them in might be no less indiscreet than to disclose Miss Tredennick's pet political aversion of the moment.)

The feet were the first to explode, then came the hands, then the heart (very loudly), then lastly the head which almost shook the foundations of Number Ten. Then a woman said in a deep-bosomed contralto, 'Now, folks, as we're in England and we may have upset some of our neighbours, I think we ought to close— this being a *vurry* English festival—with *God save the Queen.*'

While the assembly struggled half-heartedly with the National Anthem, came the real climax of the evening. A bright pink smoky glow spread slowly outwards from the top of Number Ten and hovered over the little gardens down below. Its calm radiance seemed like a thanksgiving and a benediction. The National Anthem broke off, and someone, perhaps a daughter of the house, cried, 'Well done, Miss Trewallock!', and soon a dozen eager voices, making the slogan into a chant such as one imagines might be roared out on the campus of an American university, repeated in unison, 'Well—done—Miss—Trewallock!'

Oh, if only her stiff knees were supple enough to allow her to bow her acknowledgments from the window! But how had it happened? Of course, it was Hugo,—dear Hugo, patiently watchful in the solitude of the haunted room, and judging, with a master's precision, the time to let off his one little firework. He was a boy in a thousand.

She turned to Justin and said, 'You know, it was Hugo who let off that Bengal light. He's in the roof,—in the box-room.'

Justin said, with a courtly admiration, 'What a perfect finale! How did you come to think of it?'

Miss Tredennick blushed slightly as she replied, 'But I didn't. It was Hugo's own idea. Well, everything's over now. If you'd draw the curtains, it would be most kind.'

She didn't know that two days before, Hugo had asked his friend the dustman where he lived, and that the dustman had told him he had a flat on the topmost floor of a new council-building that towered in what had been a derelict area of back-streets just off the shabbier end of Parkwell Road. 'It faces this way,' he had said. 'We can see the Square and the Crescent quite easily and I dare say we can see the backs of these houses, though it's hard to know which is which. If you could get on the roof and wave a flag, we might be able to signal to one another.' Then he looked down at Hugo's leg and added, 'But don't you go trying any larks like that.' Hugo asked, 'Would it do if I waved from one of our top windows?' The dustman said, 'Yes, I should think so. Some day I'll borrow a pair of field-glasses and make quite sure.'

So the crowning achievement of the evening was not, after all, an ingenious compliment paid to the nice Americans in Pollitt Terrace, but a summons such as Isolde, waving her white scarf in the darkness, sent out to Tristan,—though, alas, there was no guarantee that this Tristan would turn his eyes that way.

[4]

The fog thickened again, and Magda, when she was settling Miss Tredennick for the night, suggested that it might be as well to shut both the windows. But Miss Tredennick insisted that one of them should be left a few inches open at the top. However poisonous a fog might be, she never found it so suffocating as the claustrophobic sensation that came over her if she was shut up in a room that had no outlet to the sky.

She went to sleep early, but woke again about midnight and found herself listening to some slow, muffled footsteps in the street. They stopped outside Number Seven. Miss Tredennick forced herself out of bed and went to the window, where she raised the corner of one of the curtains and peeped out. Even the street-lamp was only a pale, brownish smudge and illumined nothing. But though there was nothing to see, there was something to hear,—two murmuring voices, so indistinct at first that it was impossible to give them a sex. Then one of them revealed itself as a woman's,—*that* woman's—and soon became loud enough for Miss Tredennick to catch some of the words. 'Very sweet of you. . . .' (The tone was ironical, as the next remark showed.) 'I wouldn't ask you in if you were the Duke of Edinburgh. . . . Oh, get the Hell out of here and go back to Lucy. . . . It's no use telling me. . . . Yes, I'm ever so deeply obliged to you for seeing me home, but that's quite enough. . . . I'm through with you, I tell you. . . . I hope you fall in the river and get drowned.' A door slammed, and once more there was the sound of muted footsteps, growing fainter and fainter, as they neared the Crescent.

What a fruitful entry for to-morrow's Journal! But tomorrow held more than that in store.

VIII

THE SIXTH OF NOVEMBER

On Sundays the inhabitants of Pollitt Place for the most part woke late and didn't hurry downstairs. Indeed, the first sign of life came as a rule when the news-boy made a clatter with the letter-boxes, as he delivered the papers. Miss Tredennick, who after her midnight vigil had slept soundly till nearly half-past seven, heard him approaching on the southern side of the street, while his colleague, some way behind, did the northern side. Rat-a-tat, rat-a-tat, but far clumsier than the postman's. This knock had the air of a piece of cheek or a practical joke. Rat-a-tat, Number Eleven, and the same to you, Number Nine. Then a pause, a piercing whistle and a shout. 'Harry, come here! Har-ry, come and look at this, quick!' Footsteps ran down the street and stopped outside Number Seven. 'Phew! What a nerve! Do you think we ought to tell 'em? . . . No, 'taint our business. I'm going to find Ted. Hullo, Alf! Look at this! They'll be rubbing it out in a minute!'

Once more, Miss Tredennick was at the window. The fog had almost cleared. Outside the threshold of Number Seven, a group of boys—'errand-boys' one would have called them in the old days—had sprung up as if by a miracle. Their jeering comments echoed across the street. 'That's a bit of all right! Now, Jim, you'll know where to leave your visiting-card! My word, won't old Mother O'Blahoney be wild! She'll go absolute crackers. You wait till the cops get on to it!'

Miss Tredennick almost shouted 'Stand clear!', so impatient was she to see what they were looking at. Then a fat female figure, wearing bedroom-slippers and an overcoat that implied a scantiness beneath it, waddled out of the basement of Number Fourteen and crossed the road. As she approached, the spectators gave ground, and Miss Tredennick saw, in big black letters against the dirty yellow paint of the front door, the inscription:

A TART LIVES HERE

With dark looks at the clustered boys, who were giggling and making indecent gestures behind her back, the woman pressed the bell and kept her finger on the push for several minutes. At last the front door opened a few inches and Mrs O'Blahoney's dishevelled head appeared round the corner. 'Lord! What *is* all this about, Mrs Petcham?' She drew back the door, hiding herself behind it, and the visitor went inside, where presumably a conference took place. The two newspaper boys were continuing their rounds, and the other boys had thinned out and withdrawn a little, so that they could pretend in case of trouble that they were not involved in the affair. At five to eight, the door opened again. Mrs Petcham came out first, called over her shoulder, 'Don't you forget to ring up the police, Mrs O'Blahoney,' crossed the road and went down to her basement home. Mrs O'Blahoney came next, in a man's mackintosh and a huge straw sun-hat, such as one of the would-be Bright Young Things might once have worn on Margate beach. She was followed, not by Miss Varioli, but by a tall, thin, elderly woman in a brown house-coat. Between them, they carried some sheets of corrugated paper, which they tried to fix with drawing-pins over the odious words. But they didn't find it too easy. The drawing-pins broke and the paper split, while Mrs O'Blahoney expressed her indignation in a loud monologue.

Miss Tredennick would have liked to sit and watch for ever, but she couldn't run the risk of being caught there by Magda, who might arrive any moment now with her early tea. She got back to bed and composed herself just in time. She found a slightly malicious pleasure in saying, as soon as Magda opened the bedroom door, 'There seems to have been a most extraordinary commotion outside, Magda. Do you know what it was all about? Boys whistling and shouting—on a Sunday morning too.'

Magda answered, 'Yes, Madam. Somebody painted something very offensive on the front door of Number Seven. Mrs O'Blahoney and Mrs Casey have been covering it up with paper. I hope the police will catch the hooligan.' Something prim and smug about the reply impelled Miss Tredennick to embarrass her further.

'Did you see the words?'

'Yes, Madam.'

'What were they, exactly?'

'I'd rather not repeat them to you, Madam. Perhaps you'll ask Mother, if you're set on knowing.'

The counter-attack took Miss Tredennick at a disadvantage. She parried it by saying, 'Oh, if they're really as bad as you imply, perhaps I'd better not know,—though we elderly ladies are not so easily shocked as you young ones think. Has the fog cleared?'

'Yes, Madam, it's almost gone. Oh, there's a policeman ringing the front-door bell of Number Seven.'

Miss Tredennick yawned and said, 'Well, I've no doubt he'll very soon get to the bottom of it. Thank you. Why, where's the *Sunday Times*?'

'What, Madam, isn't it there? I am so sorry. I'll slip down the road and get one. I suppose the boy got muddled.'

Miss Tredennick smiled as she said, 'No doubt the excitement was too much for him,' and complacently sipped her tea.

An hour later, when she had finished her breakfast, a strange idea came suddenly into her head. She called for Magda, who was washing up the breakfast-things, and asked to see Hugo as soon as might be convenient. Magda said, with that hint of disapproval that appeared in her tone whenever a visit from Hugo was in question, 'Well, Madam, he seemed so very drowsy this morning that Mother said she'd give him breakfast in bed, and let him stay there till dinner-time, if he wants to. But if it's anything urgent, I'm sure Mother'll make him get up at once.'

'Oh, don't hurry him on my account. Any time will do.'

But would it, she wondered as soon as Magda had gone out and shut the door. That policeman, now, was he still nosing round? The sooner she was at her post, the better. Once more in her favourite chair she looked out of the window. No policeman was visible in the street, but a small knot of people stood in a circle watching a man who was amateurishly daubing thick black paint all over the door of Number Seven. Miss Tredennick thought, 'So they'll have a respectable black door like ours. That's one thing to the good—but what shoddy work!' She noticed that Miss Varioli's bedroom curtains were still closely drawn. Was the guilty woman up there, squirming with rage and mortification, or was she sleeping through the whole business? Surely she must have been roused by the noise earlier on? It would be interesting to see her sortie that morning—if she made one. It seemed appropriate that she should emerge in a white sheet, with a halter round her neck,— but it was much more likely that she'd go to her beat flaunting her gayest colours. Then Miss Tredennick put in some hard work on her Journal.

It was nearly midday when Hugo knocked at her door. He looked tired and paler than usual and there was an apprehensiveness in his big eyes. Miss Tredennick came to the point at once.

'Good morning, Hugo. Now answer me truthfully. Did you paint those words on the door of Number Seven?'

She anticipated that he would play for time, say, 'What words do you mean?' or utter half-hearted denials—for she couldn't believe he was a hardened liar—but after he had given her one quick penetrating glance, he said simply, 'Yes, Madam, I did.'

The confession was so sudden and so complete, that Miss Tredennick didn't know how to reply. She was far too pleased with what he had done, to simulate indignation. When at length she found her tongue, all she could say was, 'But, Hugo, *why?*'

He answered, 'Because I hate her.'

'Whom do you mean by *her?* Mrs O'Blahoney, if that's the old woman's name?' (Miss Tredennick knew quite well whom Hugo meant, but she had her own end to keep up.)

'No, no. The young woman whom you can smell when she passes you in the street.'

'Hugo, what *are* you saying?'

'I suppose it's all that cheap scent she puts on herself. I think she's really wicked. Are you going to tell my mother?'

Miss Tredennick paused, while she pretended to be considering such a possibility. Then she said, 'No, I've decided to say nothing about it. But I must warn you'—she put all the sternness she could into her voice—'that if you were found out you would get into the most serious trouble. I mean, with the police. I think you've committed what is called a criminal libel. Your mother might have to pay an enormous fine, or you might be sent to a reformatory. Do you understand?'

'Yes, Madam, I suppose what I've done was very wrong.'

'Well, it was certainly very dangerous. Now tell me, what have you done with the paint-pot and the brush? If the police suspect you, they'll search the whole house.'

'I put them into a dust-bin.'

'Not *ours*, I hope! What do you think that big red-headed dustman would say, if a pot of black paint fell out when he emptied the bin? He'd have to report his find to the police at once. This affair will be the talk of the whole neighbourhood for several days. I shall be surprised if it doesn't get in the papers.'

Hugo blushed scarlet. Miss Tredennick had put her finger on a most tender spot. Had he not conceived the whole exploit with the hope of saving the big red-headed dustman from the perils of what the Sunday newspapers called 'the vice of the streets'? Miss Tredennick, misconstruing his silence, went on, 'Well, Hugo, if you've put the paint and the brush in our bin, you must get them out as soon as ever you can and hide them away till we can make some plan for getting rid of them properly.'

'But, Madam,' he said reproachfully, as if surprised that she could have thought him so stupid, 'I didn't put them in *our* bin. I carried them in a bag for a long way and put them in a bin that belongs to some flats,—council-flats, I think—near the bend in Parkwell Road. I managed to find my way there in spite of the fog, and I'm quite sure nobody saw me.'

Miss Tredennick almost clapped her hands in applause, and couldn't resist saying, 'Oh, Hugo,—well done! But what a dangerous criminal you would make. I hope you'll never do anything wrong—really wrong, I mean—not like this prank of yours— though as I said, if you'd been caught, you'd be in the most dreadful trouble. Are you quite sure nobody in the street could see you leaving this house,—or while you were busy by the door opposite?'

'The fog was so thick, I couldn't see the letters while I was painting them.'

'But you must have made some noise, going up the area-steps, or opening the basement-door.'

'Mother keeps the basement-door well oiled, so it shan't disturb you. I was very careful about the steps and about the gate at the top. It took me nearly ten minutes to get up to it.'

'Wasn't it lucky that the night was so foggy?'

'But, Madam, I was waiting for a fog.'

'So you've had the idea for some time?'

'Yes, I got the idea about a fortnight ago,—one day when *she* walked down our side of the street. I felt that someone ought to drive her away.'

'You know, Hugo, in some very odd respects you and I are very much alike. You don't understand me? Perhaps it's just as well. Now, if they ask you downstairs what we've been talking about, you must say—what will you say?'

Hugo smiled and said, 'I shall tell them you were giving me just a little scolding for letting off that firework yesterday. You could make that true, if you think it's necessary.'

'But, Hugo, it was a lovely firework. I certainly can't bring myself to scold you for that. Mr Bray and I thought it very beauti-

ful, and the Americans enjoyed it too. I'm afraid you'll have to
think of a better story.'

Hugo shrugged his hunched shoulders, as if the subject were
not worth discussing. Then he said pleadingly, 'So you really won't
tell Mother or Magda about what I've done? I couldn't bear Magda
to know. She spies on me.'

There was the sound of a footstep on the landing outside the
bedroom door. Miss Tredennick put a finger to her lips and said,
'Sh! There she is. Goodbye—and remember, you've been lucky
this time.'

Hugo made his little bow and went out of the room, while
Magda, giving him an unfriendly look, went through the sitting-
room into the kitchen to prepare Miss Tredennick's luncheon.
Meanwhile, the old woman sat full of her thoughts in her chair by
the window. Miss Varioli's curtains were still closely drawn. Could
she be lying behind them, dead of shame?

IX

THE REST OF NOVEMBER

It wasn't surprising that Magda's nerves were on edge. Since her
evening walk with Robert round Thurloe Square, she had hardly
seen him. He had just found time, the next morning, to whisper
to her on his way downstairs, 'She was in such a state when I got
back last night, I couldn't say anything. It wouldn't have been fair.
But she's going away on Thursday for a whole fortnight, and I've
got the flat in Twickenham till after Christmas. So we've plenty of
time to make our plans.'

The cause of Magda's uneasiness wasn't the doubt as to
whether Robert intended to marry her or not. She was anything
but a sacramentalist, and didn't believe that even if all the formali-
ties,—divorce, banns, marriage in church—were complied with,
they could ever wash away the fatal stain on her conscience. That
would remain—to torment her in her last illness and damn her
when dead. But her delight in Robert's presence had the power to

make the joy of the moment outweigh Hell's eternity. (She never ventured to wonder if a just God could be so ruthless as to requite a momentary sin with eternal damnation.) Oh, if Robert could always be with her, she'd be his servant, his slave, gladly losing her soul to keep his body. But, alas, he couldn't. He went to work in the morning and came back at six to spend the evening with his wife,—while she herself trudged grimly up and down stairs, looking after Miss Tredennick and Mr Bray and helping her mother and keeping an eye on Hugo.

The antipathy which she now had for Hugo almost frightened her. She had long admitted to herself that she was jealous of him, though she had done her best to repress the ugly feeling. But somehow, since she had given way to a guilty romance, her self-control had weakened in other respects as well. It wasn't difficult to excuse herself for drawing Justin's attention to the missing cigarettes. After all, he might easily have suspected her, and it wasn't fair to expect her to bear that burden for Hugo's sake, even had she been fond of him. But she knew that part of her motive was sheer malice,—the wish to discredit a mother's favourite child. She was ashamed of herself, but not repentant, and regretted that Justin himself had refused to play up. She was convinced that he was shielding Hugo, but what could she do, with the two of them against her?

What a way the boy had of getting round people! Even the hard and matter-of-fact Miss Tredennick seemed to dote on him, and was prepared to forgive almost any liberty he might choose to take. There was something unpleasant, something almost unhealthy, in the way she kept inviting him to come to her bedroom. Oh, why couldn't he be like other boys,—play with other boys or even run after girls? He was old enough, despite all those baby-ways which he shed and assumed so easily by turns.

Magda knew that she had already gone too far in her dislike of him. She had lost some of her mother's affection by urging her to send him to a school and the caution she had given Miss Tredennick against giving him too free a run of the house had not been received with favour. Quite possibly Justin despised her for telling tales about her brother. It was a mercy that the Fawleys so seldom

saw him, or he might make mischief in that quarter too. But Mrs
Fawley was always so wrapped up in herself that it was doubtful if
she remembered the existence of the cripple who lived in the basement. Perhaps dear Robert, with his readier sympathy, thought
him rather pathetic, though he had once remarked, 'Your brother
somehow makes me feel uncomfortable,—poor little chap.' (She
didn't know that Robert had said to himself, 'I think that boy's a
bloody little pervert. He looks at me as a woman looks at a man!')
    Her thoughts, as always now, when she was unhappy, swung
back to Robert hungrily. While he was with her, she could forget
her worries and her sins. Oh that Thursday would come!

[2]

    On Thursday, at half-past twelve, Dorothy came downstairs
with a suitcase. Another suitcase, which Robert had carried down
earlier, was waiting for her in the hall. Magda, coming up from the
basement at that moment, said, 'Oh, Mrs Fawley, can I get you a
taxi?' Dorothy said, 'That would be kind, if you're sure you're not
too busy,' admired herself in a Chinese Chippendale mirror, that
had come from the drawing-room at Polvannion, and sat down.
She had never taken greatly to Magda, whom she thought too shy
or too sullen to make a congenial servant, though no doubt the
girl was an excellent worker. She couldn't be having very much
of a life, spending her days upstairs with Miss Tredennick (who,
though a charming old lady, could no doubt be a tyrant when the
mood took her), or on the ground-floor, cleaning Mr Bray's beautiful things, and tied, in such free time as she had, to that stick of a
mother. No wonder she went about with a look of glum resigna-
tion. Still, just lately, perhaps, she had been looking a little more
alive, though one couldn't say she looked happy. Again Dorothy
wondered idly (as she had done on the morning of Miss Tredennick's birthday), if Magda had a young man. She might be quite
attractive if she had proper clothes and knew how to wear them.
    Dorothy surveyed her own outfit with pride. It was one of Gar-
rows' new season's models. She wanted to make a good impression
on Susan, and she'd always heard that Hove, if not Brighton, was a

smart resort. After all, she might just as well wear her best things there as hoard them for London. Robert never noticed what she was wearing, and they so rarely went out to places where clothes mattered.

It promised to be a most exciting fortnight—putting finishing touches to Susan's new flat and dressing the window of her little shop—and when she came back, there'd be only one more week of November to get through before December and Christmas. During that time, she'd have her own shopping to do, and Miss Tredennick's to finish. About Christmas itself, she was still undecided. Louise might ask her and Robert to join the house-party in Cambridgeshire, but Dorothy doubted if Robert would accept. It hardly seemed right for her to go there and leave him alone in London, though he probably wouldn't be at all unhappy. He'd find something to tinker at in his workshop, and no doubt some colleague of his or one of his Hackfield friends would ask him out for dinner on Christmas Day.

Then a more thrilling possibility occurred to her. She might persuade Susan to come to London over the holidays. Susan could sleep on the sofa in the sitting-room,—or could they turn Robert's study into a bedroom, just for those few days? (Her enterprising mind had already transformed Robert's workshop into a study.) At all events, there were two or three ways of escape from what in her heart she most dreaded,—being forced to spend dark day after dark day cooped up with Robert in the flat, with no shops to look at, no little parties to go to, and probably no friends to come and see her. That was more or less what had happened the previous year, and she was resolved to do all she could not to let it happen again.

The taxi arrived. Magda helped her in with her luggage and stood watching while the taxi turned into the Crescent. Then she sighed with relief and thought, 'If only something could happen to stop her from ever coming back here.'

In the area, Hugo was talking to Bert, and caught Magda's eye as she glanced down at him from the steps. The dustman said, 'Do you know, you've got a very pretty sister?' Hugo scowled as he answered, 'She's dull and often bad-tempered. And she's horrid to

me, whenever she gets the chance. I wish she would go away and
work somewhere else.'

[3]

When Robert came home from his office that evening, his first
thought was to make sure that his wife had really left the house. Yes,
her two suitcases had gone, and so had her toilet-things, dressing-
gown, bedroom slippers and night-dress—though he noticed with
amusement that Swinburne's *Atalanta* still lay on the bedside table.
Then he went to the sitting-room, turned out the lights, and in
unconscious imitation of Miss Tredennick, sat in a chair by the
window, keeping watch. But unlike her gaze, which moved up and
down between the front door and top window of Number Seven,
his was directed only to the area gate of Number Ten and the iron
stairway leading up to it.

He hadn't long to wait before he saw, first Hugo, and then Mrs
Muller climbing up the steps and emerging on to the pavement.
As soon as their backs disappeared at the street-corner, Robert
drew the curtains, careful to leave no chinks through which an
inquisitive neighbour opposite could spy. Then he went to the bedroom, stripped and had a bath. While he was drying himself, he
noticed a bottle of eau-de-Cologne on a shelf in the bathroom,
and like a young schoolgirl who tries the effect of her mother's
lipstick for the first time, he took it down and dabbed the scent all
over his chest and under his arms. Then he walked naked into the
bedroom and was about to dress himself, when he felt a sudden
distaste for his travel-stained clothes and wondered if they smelt.
He bundled them impulsively into a drawer and took out a pair
of clean pyjamas and a thin silk dressing-gown (a gift from Dorothy the previous Christmas, though he had never yet worn it), and
put them on. Then he went back to the sitting-room and without
switching on the light he opened the door a couple of inches and
listened for Magda's footsteps on the stairs.

She came up from the basement soon before seven. When she
reached the first landing, he saw her pause just outside the door,
looking uneasy and puzzled because it was ajar. He flung it wide

open, and seizing her in his arms, carried her over the threshold into the dark room and kissed her passionately. She made no effort to struggle from his embrace, but whispered to him, 'I've got to get her dinner ready first. She's only having a little soup—which is ready—and an omelette. I'll come to you on my way down, but I shan't be able to stay more than twenty minutes, as I shall have to go upstairs again and wash up and settle her for the night.'

He said, 'And after that, darling? What is the earliest your mother and Hugo will be back?'

'They can't be back before a quarter to eleven, if they stay for the whole film. Of course, if Hugo says he's feeling ill or bored—and he might easily—they might be back any time.'

'We shall have to risk that,' he murmured. 'I'm so excited to-night, I'm prepared to risk anything—and to make you risk it. I should like to walk hand in hand with you down the street and let those prying people at the windows see us together and point at us and hiss their silly disapproval. It's all your doing. I've never been like this before.'

She said, 'I must go now,' drew herself gently away, smoothed her hair and her dress and went upstairs.

When she came down again, she found that he'd made some coffee and laid a tray with potted shrimps and brown bread-and-butter.

He said, 'I don't see why you shouldn't have your dinner while she's having hers.' Magda smiled happily and answered, 'But what will Mother say when she comes home and finds I haven't eaten my supper in our kitchen?'

'Is she bound to know?'

'Well, I think I can make it look as if I have. But, Robert, how long shall we have to go on pretending like this?' The moment she had asked the question she regretted it, but he answered readily, 'We're not even going to consider that question to-night—or any other question. There's a whole lovely fortnight ahead of us. Now, tell me honestly—can you cut bread-and-butter quite as thin as I can?'

She laughed outright. 'Yes, much thinner. When Miss Tredennick has it for tea, it's almost as thin as tissue-paper.'

They chatted gaily, but with a nervous eagerness, as if both of them, knowing that this interlude must be short, longed for it to be over. When it was time for Magda to go upstairs again, Robert said, 'I don't know how I shall bear waiting for you. You must hurry and skimp your work, or I shall go mad!'

When she had gone, he cleared up the remains of their little meal and paced up and down the room, with his eye on the clock. The strain of his inaction was so great that every nerve in his body began to quiver in an agony of frustration, and he had a feeling of panic. What was the matter with him? Was he losing his grip on himself? Was this the way that nervous breakdowns started? Would he soon find himself shouting or sobbing or tearing his hair, or, worse, ringing up for a doctor?

Then suddenly it occurred to him to wonder what he would do if Magda didn't come to see him again that night. Suppose, for example, Miss Tredennick felt ill and wanted Magda to sit up with her? If that happened, he thought he would really go mad. He'd rush upstairs, seize the selfish old bitch by the shoulders and fling her out of the window, like Jezebel. Or he'd strangle her quietly or smother her with a pillow. Anything to rid the world of such an incubus. As it was, he'd half a mind to storm into her bedroom and let her know what would come to her, if she showed any sign of interfering between him and Magda.

Again, he wondered what was the matter with him. Was this the normal result of being in love? He'd never felt like that about Dorothy, with whom—evidently—he'd never been in love at all. Perhaps it wasn't surprising that theologians and sociologists disapproved of passionate love, the former declaring that it came between man and his Maker, and the latter discouraging it as apt to impair the smooth working of the social organism. Well, let the theologians and sociologists rant as they would, he was in love with Magda, and that was enough.

When she came down and tapped softly on the door, these and other perplexities troubled neither of them for two splendid hours.

On the floor above, Miss Tredennick was lying awake. She had tried to sleep, but for some reason her mind was restless. She switched on the light and picked up the book by her bed,—some nineteenth-century memoirs—but they failed to hold her attention and she turned the pages mechanically, hardly taking in a word of what she was reading. The whole time, she was waiting for something to happen in the street or in Number Seven, and she interpreted every faint noise that reached her ears as signal that some drama was about to begin. But nothing rewarded her wakefulness that night.

Justin too was in bed and sleepless. He had dined early with his publisher, who lived at some distance from London, and had been told, rather brutally, that *Seven Silent Sinners* had been a failure from the financial point of view and that there had been no gain of prestige to justify the expense. As for Justin's new book, his publisher didn't even ask what its title was to be.

But this was only one of Justin's worries. The rather odd sensation near his heart—not exactly a pain, though no doubt it would soon become one—was troubling him again, although he'd come home in a taxi. On the way, he had also noticed a dryness at the back of his throat and nose which meant that another cold was in store for him. One of his two remaining teeth was aching a little, and if that had to come out, there would be no escape from a new and much more cumbersome sort of denture. The political news was poor and the Government was every day losing its popularity, while prices were dwindling on the Stock Exchange. Suppose Labour got in and really put their new programme into force? How would he live? Twenty years before, he might have subsisted on his royalties, but now they would hardly pay for his sherry. He was getting too old and tired to struggle on much longer. How right Lord Hervey was when he said to his friend Lady Mary Wortley Montagu, *The last stages of an infirm life are filthy roads.*

And more than once, when Justin heard a slight noise overhead, he looked up at the ceiling and thought of the Fawleys, and envied them for their good health and comparative youth, their adaptability to a changing world and, above all, for the companionship which they had with one another.

[4]

The fortnight that followed was for Robert and Magda a period of rapture such as neither of them had conceived to be possible. Their appetite grew on what fed it. Magda's scruples and doubts were banished for a while by the ecstasy of her first emotional awakening, and even for Robert the experience was almost as rich. Dorothy's response to his love-making, though genuine in its way, had always a kind of archness about it, as if something impelled her to transform her passion into a pretty bedroom-ornament, and he now found in Magda's love a single-mindedness and an intensity of which he hadn't guessed women were capable.

Love may indeed ennoble a character, but it may also play havoc with old moral values and make a stubborn sense of duty appear in the guise of a neurotic inhibition. For the first time in his life, Robert took to excusing himself for leaving his office early on the score of a chill or a headache, and for the first time in hers, Magda made it clear to her mother that her long hours of work must be shortened and that, above all, her free time must really be her own to use as she liked. In vain, Mrs Muller kept saying interrogatively, 'Well, Magda, I know I can trust you and I don't want to spoil your life, but I think you might trust me,' but Magda replied, 'I really don't know what you mean. All that work, all that staying indoors, was getting me down. You noticed it yourself.' So her mother spent more of her time looking after Miss Tredennick (who asked a sly question or two, but didn't press too hard for an answer), and got in a charwoman to do the rough work downstairs.

Robert and Magda found the flat in Twickenham an irresistible attraction, and slipped off there whenever they could, even though the journey might take much longer than the time they could spend there together. Robert had a spare latch-key cut and gave it to Magda so that she should have access to the flat whenever she wished. Sometimes she arrived half an hour before he did—they made a point of travelling separately, for part of the way, at least—and her keenest delight was to sit waiting for him, as if by some miracle she had the privilege (shared by a million suburban housewives, and shared too by Dorothy,—though Magda preferred not to think of this), of expecting the punctual return of her husband, the bread-winner, as soon as his day's work was over. To heighten the illusion, she bought a few knicknacks, a vase, an earthenware dog, a cheap colour-print, and put them about the flat, which henceforward became symbolically her home.

Meanwhile, the day fixed for Dorothy's return approached, and almost at the last minute was deferred for another week. She had caught a touch of 'flu and Susan insisted on her staying in Brighton till she was really well enough to face the fogs of London. Both Robert and Magda were now living in such a world of fantasy, that this reprieve seemed hardly remarkable. It is true that Robert, less fatalistic than Magda, did sometimes in his more cool-blooded moments consider what he would do when Dorothy came back. The evening when he had almost promised Magda in Thurloe Square that he would have things out with his wife, as soon as he got home, and then had been thwarted by her fit of hysterics, made him distrust his power to launch his thunderbolt out of the blue. He was confident that if she gave him the slightest opening, he would be able to make it into an effective breach between them, but the opening itself must be made by her. If ever she reproached him for being uncompanionable, for neglecting her, for being restless or moody, he would speak out at once. It seemed unlikely that she would ever suspect him of being unfaithful to her, but if she did, either intuitively—though he'd never believed in woman's intuition—or because some accident had put her on her guard,—if ever he caught her playing the detective, asking artless but awkward questions or spying on him, he would hide nothing from her except Magda's name. Far the best solution would be that Dorothy should find herself so much happier with Susan or some other friend of hers, than she was with him, that she would take the initiative herself, and ask him for her freedom. He knew that as it was, he often bored her. Very well, in future he would be ten times more of a bore, exasperate her by asking ignorant questions almost on the crude level of 'What are Keats?', and not listening to her replies. This was the nearest he could bring himself to actual cruelty. It wasn't in his nature to shirk his share of the housework, cooking or washing-up, however politic it might have been to do so.

Perhaps the weakness and the cowardice inherent in such a compromise might have come home to him, if Magda had even once thrown out a hint that it was time for him to 'make an honest woman' of her. But she still believed that more than marriage was needed to make a woman honest.

[5]

It was the night before Dorothy was to come back from Brighton, and Robert and Magda were spending it in Twickenham. Robert seemed even brighter and more self-assured than usual, and Magda, who, for the first time since the three weeks' idyll had begun, found her happiness invaded by sad apprehensions, was a little alarmed to see him so gay. Was it possible that in some curious way he was looking forward to Dorothy's return? Had he felt lonely while she was away?

When they had finished their little supper, Magda said wistfully, 'Well, I suppose we ought to begin packing up, just in case we can't come out here again before your friend gets back from America. I wonder what he'd think of those things of ours, if he found them here.'

She looked round the flat, letting her eyes rest on her treasures—the colour-print, the earthenware dog and the vase which she had filled with some fresh anemones that evening. Robert got up very quietly and, standing behind her, put his hands on her shoulders and kissed her hair.

'Darling, don't look so sad. I've some splendid news and it was naughty of me not to tell you at once. But I wanted to keep it as a lovely surprise. Guess what it is!'

It was on the tip of her tongue to say, 'You've heard from Dorothy and she wants to divorce you,' but she was prudent enough to leave those words unspoken, and shook her head in bewilderment.

'Come on, guess. I'll give you three guesses.'

'Mrs Fawley's staying in Brighton another week?'

'No. She'll be back to-morrow, so far as I know. It's something much better,—more far-reaching than that.'

She turned her head round. He kissed her lips and went on,

'In about six weeks, or sooner, if I can manage it, this flat will be ours,—ours, darling, our very own.'

'Robert, what do you mean?'

'I had a letter from Hamilton this morning and he says that when he gets back from America he has to report straight to our new place in Scotland, where he's going to be second-in-command. It's a very good job, by the way. I rather think, though he didn't actually say so, that he's going to get married. He's been dangling some adoring girl on a string for a good many years and I dare say he feels it's time he settled down. At any rate, he'll be living up in Scotland and has asked me to get rid of this flat for him. I told him how much I liked it, and he said he'd be delighted for me to take over the lease—there's still fifteen months to run. It's very decent of him, because the rent is so low by present-day standards that he could get something by way of premium. We can have the fitted carpets and the curtains at a valuation, if we want them. He asked me to have the other things sent to some furniture-people in Inverness, to be ready when he gets his new house. (The Government are giving him one, of course.) So we shall have to do our own furnishing. Well, I don't mind that, do you? I think the bed is perfectly frightful. That's the first thing we'll buy,—a really lovely, comfortable bed.'

He kissed her again. For a short while she was too dazed to speak. Then she said, 'But, Robert, have you thought about—the money—and other things?'

'Don't worry about the money. I've got quite a lot in the Post Office and some Savings Certificates. I'll draw it out as we need it. I've never spent very much on Dorothy. She's got more than I have, and whatever bad qualities she may have, meanness isn't one of them. Of course, I shan't sponge on her or cut down my contribution to Pollitt Place—while that still goes on. Believe me, darling, I've thought it all out, and this is the best thing that could have happened. Far better let the future take gradual shape than have a thundering row and screams in the house, with Miss Tredennick peeping over the stairs and asking what it's all about. I don't intend to be tied to Dorothy's skirts as I used to be. When I want to go out on my own, I shall go. You've set me a good example. I do admit, I don't want a sudden flare-up and shall do my best to avoid one.

But if one comes—on Dorothy's side—I shall know how to deal with it. But I don't expect that kind of thing at all. I can almost guarantee that within a week of coming home she'll be looking for some excuse to go away again. Very well, let her go,—and if one day she writes to me and says she's never coming back, *our* flat will be waiting for us. That's all that matters,—having our flat and being together in it. But don't let's waste any more of our precious minutes looking ahead. Oh Magda, my beautiful darling——'

X

THE FIRST WEEK OF DECEMBER

THE approach of Christmas brought more perplexities than promise of pleasure to those who lived at Ten Pollitt Place.

Justin wished he could hibernate throughout the festive season. His club would be closed. An old friend who usually asked him to stay for two or three of those dreaded and difficult days, had died during the year, and most of Justin's other old friends were either too busy struggling through their dotage to remember him or were being entertained by younger members of their own families. Lady Victoria had already gone to a niece in Bournemouth. Lady Beatrice had cadged an invitation from some Americans to spend Christmas with them on the Riviera. Lady Farless was giving an ambitious house-party in Cumberland, and even had Justin been asked, he couldn't have faced it, let alone the long journey. If he didn't bestir himself he would be reduced to nibbling biscuits alone in his room. Perhaps the Fawleys would be free on Christmas Eve? He had only a nodding acquaintance with either of them and had never sought to enlarge it, but surely the spirit of Christmas would excuse a belated outburst of friendliness. He might rake up, from among his less cherished acquaintances, half a dozen guests to meet them. It could be a kind of cocktail-party, from seven to nine, with those slender but insidiously filling things to eat that Garrows supplied ready-made at their delicatessen counter. Mrs Muller would know what to get. On Christmas Day,

Miss Tredennick was certain to be at home to him and a few of her friends for an old-fashioned tea, followed fairly soon by drinks. He needn't bother about dinner that night. As for Boxing Day and that diabolical invention the super-Boxing Day which followed it—for Christmas that year fell on a Sunday—if nobody asked him out, he'd just have to ring the changes between some of those goodish, semi-residential hotels in which South Kensington seems to specialise. But what a bore,—what a depressing bore the whole thing was! He reminded himself of a sentence he had used in one of his own novels. *In the winter one can always cheer oneself up by imagining that one will be happier in the summer: but in the summer one has no such consolation.* But the epigram didn't make him any happier.

Miss Tredennick, to whom the passing of every day was a problem, felt no special apprehension over Christmas. She would have her usual little tea-party on Christmas Day,—the descendants of various uncles and aunts of hers, who would come from a sense of duty or, to put it less kindly, for mercenary reasons,—after all, the old lady must leave her money to somebody—one or two half-forgotten friends and of course Mr Bray. She had considered asking Mrs Fawley but had decided that it wouldn't be wise to become too friendly with her. Besides, her husband, though no doubt a most excellent man, was hardly suitable for a drawing-room. But the success or failure of her party didn't weigh very much with Miss Tredennick. Whether she enjoyed her Christmas or not would depend on events outside the house,—particularly those which occurred at Number Seven across the way.

Since the glorious morning when she had seen Hugo's handiwork on the yellow door, very little had rewarded her vigilance, and her Journal would have been miserably dull if she hadn't taken to interlarding the lean narrative with more and more daring scraps of poetry.

'*Where are you going, my pretty maid?*'
'*To buy something useful, Sir,' she said.*
'*The strongest incentives require preventives,*
    And a maid is quickly betrayed,' she said.

She wished she could remember her father's spicy continuation of the ditty. Originally she had hated Y.V. for her wanton behaviour. Now she hated her twice as much because her behaviour was not wanton enough.

Mrs Muller's problems were for the most part domestic. Like Magda (and unlike any of the other five people in the house), she was not without some feeling for the religious aspect of the Festival, but her chief preoccupation was the need to do the shopping for so many days in advance and to plan her time so that she could cope with the extra work which the season would thrust upon her. Miss Tredennick would be sure to give her usual party and Mr Bray had already announced that he didn't expect to be going away for Christmas this year. Even though he had no claim on her for extra service, it would not be right to let the old gentleman fend for himself. And she couldn't rely on Magda as fully as she had done the year before. However, at all costs, she must plan a treat for Hugo. He should have his little Christmas-tree of course, but he ought to have a little party as well. Perhaps she could manage one on Boxing Day. But whom should she ask to it? He wouldn't care for such few friends as she had, and he didn't seem to have any of his own.

She needn't have worried about him. On that very morning, the dustman had asked him what he was doing over Christmas, and Hugo had said, in a pathetic voice, 'Nothing. Nothing at all.' 'Why, aren't they taking you to the pantomime, or letting you ask some of your pals into tea?' Hugo shook his head and said, 'I haven't any friends. You see, I can't play games like other boys, and I don't enjoy being with them.' The dustman frowned thoughtfully and then said, 'Well, the wife and I are having some of her nephews and nieces to tea at six on Christmas Day. You'll be most welcome if you'd care to come,—that's to say if your mother would let you, which I don't suppose she would.' Hugo beamed with pleasure. 'What, come to tea with you? Oh, I should love to. But you will talk to me, won't you?' 'Oh yes, I'll do that, all right. But be sure to ask your mother. Otherwise I might get into trouble.' Hugo was saying, 'Oh, I can manage Mother all right,' when he looked up and saw Magda scrubbing the front-door step, which some dog had fouled for the second time that morning. Though she was on her knees and had her back turned to the area, he was sure she had been listening. He whispered, 'Yes, I'll ask Mother. Magda might try to stop me, but Mother wouldn't.' So for Hugo, Christmas already held the promise of a treat such as his mother could never provide for him. He was already filled with happiest anticipations, not only of the party itself, but of its aftermath—the glowing memories it would leave behind, and the chance it might give him of playing the host in his turn, though he hoped *his* party would be a party for two.

Magda had indeed overheard the conversation, but judged it wiser not to mention it to her mother there and then. Having plans of her own (or hoping she had), it would be risky for her to interfere with the plans of other people. All her hopes of a happy Christmas centred round two days,—the evening before Christmas Eve and Tuesday, the second Boxing Day. Robert had vowed that by some means or other—even if he had to invent an emergency-call to his office—he would break loose from Dorothy on one of those evenings, if not on both. Could Magda keep them both free? She promised she would, and was even then seeking for some excuse which would spare her telling too downright a lie. She had a girlfriend, who, if approached with tact, might give her an alibi without asking too many questions. The subterfuges to which intriguers are driven ill accorded with Magda's true character, and at any other time would have sat heavily upon her conscience. But having already committed, as she thought, the awful sin against the Holy Ghost, for which there is no forgiveness, she could now think more lightly of what in the past would have seemed an enormity.

Meanwhile, Dorothy, on whose intentions and movements the happiness of two people was so closely hinged, was more at peace with herself than she had been for a very long time. It was true that her bolder plans had fallen through. She could not tear Susan away from the flat in Brighton, and Louise showed no sign of asking her and Robert to join them in Cambridgeshire. (That was Robert's fault. He'd been so boorish the last time he had stayed there. One had to be his wife to understand him and make the necessary allowances.) But she wasn't sorry to be back in London. She had found dear Susan difficult at times, and far too energetic. Besides, she still had a good deal of shopping to do for Miss Tredennick, not to mention her own.

It was with the best excuses that she had lunch at Garrows nearly every day. When she went up to the restaurant on the third floor, she looked with contemptuous pity at the people lolling in the big lounge which Garrows provided for their wearier customers. Little did Garrows know, she thought, what sort of people made so brazenly free of it. They looked like a collection of refugees harried from one end of Europe to the other. Here was an old man with big holes in the soles of his shoes, leaning back in a chair and munching sandwiches bought at a coffee-stall. There, a fat woman, with a nose so red that you'd think she was pickled in port, was snoring, stretched out at almost full length on a sofa. And as for those three young women sitting near her—Dorothy shuddered and turned away fastidiously, thanking God that she was in Garrows on genuine business, and was not yet reduced to such undignified shifts to get through the unwanted hours of the day. (To reassure any nervous shareholders, it may be said that Garrows are as well informed as Dorothy of what goes on in their rest-room, and know to a penny what contribution it makes towards their dividend.)

How blessed a thing it was to join legitimately the sisterhood of eager purchasers, whose gossip, at this season of the year, had an especially piquant quality. 'I'm looking for a pair of gay but cosy bedroom-slippers for a gentleman. . . . Do you think this game will be quite noisy enough? Remember, the three Arbuthnot boys are coming! . . . But surely, blue is not a Christmassy colour? Green and red, perhaps, like holly and holly-berries, with silver splashes for the mistletoe. . . .' Dorothy listened, not mockingly or censoriously as Aldous Huxley might have listened,—for such observations were always apt to remind her of his famous phrase about the children who never needed a laxative—but with a delight in which she felt no shame, almost persuading herself that she could discern a hidden beauty in this great annual parade of individualism, so blandly aloof from any kind of moral, social or economic theorising. Floreat Garrows! So she shopped and lunched and shopped again, and the short days passed by with a succession of thrills.

Of course, there were the evenings to get through, when the shops were shut,—long evenings with Robert. But the change in him, which she had begun to notice before she went to Brighton, had gone still further. She now detected a trace of something spiritual about him. His face seemed less coarsely drawn, his mind less wooden,—almost as if he had been refined by suffering, while she was away. Had he been pining for her? Had there been too much *take* and too little *give* on her side of the marriage? Henceforward, she would really make an effort to adapt her life to his. She would try to take an interest in broken watches and his irksome little hobbies. When he talked to her about what went on in the middle of the atom—though he hadn't done so for a very long time—she wouldn't change the subject at once and say, 'I've just read such a good book about Shakespeare's Sonnets. I do wish, for once, you'd read something like that. It's so uncivilised to cut oneself off from everything that makes life worth while.' (Oh the long wrangles that they used to have! 'At any rate,' he'd say, 'the things *I* do and like are *useful* things.' And she would try to explain that the cultivation of the mind was valuable for its own sake, and had a higher form of utility than any tinkering with material objects. '*You'd* say a bathroom is more useful than a drawing-room. *I* say it's only use is to fit people for living in a drawing-room. It's on a lower plane.' But he wouldn't or couldn't see her point, and would walk away glumly while she was still talking.)

No, there must be no more silly quarrels like that. She was right in her views, of course, but she must accept it that he couldn't share them. After all, he had many sweet qualities. He'd never caused her the slightest anxiety so far as other women were concerned—though, if it came to that, she'd kept her own side of the bargain no less faithfully. But men were more naturally promiscuous than women,—or so people said. Ought she to make it clear that if he wanted her to be what she had been to him in their early life together, she wouldn't refuse?

XI

THE THIRTEENTH OF DECEMBER

WITH a peculiar instinct Hugo knew exactly the type of man he could get round most easily,—a man of about fifty, with greying hair and a kind but slightly sad face. If the man were married—and he probably would be—he would have married quite early in life, not so much because he wanted a wife as because he wanted a home and couldn't afford to keep a servant to run it. Most likely he would have three or four children, whom he had spoilt for the sake of peace and quiet, but by now they would be grown up, perhaps with children of their own, and would only bother him when they were in trouble. His wife would have taken to nagging, and though he spent the whole of his leisure with her, he was always relieved to get away from her and set out for his work.

Hugo, looking small and clean and neat, shuffled towards a rank of taxi-cabs near a bus stop and studied the faces of the drivers. The one in front was a debonair young fellow with a thin, pointed moustache and close-set eyes that looked as if they were staring at the main chance the whole time. Quite useless. The second one was very old indeed, with a lined, cantankerous face and big tufts of white hair growing out of his ears. Hugo thought, 'Rather better, but none too good.' He looked at his watch, walked down the road a few paces and then summed up the third driver. This one seemed perfect, especially when, without any provocation, he gave Hugo a shy, fatherly smile.

Hugo gave him a shy smile in return and waited. A woman laden with parcels gave a wave from the far side of the road, and the first cab moved off the rank. Two minutes later, the telephone-bell by the shelter began to ring. The old man climbed wearily out of the cab to answer it, and Hugo seized his chance. He hurried to the middle of the road as fast as he could, and beaming into the face of his chosen driver, he said, 'I want you to do something very special for me. Can you pull off the rank and stop just down the road, near the bus stop?' The man looked a little doubtful and said, 'Why, sonny, what's up? Hadn't you better tell me straight out what you want?' and Hugo replied with a childish grandeur that amused the man, 'I want to hire your cab. Look, I've got four pounds ten!' As he spoke, he unclenched his left hand and showed the notes. 'All right, guv'nor, get inside. The traffic's a bit of a problem, but I'll park as near the bus stop as I can.'

When the taxi had taken up its new position, Hugo opened the window between him and the driver and said, 'It's like what happens in detective stories. I'm expecting a woman to get on a bus over there in five minutes, and I want you to follow it so that I can find out where she gets off. I don't know how far she'll go, but go on till I've spent all my money. How far will it take me, allowing for your fare back again?'

'Oh, a long way. As far as Staines, I dare say, or even Windsor. Do you know the number of the bus she's likely to take?'

'I'm not certain, but I think it'll be a 27. I followed her as far as this before.'

The driver said, 'The 27 stops at Teddington station, except on Sundays in summer, when it goes on to Hampton Court. So that'll be well within your means—unless, of course, she gets off somewhere and takes a Green Line and goes right on into the country. In that case——'

He broke off, looking puzzled and apprehensive. After all, very nasty things happened these days. There were gangs which made a point of robbing drivers and sometimes blackmailed them. Was it quite safe to put himself in the hands of this queer little kid, though he seemed a decent chap and nicely spoken?

As if Hugo could read his thoughts, he said, 'Perhaps I'd better tell you, it's my sister. I think she's going to meet a man and she hasn't told Mother or me anything about him.'

As always, when Hugo spoke the truth, his words carried full conviction. The driver smiled and said, 'My word! It's like that, is it? It struck me as rather rum that a fellow as young as you are should be chasing women. But don't you think it's a bit—what shall I say?—a bit low-down and sneaky to go spying on her?'

Hugo affected to consider this point, then answered, 'No, I don't think it is. I think I ought to know where she goes. She's never been one to have men-friends before, and I don't suppose she knows how to look after herself.'

The driver chuckled. 'Meaning, of course, you do! And I dare say you can, though one wouldn't think it, to look at you. Well, I'll do my best.' Then he added, 'Have you no father?'

Hugo shook his head, 'No, he was killed in the war. There's only Mother and Magda and me.' In his pedantic way, he would have liked to say, 'There are only Mother and Magda and *I*,' but he thought the bad grammar would be more endearing.

Five minutes passed, then Hugo said, 'There she is, in her dark blue coat. It's her best. I think I'll crouch down a bit, till she gets on the bus.' And he made himself so small that the cab looked empty. 'Yes, it *is* a 27. Now we shall see.'

The chase began. Both Hugo and his driver found it much more difficult than they had supposed it would be to keep track of the bus without getting too far ahead or too far behind. In books, such exploits often appear very simple. 'Driver, follow that car, and there'll be a guinea for you!' And he gets the guinea, how-ever skilfully the car he's pursuing dodges through the traffic and twists down side-streets in an effort to throw the sleuths off the scent. But Hugo's driver was cast in a different mould. He was not one to whom an adventurer would have entrusted a confidential mission,—not because he was unreliable, but because he was too slow-witted and innocent.

The homeward rush to the suburbs had started already and the traffic was thickening. He began to sweat under the strain and said through the window, 'I'm taking your money under false pre-tences, sonny. I'm no hand at this game. Hadn't we better call it a day? I'll drive you home free of charge.'

Hugo said, 'No, please go on. I've a feeling we shan't lose sight of her. But if we do, I shan't blame you.'

The task would have been hopeless if the bus had been a crawler,—one of those that exasperate the passengers by loiter-ing at every stop and getting themselves caught deliberately in every traffic-block and at every change of the lights. (The ignorant public, instead of blaming the driver, who wants his cup of tea as much as they do, should remember that buses run to a time-table, and that if they've made too much ground, they must contrive to lose it before they reach the inspector at the control-point.)

But the particular bus that Hugo was following, was in the opposite predicament. It was behind its time. This meant short waits at the compulsory stops and perhaps a blind eye turned towards the request stops. The great thing was, it kept on the move as steadily as it could, which made the pursuit very much easier. Once or twice, the taxi-driver said pathetically, 'I couldn't see that stop: she may have got off,' but Hugo answered, 'I'm almost sure she didn't. Besides, I think this street is rather too shabby. Let's go on.'

They had an anxious moment at Kew Bridge, where a great many passengers got out, but Hugo declared that Magda was not among them, and they drove down the long road past Kew Gardens. Much the same happened when they crossed the river again by Richmond Bridge. In fact, the driver said, 'There she goes,—blue coat and black hat. We'd better turn round.' But Hugo said, 'That woman's too fat for Magda. Magda's skinny and taller. Please do go on.' So they went along Richmond Road, past Marble Hill Park and right into Twickenham, where they had their reward. Hugo clapped his hands like a child and shouted, 'She's out! She's got out! She's turned up there to the right. Now all we have to do is to go very slowly and find where she goes to.' The driver said, 'Yes, but we mustn't let her notice we're following her, or she might suspect something.' Hugo shrewdly replied, 'Oh, she'll be far too busy thinking of the man she's going to meet, to notice us. Still, I'll keep out of sight, just in case she looks round.' And he crouched down again, with his eyes on the level of the bottom of the window.

Magda was walking quickly, and her course zigzagged into a residential quarter some way from the river. Then she paused in front of a not very modern block of flats, took a latch-key out of her bag and went straight in, through a side-door.

Hugo said, 'Well, this seems to be it.' Then the driver, prompted by his reading of detective-stories, said, 'If you'd like to look round, I can always pretend to be doing something to the cab.' He got out, opened the bonnet, bent down and in traditional fashion presented such a view of his ample rump that it could hardly fail to convince a watcher at a window above that heavy repairs were in progress down below. Hugo too got out, by the door on the far side, and crept round towards the flats in the shadow of some laurels.

A notice-board by the road proclaimed the block to be Under-bourne Mansions. It needed repainting badly, and so, if one could judge in the stingy light which shone above the three entrance-doors, did the building itself. Between it and the road there was a strip of garden, ambitiously laid out as a rockery, but the effort or the expense of keeping it up must have been too great: for it was full of half-dead weeds and sickly-looking shrubs.

'Not very posh,' said the driver and straightened himself, rub-bing the small of his back, where the bending had caught him. 'Now what do we do?' Hugo hung his head thoughtfully, feeling suddenly rather forlorn and helpless. 'I don't know. What do you think?' The driver scratched his head in perplexity. Here again, Hugo's choice of a chauffeur, though in other ways admirable, proved at fault. Most taxi-drivers—at least, most London taxi-drivers,—are supposed to be men of the world, closely acquainted with every variety of amorous intrigue that the city has to offer. Some of them—for a suitable fee—would have played the private-detective quite adroitly,—questioned hall-porters, chummed up with chars, invented errands to gain access to the building and memorised the lists of names by each entrance. But Hugo's driver could only scratch his head and say after a very long pause, 'Well, you *could*, I suppose, go inside and tell the porter—though I must say, I haven't seen one about—that your sister's in one of the flats and you want to see her on—on very urgent family affairs!' As he produced the last phrase—a formula that he had learnt in the First World War,—he smacked his lips at its appropriateness.

Hugo said, 'But I don't want to see her at all. I think I'd better get back into the cab. Why, it's after six!' The taxi-man nodded and said, 'Yes, that's why there's nobody about just now. They'll all be listening to the six o'clock news. Credit squeeze to be tighter—no more hire-purchase—and a wife who won't give me any peace at all till she gets a new washing-machine.' Hugo asked, 'How much have

I spent up to now, if we go straight back?' The driver looked at the meter and did some calculations. 'Well, we'll call it thirty-five bob, all in, if that's all right.' Hugo told him it would be quite all right, but added, 'Mind, I want you to treat me like a proper customer. Well, I suppose we'd better be off. I wish there were a seat in front. It would be so much easier to talk to you.' The driver said, 'Oh, in my job, you have to learn to talk backwards through the window.'

He opened the door of the cab, helped Hugo in, then hoisted himself into the driver's seat and started the engine. While they were rumbling in bottom gear up a slight incline, a man hurried past them towards the entrance of Underbourne Mansions. He paused for a second in the light of a street-lamp to look at his wrist-watch, while Hugo put his head through the side window and stared back at him. Then, as soon as they were over the brow of the little hill, he shouted through the partition, 'I've seen the man! I know him! It's—no, I'd better not tell you, but, my word, what *would* Mother say—what *would* she say!'

'You don't want to go back and have it out with him?' the driver asked rather apprehensively. He had seen the man and noticed his vigorous stride and thought he looked a tough customer.

'Oh no,' Hugo crooned. 'You don't understand. It isn't like that at all. I know everything now,—all I wanted to know.' And he concluded, like a distinguished guest complimenting his hostess, 'This afternoon has been a great success!'

They didn't speak to one another again till they had got through the Hammersmith bottle-neck. Then the driver said, reflectively and sadly, 'You know, sonny, if I was you, I shouldn't be too hard on your sister. You're only young once and there isn't very much left for you afterwards, whatever people say. I had my chances and I didn't take them—and look where it's landed me. Don't blame your sister, if she's making the most of her chances while she can.'

Hugo said, 'I don't blame her, exactly.' Then he added, in a voice which sounded as if his emotions were stirred, 'But it's so unfair. *She* can go out and have men whenever she likes, and I—I've got to potter about at home and see nobody but the people who come to our street——' He stopped suddenly, realising that this remark might be disloyal to his friend the dustman.

The taxi-man did his best to be sympathetic. 'But, sonny, when I talked about being young, I didn't mean being as young as you are. You wait another five years or maybe less, and you can be sure some nice girl will come along and take a fancy to you.'

Hugo shouted, 'I don't want what you call a nice girl.' Then he added more softly, 'You forget, I'm a cripple. A lot of funny things may happen to me, if I live, but there's one thing I can promise you—I shall *never* marry.'

The driver, who felt sore at having his well-meant advice so roundly rejected, didn't speak again till they reached Olympia. Then he said, rather shortly, 'Now, Guv'nor, where would you like me to set you down?'

'Where Pollitt Crescent turns into Pollitt Square. I live quite close, but it wouldn't do for me to be seen coming home in a taxi.' The driver said, 'Right-ho,' and then added in a lower, yet audible tone, 'That's still one of our swanky neighbourhoods,—full of old cats with daughters going astray.'

But when Hugo got out, looking tense and very tired, the man's heart melted, and he said, 'Look here, sonny, I don't want to be greedy. It's been an interesting afternoon for me—something I've never done before—far better than the pictures. Thirty bob will pay my expenses all right. You keep the rest. I expect you can do with it.'

Hugo looked at him gravely, as if weighing up his moral attributes, and said, 'No, that won't do. You've been good to me, and I want to show you I'm grateful. I'm going to give you two pounds. If you don't take it, I shan't wish you good night. I can afford it. Please?'

The cherub-face smiled, the taxi-man hesitated, then took the money and shook Hugo's hand.

[2]

Hugo had a late supper with his mother that night, since, in Magda's absence, she had to look after Miss Tredennick. They didn't talk very much to one another; for both of them had a good deal to think about. But Mrs Muller's thoughts had a way of uttering themselves aloud, and towards the end of the meal one of them came out.

'Well, I hope she doesn't bring it back with her!'

'What did you say?' asked Hugo, abstractedly.

'I was thinking of Magda. I knew she was seeing Josephine tonight, but she didn't tell me till just before she went out that Josephine had the 'flu. It would be a business if we all caught it—just before Christmas, too. This Josephine has got plenty of other friends, and she never used to bother with Magda very much. She shouldn't have sent for her. And Mr Bray so frightened of microbes. I don't suppose he'd let Magda do his room, if he knew.'

Hugo said, after a short silence, 'Mother, do you think I ought to give a Christmas present to Mrs Fawley?'

'To Mrs Fawley? Why ever should you, Hugo? She gives me and Magda a little present—some cheapish handkerchiefs, or something like that—and we send her a card, but she's never given anything to you. Or if she has, you've never told me about it.'

She looked at Hugo suspiciously, but he answered, 'No, Mother, she hasn't. But I feel I should like to give her something this year, or at least send her a card of my own. I'm quite old enough to do that now.'

His mother said grudgingly, 'Well, I suppose there wouldn't be any harm in that—though, of course, you must address it to both of them—Mr and Mrs Fawley. But I shouldn't waste the money if I was you. You'll be sending Miss Tredennick a card, of course, and it might be nice to give her a little present. She's been very good to you this year. And you could send a card to Mr Bray. You remember, he gave you ten shillings last Christmas, and I expect he'll do the same this year. But those Fawleys,—they've never seemed quite to belong to this house, like the other two do. Perhaps it's because we don't do anything for them, excepting the hall and the stairs. But they take that for granted, as it's in their lease. Won't you have some more pudding, dear? It'll do you good.'

'No, thank you. I'm not very hungry to-night.'

'You're tired, dear. You've never really told me what you did this afternoon.'

'Yes, I did. I told you I went exploring.'

'Where did you go?'

'In the Hammersmith direction.'

'But, Hugo, that's a horrid, rough part. What could you find to interest you there?'

'The river's pretty, with the lights on the bridge.'

Mrs Muller began to clear the dishes away, while Hugo sat silent, folding his table-napkin—his mother had always brought him up to use one—in a fantastic pattern. Then, when she had started to wash up, he said, 'Mother, what were those papers I saw in the sitting-room—on Magda's desk? I saw the envelope they came in this morning. It was addressed to her, but it had printed on it, *The Albany Secretarial College*. Is she going to stop doing house-work?'

'No, Hugo. I meant to tell you. She got those papers—the—what do they call it?'

'The prospectus?'

'Yes, the prospectus—for you. She's been on at me for some time about it. At first I said no, but she said, well, there couldn't be any harm in her just writing for particulars and I had to agree. You see, she thinks you might be very much happier if you began to learn how to make a living for yourself. It isn't like an ordinary school. They don't have masters or games or anything of that sort. They have tutors who coach you—like Mr Middleton does, only he doesn't seem to teach you anything useful. Don't you think you might like to try it, just for a term? Even if it didn't turn out to be much use, it would give you something to do, instead of sitting and reading alone and going out for your little lonely walks. The other boys would be very nice to you—they wouldn't be at all like ordinary schoolboys. And you need hardly see them unless you wanted to.'

Hugo's face had gone very pale, and he raised his upper lip, showing his teeth like an animal that threatens to bite.

'So it was Magda who wrote to this college?' he asked.

'Yes, dear, but I knew she was going to. After all, she's quite right. You see—it's horrid even to speak of such awful things, but you won't always have me. People have accidents and sudden illnesses and—oh, Hugo dear, I hope you'll never *need* to work, and as long as I live and can work, I'll do my best to save you from that—but I shan't live for ever.' She shuddered as she spoke those gloomy words, which suddenly put her in mind of Hugo's prophecy about someone dying in the house before the end of the year. Then, with an attempt at cheerfulness, she went on, 'Besides, when you're grown up—and that won't be so very long now—you can't just go to Mr Middleton in the mornings and hang about the house for the rest of the day. Why, darling, what's the matter?'

He hid his face with his hands, so that nothing but his blond little head was showing, and began to sob loudly. His mother left the sink and put her arms round him. She could feel him trembling, while he nestled against her.

Between outbursts of tears, he gasped, 'I want to stay as I am—I don't want to grow up. Nobody loves a grown man—at least, not the kind of person I want to love me—and not in the way I want to be loved.'

She stroked his hair and said, 'Never mind, Hugo darling. You may feel different about it all some day,—but till you do, you can go on just as you are. But you know, you're a clever boy, and you oughtn't to waste your gifts.'

He broke free from her embrace and said defiantly, 'I shan't ever feel different from what I am now,—really different, that is. And I don't want to learn the kind of things they teach you at these schools,—useful things, they call them, like bookkeeping and shorthand. Mr Middleton calls them competitive things. I want to learn exquisite poetry, like Tennyson and Byron and Milton. And I want to go on with my Latin. I want to read Catullus and Virgil and Horace—you wouldn't know who they are, but Miss Tredennick knows. Her father used to read Horace, and she's recited some of it to me. And I want to write—like Mr Bray, but much better—Mr Middleton says his novels are middle-brow—and to draw—but the kind of pictures I like, not pictures to sell.'

Delighted to find him more rational, Mrs Muller said, 'Well, of course you might make a name by writing—some wonderful play, that they'd do on TV——' Hugo gave her a look of contempt, but she went on bravely, 'Still a day may come when you'll have to earn your own living and for your own sake you ought to be prepared for it.'

Hugo answered grimly, 'I'd rather starve to death than earn my living by painting and writing things to sell.' Then, taking his mother's red and slightly damp hand, he said coaxingly, 'Darling Mutti, promise me you'll burn that prospectus before Magda comes home. Or will you let me burn it? I can light it in the dustbin, so there won't be any mess with the ashes. Darling Mutti, please say yes.'

She sighed in surrender and said, 'Very well—if you want to.'

Hugo went out all smiles into the sitting-room, where he found a candle, lit it and took the detested envelope and prospectus from a small fumed-oak bureau, and carried them into the area. He laid the lid of the dust-bin very quietly on the stone floor and then, holding the papers with his left hand inside the bin, which was less than half full, he lit each page separately, and as he did so,— invoking the Genius who presided over all dust-bins,—he chanted, 'I make this burnt-offering of my future to *you*!'

XII

THE WEEK BEFORE CHRISTMAS

By now, the trappings of Christmas had made their way from the shops into private houses. In the Pollitts, a hundred front doors had opened to welcome bundles of holly and mistletoe, with their trails of dropped berries, soon to be squashed on carpets. Mantelpieces were decorated with calendars and cards that fluttered or fell in a draught. Drawers and odd corners were filled with gifts, gay gummed labels, coloured string, wrapping-paper, boxes of crackers and festive novelties. Store-cupboards were crammed with delicacies in cartons and tins and jars. The great orgy of spending was under way, though the great orgy of consuming was yet to come.

Nor did this spirit of enterprise confine itself to the privacy of the home. It had a public aspect. The nice Americans who lived in the Terrace, and had given the firework party on Guy Fawkes Day, were the first to hang a big garland of holly and mistletoe, tied with red satin ribbon, to the knocker of their front-door, while if one was lucky enough to have a view of their small garden at the back of the house, one could see them decorating a well-grown Christmas-tree with fairies, gnomes, butterflies, glass ornaments and coloured lanterns, all guaranteed to stand the English climate. Mrs Muller described it minutely to Miss Tredennick, who struggled into her sitting-room to inspect it. On the floor below, Dorothy whiled away many happy moments in the same fashion. Justin, from his bedroom window, had a glimpse of its higher branches waving above the level of three garden-walls, but the sight increased his seasonable gloom. Only the Mullers in their basement-kitchen had no view of it at all.

However, Ten Pollitt Place was not altogether eclipsed. Those who peeped down through the area railings could see, in the Mullers' sitting-room, a miniature version of a very Protestant Crib, with the chief emphasis on the animals, and illuminated by fat Swedish candles. Mrs Muller would have liked a garland on the front door, but Miss Tredennick feared it might damage the paint.

But it was Dorothy who gave the house its *cachet*. Inspired by the Americans' example, she asked Robert to fix up a small Christmas-tree on the balcony, for the benefit of anyone passing by in the street. As always, he was only too glad to have an excuse for using his hands, and did the work well. The tree was lit up by minute electric lights which went off and on and changed colour in rotation. A disadvantage was that the carol-singers made a bee-line for the house and loitered by it long after they had exhausted their repertoire. Miss Tredennick told Mrs Muller to give five shillings— in five separate instalments—to singers who showed real talent. If they showed none, instead of getting a penny to go into the next street, they got a scolding for the inadequacy of their performance. Miss Tredennick had said, 'I will *not* be blackmailed by mere cacophony,' and Mrs Muller had to translate the dictum as best she could. Poor Justin, who was the chief sufferer from these assaults, was capricious in his reactions. Sometimes he opened his window and shouted, 'Stop that filthy row!' while at other times, if the singers looked really cold and miserable, he darted out with an offering of half a crown. Dorothy, who was enchanted to see their eyes turned upwards to her Christmas-tree, would throw down a sixpence from the balcony. This often led to scuffles in the gutter.

She had now settled her programme for the five nights round Christmas. On the Friday, she was to take a married couple and a spinster to the theatre, after which the four of them were to have a light supper in the spinster's flat. (Robert couldn't come. He said that there was to be a party at the Research Station, and that he was more or less bound to be there. He could have got an invitation for Dorothy, of course, but he knew it wasn't in her line. She would hate it.)

On Saturday, Christmas Eve, she was to lunch with Susan, who was coming up for the day, at Garrows, who were remaining open till three o'clock that afternoon. In the evening, nothing—in other words, she would be spending it alone with Robert. Perhaps he would take her out to the West End to see the decorations. (Justin, who had thought of asking her and Robert to his cocktail-party that night, had decided against it. It might involve him in too many smiles and chats when he met the Fawleys in the hall.)

Sunday, Christmas Day. A tedious journey and a still more tedious luncheon—or 'dinner', as she knew the meal would be called—with some friends at Hackfield. They were really Robert's friends, not hers. He would talk to the husband about motor-car engines and probably retire with him to the built-on garage, to lend a hand at some messy repair, while she would have to sit and listen to her hostess explaining how she made her atrocious cakes. In the evening, another blank.

Monday, the first Boxing Day. A little party at Number Ten in the late afternoon. She had scraped up seven rather incompatible acquaintances, one of whom was nearly deaf and refused to wear an appliance, but any guests were better than none. It would have been intolerable to let the festive season go by without giving some sort of entertainment at home. Besides, it provided a good excuse for titivating the drawing-room.

Tuesday, the second Boxing Day. The married couple whom she was taking to the theatre on the Friday were giving a theatre-party in their turn. The show began early, and the treat included supper afterwards. Robert, who had been asked, refused to go with them to the theatre, but after great pressure from Dorothy (herself greatly pressed by her hostess who had an unrequited fondness for Robert), he agreed to come on to the supper. Yet even this concession was qualified. They mustn't wait for him if he was late, and so on. 'But, darling, why should you be late?' Oh, there was a film about a submarine he'd thought of going to see, and it didn't begin till nine-thirty. But surely he could go to the film any night? They might go to it together. No, it was technical. She would be bored by it. Had it not been for her new policy of appeasement, they might have had a little row over this.

She sighed, with the lukewarm satisfaction of a general, who hopes he has deployed to best advantage the somewhat second-rate troops at his command.

XIII

THE NIGHT OF THE TWENTY-THIRD OF DECEMBER

(pianissimo)
Doodle 'em, me doodle 'em, me doodle 'em, me doodle 'em.
    Non, non! me doodle 'em. Oui, oui! me doodle 'em.
Doodle 'em, me doodle 'em, me doodle 'em, me doodle 'em.
    Yip, yip! me doodle 'em. Hiya! me doodle 'em.

Miss Tredennick stirred in her light sleep. Her dreams were accompanied by the same outrageous lilt which had disturbed the silence of Pollitt Place on that memorable night of mid-September. But now the music was more than merely audible; it had the visible form of a panorama of a thousand night-clubs, a thousand band-leaders dispensing sexual aperitifs as they tapped the polished floor with their glossy patent-leather toes, wriggled their slender black thighs and smirked like sophisticated monkeys. Round each one were concentric circles of naked female shoulders and bosoms indecently revealed. Oh for a thousand barrels of vitriol to pour down upon them! St Thomas Aquinas said that one of the pleasures of the blessed would be to watch the torments of the damned writhing in Hell. Well, it would be fun to watch the fat flesh of those women sizzling! With this thought, Miss Tredennick awoke.

(più forte)
Doodle 'em, me doodle 'em, me doodle 'em, me doodle 'em.
Nein, nein! me doodle 'em; Ja, ja! me doodle 'em . . .

The refrain still throbbed in her ears, and try as she would, she couldn't banish it. It was so real, so insistent, though soft and muffled, like music heard through the chink at the top of a window. Then, in a flash, the truth became clear to her. However unreal her vision of band-leaders and naked shoulders might have been, the music was real, and it *was* coming through the chink at the top of her window. Quivering with excitement, she bundled herself out of bed and into the chair from which she kept her daily watch. Then, drawing a corner of the curtain aside, she peeped out.

There was a mist in the street, but she could see a car in front of the door of Number Seven. It looked like the very car which had been the first offender. There was no light inside. Had the driver gone indoors with his companion and forgotten to switch off the radio in the car? It was far too cold a night to loiter in the street—too cold even to dance there. But there was a chance they hadn't yet got out. The car might have a heater—Miss Tredennick had heard that some cars had them nowadays—to keep them warm during their love-making. If only she could hear what they were saying, or better still, see what they were doing! Her imagination rose to great heights—or perhaps one should say, sank to great depths—as she pictured lively scenes enacted within that small area of snug darkness. Yes, they were still there! A cigarette-lighter, flaring for a moment behind the off-side window, revealed a male hand and a pair of female lips.

Doodle 'em, me doodle 'em, me doodle 'em, me doodle 'em . . .

It seemed as if the car itself was vibrating to the muted rhythm, —and not only the car, but the street-lamp, the area-railings, the street itself. The throbbing had reached Number Ten, the floor of Miss Tredennick's own bedroom, her own legs, her own body, which rose to fever-heat, while a sudden tremendous buzzing in her head drowned the music. At all costs, she must fight it, keep her ears and eyes at the extremest tension they could bear. She began to count, as people sometimes do when the dentist takes a grip of a tooth and begins to tug. One—two—three—four—then something seemed to snap—it might have been a tooth coming out inside her brain—and she shouted, 'Help! Help! Quick! Come and help me! I'm dying!'

The cry was so loud and desperate that Dorothy heard it, although it had to reach her bedroom obliquely. She had been awake for about half an hour, regretting that she hadn't taken her sleeping tablets, but she had gone to bed feeling so calm after the little theatre-party, that she hadn't thought she would need them.

She listened intently, and the cry was repeated, but more faintly. In the bed opposite, Robert was snoring gently, in that healthy sleep which is the aftermath of satisfied desire. Dorothy got up and shook his shoulder. He turned his face towards her with a smile and said, 'Yes, darling—what is it?' Then, opening his eyes he gave her a look of alarm. 'Why, what's the matter?'

'It's Miss Tredennick. She was shouting for help. Oh, Robert, what ought we to do?'

'Shouting for help?'

'Yes, it sounded like that. Could it be a burglar?'

'Are you *sure*, Dorothy?'

'Oh yes. I was wide awake when I heard the scream.'

'Then I'd better go up.'

He jumped out of bed and reached for his thick dressing-gown, which was hanging from a hook on the door. As he did so, his wife thought how young and almost beautiful he looked, with his boyishly tousled hair, his smooth chest revealed by his unbuttoned pyjama-jacket, his slender hips and long straight legs. Yet even in that moment of urgency, she wished he would wear the silk dressing-gown which she had given him as a Christmas present, instead of the drab woollen one he was putting on.

'You ought to take something, in case it *is* a burglar.'

'Oh, I don't suppose it's anything more than a nightmare. Still, I might as well take a hammer.'

He darted into the workshop, came back armed, and opened the door on to the landing.

'Just a minute, while I slip something on, and I'll come with you.'

But he was already upstairs and knocking on the door of Miss Tredennick's bedroom. There was no reply. He knocked again, opened the door, and finding the room in darkness, switched on the light. Miss Tredennick wasn't in her bed, and at first glance he thought the room was empty. Then, going into the middle of the room, he saw her body on the floor, not prone, but propped up, almost comfortably, against the far side of the bed. She was breathing heavily.

'Who's that?'

The words came slowly, but distinctly enough.

'It's Robert Fawley. Aren't you well, Miss Tredennick?'

'No. I'm—I'm very ill. I think I must have—had a kind of—stroke. My father had one. Will you put me—on the bed—and send for the doctor?'

As she spoke, her speech gained in fluency. He turned down the bedding, picked her up in his arms and laid her on the mattress, then quickly covered her with sheet, blankets, and eiderdown.

She said, 'You know, I can't see you. I've gone blind. My father didn't—at least, not till just before he died—but they say it happens like that sometimes. Will you get the doctor—Dr Jamieson, I mean—at once? There's a telephone by the bed—on the pedestal-cupboard. You'll find the number in the little green leather book. Who's that?'

It was Dorothy, who had 'slipped something on' and had made her way, with timorous curiosity, upstairs.

'Oh, Robert, what is it?'

Miss Tredennick said fiercely, 'Don't interrupt Mr Fawley. Ring up the doctor.'

Robert dialled the number, and after a very long pause, a sleepy voice answered, 'Who on earth are you?' Dr Jamieson's practice was largely confined to well-to-do private patients, most of them suffering from senile decay, and he wasn't used to emergency calls in the small hours.

Robert said quietly, 'I'm speaking from Ten Pollitt Place. Will you please come round at once? Miss Tredennick has suddenly been taken very unwell.'

'Oh dear, I am sorry. Could you describe the symptoms at all— so that I shall know what I need to bring with me?'

Robert turned to Miss Tredennick and said, 'Dr Jamieson has asked me to describe the symptoms. Do you think you could——?'

'Yes, give me the telephone. . . . Thank you. Dr Jamieson, this is Miss Tredennick speaking. I've gone blind. I suppose it's a kind of stroke.'

'My dear, dear lady, I'll be round in ten minutes.'

Robert took the telephone and put it back on the pedestal-cupboard. Then Dorothy said, 'Oh, dear Miss Tredennick, can't I do anything?'

'Mr Fawley, would you now be kind enough to go downstairs and fetch Mrs Muller? I don't like to use the bell, in case it wakes Mr Bray.' Miss Tredennick put sufficient emphasis on *Mr* Fawley to make it quite clear that the best thing *Mrs* could do was to go back to bed at once. Robert said, 'Certainly,' and ran downstairs, and Dorothy, lacking the courage to make another offer of help, went back to her bedroom, where she did her hair and put on a boudoir-gown.

Robert had only twice been down to the basement—each time to do some urgent repairs in the kitchen. He knew that the mother and daughter slept in two tiny rooms adjoining it, but didn't know which had which, and as it happened, it was on Magda's door that he tapped. She, like Dorothy, though full of very different thoughts, had been lying awake and heard the quick footsteps on the stairs, though it didn't occur to her that they could be Robert's. When she opened the door and saw him, she gave a gasp of pleasure, that was immediately followed by one of dismay. She whispered, 'But this is *mad*—my mother's next door!' Then, noticing the hammer which he was carrying absent-mindedly in his hand, she shrank back in horror. Had he really gone mad? Had he repented and come down to kill her?

Robert at once stepped back into the passage and said rather loudly, 'Oh, I'm most terribly sorry. I thought this was your mother's room. Will you wake her? Miss Tredennick is ill. My wife heard her shouting for help, and we thought it might be burglars. Dr Jamieson will be round very soon. I'll let him in when he comes. In the meantime, Miss Tredennick would like your mother to go up to her.'

Magda sighed with relief, pulled herself together and said, 'Of course, Mr Fawley. I'll call Mother at once.'

Robert watched her with rekindled desires, as she came out of her room and went to the adjoining door. Then, at a sound from the sitting-room behind him, he looked round and saw Hugo bare-footed and in white pyjamas, peeping out at him slyly. Robert thought, 'What a prurient-minded little brat he is!' Aloud, he said firmly, 'Hugo, get back to bed, or you'll catch a cold.' Instead of obeying, Hugo stood looking at him with a smile that was both derisive and sweet. Robert shrugged his shoulders angrily, walked up to Mrs Muller's door, behind which he could hear the sound of voices, tapped on it and said, 'I'll let Dr Jamieson in, Mrs Muller. Don't worry too much. I can't think Miss Tredennick is very ill. And by the way, before you go up, if I were you I should order Hugo to get back to bed. He'll only catch a cold or make a nuisance of himself. Good night, in case I don't see you again.' He walked down the passage to the foot of the stairs. As he passed the sitting-room door, Hugo, who was still standing defiantly there, said, 'Good night, Mr Fawley,' but Robert didn't answer or look round.

But when he reached the foot of the stairs in the hall, he paused and, deciding to wait where he was for the doctor, sat down in a chair. His memory of the earlier part of that night was still tormentingly vivid. Never before had his and Magda's love-making been so ardent on both sides, so inevitable, so satisfying, so timeless. What a come-down it would be to exchange the ecstacies of Twickenham for the flood of inquisitive small-talk which his wife would pour out as soon as she got him alone. (He hadn't seen her that evening till she awoke him, as he had reached home half an hour before her and by good luck was asleep when she arrived.)

He could picture her, sitting on the edge of her bed,—or had she perhaps gone to the sitting-room?—her eyes protruding with excitement and a ghoulish half-smile playing round her thin lips. Any moment, she might call over the banisters to know what he was doing. If she did, he would say he was waiting in the hall to open the door for Dr Jamieson before the bell rang, so that Mr Bray shouldn't be disturbed.

Besides, while Mrs Muller was upstairs, he might manage another delicious encounter with Magda,—might even go into her bedroom and kiss her there. The risk inflamed his passion. If only someone would smother that horrible boy! His feelings towards Hugo were becoming quite murderous, when both Mrs Muller and Magda came up from the basement. Mrs Muller went straight on ahead. Magda turned round for a moment, gave him a nervous smile and then followed her mother. Five minutes later he heard Dr Jamieson's step on the threshold and opened the door, and, as soon as the old man was in the hall, took his coat and hat and told him what had happened. He concluded by saying, 'I noticed that when she held the telephone, though her hand was trembling, her grip was quite firm. Mrs Muller and Magda are upstairs with her now. I'll be about when you come down, in case there's anything I can do to help. And we'll be most happy to give you a cup of tea, or something stronger, if you fancy it.'

Dr Jamieson, who looked not only sleepy but rather ill, gave a tired smile and said, 'That's very good of you. If coffee wouldn't put you to too much trouble——' Robert said, 'Not at all,' and followed him as he climbed the stairs. When they reached the first landing, Dorothy came out, but Robert pushed her gently back into the sitting-room, went in after her and shut the door.

As he anticipated, she was agog. 'Oh, Robert, what *do* you make of it all? Is she really ill? What did Dr Jamieson say?'

'He said he'd like some coffee when he comes down. I'll go and get it ready.'

Despite the precautions which Robert and Miss Tredennick had taken that Justin's sleep should not be broken by the ringing of bells, he was awake. Though he hadn't heard the cry from Miss

Tredennick's bedroom, he had heard steps on the stairs, voices below him in the basement, more steps, then the opening and shutting of the front door and voices in the hall. His first thought had been that he ought to get up and investigate. Had something gone wrong with the plumbing? Was a cascade of water pouring down from the top of the house? Or was someone ill? But he shrank from stirring, partly from laziness and partly because he felt sure that he would be useless, whatever form the crisis might be taking. (Besides, he would have to put in his teeth and brush his hair.) Then he recognised Robert's firm voice and was greatly relieved. There was a lot to be said for having a real man about the house. It didn't occur to him to put himself in such a category.

'Milk?'

'Yes, please, half and half.'

'And sugar?'

'Yes, three lumps, if I may.'

'Well, Doctor, how is she?'

Dr Jamieson looked at Dorothy reproachfully. (Must have been quite a pretty woman in her day. A bit faded now, and nervy, and much too excited. She ought to have known better, at her age, than to start questioning him about a patient.)

He sipped his coffee reflectively, and said at length, 'Oh, I've every hope that she'll soon be quite all right.'

'You're sure you wouldn't like me to sit up with her?'

'Oh no. I've given her something to make her sleep, and Magda's going to sleep on the sofa, in the drawing-room, just in case of need.'

'But, Doctor,—this sudden attack of blindness—has she really gone blind?'

He took another sip and said, 'I hope when I've seen her tomorrow morning, I shall be able to issue a favourable bulletin.' He smiled, yawned, apologised for yawning, and went on, 'These things make one feel one's age. I've got quite out of the way of sudden calls like this. I suppose it's a sign that I ought to be handing over my practice to a younger man. But no young man would want it. It's dying as fast as my patients, and even if some of them survive me, my practice can't hope to, if we're going to have another Labour Government.'

Dorothy gave Robert a quick glance of apprehension; for she knew that Tory talk nearly always made him truculent. But instead of reacting, he said, 'Dorothy, do you think we could offer the doctor a drop of brandy? There used to be a bottle.' Then he added, for Dr Jamieson's benefit, 'In this house, it's my wife who has charge of the wine-cellar.'

Dr Jamieson was protesting unconvincingly, when Dorothy jumped up from her chair and said, 'Oh, Robert, how clever of you to think of it. I got a bottle this morning—for our small party next Monday. It's in the cupboard in the bedroom. I'll go and fetch it.' While she was out of the room, the doctor leant confidentially towards Robert and said, 'Of course, I shall call in a second opinion.' Robert nodded and said, 'Yes, of course,' while he thought what a ramp private practice could be.

Just as Dorothy was coming back with the bottle, three small glasses and a corkscrew, there was a tap on the door. It was Mrs Muller, surprisingly followed by Hugo, with his hair neatly brushed, and wearing a blue silk dressing-gown and blue bedroom-slippers. Mrs Muller said, 'I do beg your pardon, I'm sure, for intruding like this, but Hugo has told me something he thinks the doctor ought to hear. May he come in?'

Robert said, rather stiffly, 'Yes, of course he may. But don't you think he had better speak to the doctor alone?' However, Dr Jamieson seemed far too comfortably settled in his chair, to wish to move from it there and then, and Dorothy said, giving Hugo a smile, 'Yes, of course,—come in, Hugo—and you too, Mrs Muller. That is, if the doctor doesn't mind such an audience. Or would it be better if Robert and I went into our bedroom, just for a minute? I promise you, I'll do my best not to listen through the door!'

She smiled again. (Really, this beat any party!) Mrs Muller said, 'It's very good of you, Madam, but I think I'll wait for Hugo downstairs,' went out and shut the door. Dr Jamieson said ponderously, 'Well, I hardly think there can be any harm in your hearing whatever disclosure this young man has to make. Now, Hugo, what's this about?'

After giving Dorothy a look of gratitude and Robert a much more complex look, Hugo began, with complete self-possession.

'I know what woke up Miss Tredennick to-night. It was a car radio in the street, and it played the same tune as it played that night in September when she was ill before. I heard it both times. The tune is called, *Will you do the doodle 'em with me?* It's very vulgar.'

The doctor turned towards Hugo with new interest and asked, 'But what do you think was specially upsetting about this tune? You must have a lot of—er—vulgar music in this street. I know we do in the Crescent.'

Hugo looked at the old man cautiously and said, 'I don't suppose it was so much the tune, as the car that played it. You see, it was the same car that played it in September.'

'Hm, most inconsiderate. If I had my way, there'd be a curfew for all street-noises from midnight to seven a.m. But I fail to see——'

Then Dorothy interposed. 'Tell me, Hugo, where did the car stop?'

'Outside Number Seven. That's where it stopped before. You know the woman who lives there,—the young one, not Mrs O'Blahoney or one of the other three old ones—some man brought her back. The first time, they danced on the pavement. This time, they just sat in the car and talked—at least I suppose they talked—for quite a long time. Then the woman got out alone and went indoors.'

Dorothy said, 'Oh yes, I know the woman Hugo means. She's one of our rather flashier neighbours, Doctor, if you understand me.' Meanwhile, Robert was blushing, half ashamed to remember that there had been days when the mere sight of the culprit had represented the sum-total of his sex-life.

Hugo said, 'I don't think Miss Tredennick likes the woman very much. I don't like her either.' As he spoke the last words, he looked straight at Robert, who blushed still more deeply. There was a short silence. Then Dr Jamieson said, 'Thank you, Hugo. You were quite right to tell me this. It certainly might explain things up to a point, though of course—hm, hm,—well, it's nearly four o'clock and to-morrow's Christmas Eve, so the sooner you get back to bed the better, my boy.'

Hugo got up, gave the three adults a comprehensive bow, and said, 'Good night, Mrs Fawley. Good night, Dr Jamieson. Good night, Mr Fawley.' Once more he looked straight at Robert, baring his teeth a little, while his eyes radiated contempt, unwilling admiration and hatred.

When he was out of the room, Dorothy said, 'What a very strange child he is. He somehow makes you feel as if he could read your thoughts.'

XIV

CHRISTMAS EVE

CHRISTMAS EVE began with a breakfast of bread and milk for Miss Tredennick. Dr Jamieson had said to Mrs Muller, 'Unless her sight has come back to her by the morning—and it may—don't give her an ordinary breakfast. She'd either have to fumble about for things on a tray—and make a mess of it—or Magda would have to feed her, which would be rather trying for both of them. Of course, in time, it would be different. But for the moment, I recommend bread and milk, which she can eat without help. Say I ordered it.'

He came round at a quarter past nine and found his patient perfectly well, except that she was still unable to see. She said, 'Have I had a stroke?' and he answered, 'If you have, it was a stroke of a most peculiar kind, and the B.M.J. will have lots to say about it.' She went on, 'How am I to get through the day? It was bad enough getting through them before, but now—I can't read, I can't do embroidery, I can't even look out of the window. I can't do anything but listen to the wireless, which I hate. I think I'll have Hugo to sit up with me and tell me what's happening outside in the street. My body's like a coffin. I need taking out of it.'

Dr Jamieson said, 'You'll be much too busy for that. Sir Claudius Catchpole is coming at half-past ten, and I've asked Mr Julius Augenblick, the ophthalmologist, to stand by for half-past eleven, in case he's needed. I've also booked Sir Willoughby Wakenot, who's one of our leading neurologists, for half-past one—it was his only free time—and at a quarter past three, I'd like you to have a talk with Fortescue Faring, a young psychiatrist who is highly thought of. So you see, you've a very full day ahead of you.'

He went, and Magda came in to prepare the room for the specialist's visit. Miss Tredennick said, 'Magda, I want to see Hugo for a moment. Will you fetch him? I don't suppose he's going to Mr Middleton to-day.' Magda said, 'No, Madam, he isn't, but after last night he's having breakfast in bed. Mother said he was very tired.'

'What do you mean, when you say "after last night"? Was *he* awakened? Yes, poor boy, I suppose he was bound to be. Well, send him up as soon as there's a gap between all these visitors. Don't forget. It's important.'

Sir Claudius Catchpole came and examined her and conferred at length with Dr Jamieson in the entrance-hall. 'Quite so,—no sign at all,—subject of course to what Augenblick has to say—and Willoughby Wakenot. . . . My dear fellow, in such a case, one can't take too many precautions. In the end—as you suggest—we may have to rely on Fortescue Faring, though to my old-fashioned way of thinking that would be a sad comedown for British medicine.'

Dorothy, who was watching from the window above, saw him leave the house, and thought, 'What a handsome man! He looks every inch a genius.' She thought much less of Julius Augenblick, a drab little man in a snuff-coloured overcoat and without a hat. His head was redeemed from baldness by scattered, irregular patches of thin black hair, which made it look like a map. He carried a very large and shabby brown bag. Forty minutes later, when he left the house, her opinion of him was even lower. He looked like a punctured balloon, as if his professional ego had been deflated.

She was still watching, when a nurse arrived. She was a smart, cheerful little body, but Dorothy wondered how long her resilience would maintain itself against Miss Tredennick's barbed arrows. The nurse's reception was certainly inauspicious; for Hugo had anticipated her upstairs by hardly more than a minute, and when Magda tapped on the bedroom door to announce her,

Miss Tredennick called out, 'I'm busy. Please ask her to wait in my sitting-room till I send for her.' Then turning her sightless eyes towards Hugo's voice, she continued, 'So you heard the music too. Did you *see* anything?'

'Yes, Madam, I saw the woman get out.'

'And the man,—what did he do?'

'The man stayed in the car. She shook her fist at it as it drove away and went indoors.'

'Did you notice what time that was?'

'Yes, a quarter past two.' He paused, then went on with a trace of embarrassment, 'You know, Madam, I spoke to Dr Jamieson last night and told him I knew what had upset you. Was that wrong of me? I thought it might help in your cure.'

She said, almost angrily, 'Oh, you shouldn't have done that. I wish you hadn't. However, I suppose it makes no difference now. But I should have liked it to be a secret between us. If you notice anything else—you know what I mean—don't tell *them*—just tell me. Do you understand?'

'Yes, Madam. I didn't tell them about her waving her fist at the car. I kept that for you.'

'Keep everything for me. Oh, my dear Hugo, you'll have to lend me your eyes till mine recover. Keep a good watch, and write down everything you see in a private book and come up and read it to me. Oh dear, now I've got to face this new woman. Will you send her in?'

'Yes, Madam. Goodbye for now.'

'Goodbye, Hugo.'

He went out on to the landing, then opened the sitting-room door and found the nurse bridling by the back window. He gave her a condescending little nod, said, 'Miss Tredennick is ready for you, Nurse,' and went downstairs.

When Dorothy got back from her lunch with Susan at Garrows, she met Sir Willoughby Wakenot leaving Number Ten. He was big and sleek, with a bushy ginger moustache. She tried to read a diagnosis in his expression. It was slightly peevish, despite the artificial smile he gave her as he made way for her to go in. 'It's really too bad,' she thought. 'We ought to be told something *definite* by now. After all, it is Christmas-time and we have our plans to consider.' And she wondered again whether she ought to cancel her Boxing Day party. Of course, she wouldn't think of giving it, if Miss Tredennick turned out to be seriously ill. She made a resolve to ring up Dr Jamieson late that evening and ask him for his advice.

Justin, whose problem was even more urgent than Dorothy's since his party was to take place that very afternoon, had done so already. The reply had been, 'Go ahead, by all means.' As a next step, he consulted Mrs Muller. Would she think it inconsiderate of him to inflict so much washing-up on a household already burdened with extra work? But she assured him that they could take it in their stride. Besides, she had already sent Hugo out to buy the refreshments. He loved shopping and was so clever at it. So Justin began to make his small preparations. What a pity it was that his guests were going to be such a very dull lot!

Mr Fortescue Faring, the psychiatrist, arrived a few minutes before he was due. It was one of his principles to catch his patients off their guard when he could. He didn't realise that if Miss Tredennick had been able to see the time, she would have been quite capable of keeping him waiting, so as to give him a lesson in true punctuality. He had only been talking to her for five minutes when he said, 'As you've never been treated in this way before, I ought to warn you that you'll probably find yourself falling in love with me. If you do, it'll be of no consequence at all. It's merely a stage which we call a transference.'

She answered tartly. 'I hardly think that's likely,—at least, until I can see you. You have a nice voice and I like the type of eau-de-Cologne you use, but for all I know, you may be hideous.' Faring, whom some of his more romantic patients compared to pictures of the youthful Shelley, and who didn't dislike the comparison, said wittily, 'Well, that remains to be *seen*', but his expression was not very amiable.

Then he started to probe, very delicately at first, into the depths of her mind, but he soon found that his caution was quite unnecessary. It was amazing how many intimate things came pouring out during the next half-hour. At the age of twelve she had seen her father relieving one of nature's innocent needs—she didn't put it in this mealy-mouthed way—behind the potting-shed in their garden in Warwickshire, and she volunteered that she had rather enjoyed it. Indeed, Faring had to admit that never before had he come across a patient with so few inhibitions. It was only when (in accordance with Dr Jamieson's priming) he approached the subject of the car belonging to Miss Varioli's admirer, that he came upon a certain evasiveness,—an unwillingness to co-operate, the breaking-down of which might be, in two senses, not unlucrative. When the session was over, she said, 'Well,—how soon shall I know whether you're ugly or not?', and he answered, 'I hope it won't be so very long now. But we must have patience. Any attempt to hurry things too much only makes them worse, and might enlarge the area of psychotic trauma. Tell me, frankly, have you enjoyed our talk?' 'Yes and no, Mr Faring.' 'I hope it didn't distress you?' 'Not in the least. I hope it didn't shock *you*.' He gave her a smile of pity, then recollecting that she couldn't see it, transformed it into a slightly forced little laugh.

Dr Jamieson paid another visit at half-past six. Miss Tredennick said, 'Well, Doctor, this has been an expensive day. What's the verdict?'

'There isn't one. None of us—and when I say *us*, I don't of course include Mr Faring—can find anything wrong with you. Faring seems pretty confident that given time he can cure you completely,—but I'm hoping you'll cure yourself long before that. Of course, if the symptom persists, you'll have to go to a clinic after Christmas and be properly investigated. Quite possibly a course of shock-treatment would do the trick. Meanwhile——'

She interrupted him. 'Be patient, take things quietly, rest as much as you can and Nurse will give you a nerve-sedative every four hours. Is that what you mean?'

He laughed and said, 'You're a wonderful old lady. I'm sure you'll live to be at least a hundred.'

At a quarter to nine, the last of Justin's guests said good night, and he went and sat in his bedroom while Magda cleared up in the sitting-room. He was rather tired—so was Magda, though he never noticed it—and his tooth, about which he had forgotten during the party, began to nag him again. As soon as Christmas was over—or at the latest, early in the New Year—he must have it dealt with, whatever the fuss and discomfort he might be let in for. Was that a little abscess near the root? Better dab on some iodine, just in case. He did so, spilling some on a clean towel and staining his fingers a disgusting colour. Still there had been times when he'd been more unhappy, and he felt better for having made a social effort. His guests, in their somewhat second-rate way, had been quite agreeable and seemed to enjoy themselves. It was a good thing to bestir oneself now and then. Sixty-eight wasn't very old after all. General Drumwell at the Club was over eighty, and his life was one long succession of blood-sports. Not of course that one would think of taking to them, even if they promised eternal youth. Well, another Christmas Eve was nearly over. He would go to bed early and hope that in his dreams Santa Claus would make him the present of a perfect plot and the skill to turn it into a masterpiece that would rank both as a best-seller and a classic.

'Good night, Magda, and thank you so much. I'm ashamed to have given you all this extra work at such a time. Oh, by the way, will you give this envelope to Hugo? It's a little present. I meant to give it to your mother this morning.'

'Yes, Sir. It's very kind of you. Good night, Sir.'

As she went out, the Fawleys came down the stairs. Dorothy said graciously, 'What, Magda, are you still busy? You must be exhausted, poor girl. Tell me,—is there any news from the top floor?'

'No, Madam, no news at all. I think Miss Tredennick is quite well in herself,—apart from——'

'Yes, of course. What terrible things can happen to one in the twinkling of an eye. I managed to catch Dr Jamieson for a moment on his way down, and he said there was no need at all for us to put off our little party on Monday. If the news had been bad, I shouldn't have dreamt of giving it. Well, we must be going. My husband insists I shall go out with him and see the decorations. It makes me feel quite like a schoolgirl again! So good night and sweet dreams!'

'Good night, Madam. Good night, Sir.'

Robert who had been standing by in an embarrassed silence, said gruffly, 'Good night,' and without looking round followed Dorothy into the street.

Hugo went to bed early. At half-past eleven his mother tiptoed into his room and found him asleep. She was glad to find that he had remembered to hang a stocking at the foot of the bed. She detached it carefully and carried it into the sitting-room, where she filled it with presents,—a box of Turkish Delight, a bottle of green ink, a case of pencils, a small book entitled, *A Hundred Great Poems*, a five-year diary, an empty photograph-frame, and a gay figure of Puck, with tinsel wings and its body full of sweets. It had been hard to find things suitable to his age, and next year it would be still harder. She sighed as she thought that a year or two after that he would be really grown up.

Once more in his bedroom, she replaced the stocking and stood watching him in the dim light that came round the door, which she had left ajar. He was lying as he usually did, with his knees drawn up towards his chin and his face buried under the clothes,— a small, almost circular mound beneath the quilt, showing nothing except a patch of white skin at the nape of the neck, the tip of an ear and the flaxen hair on the dome of his head, which she longed to kiss. Tears gathered in her eyes, and fearing that if she stayed by him any longer she might break into sobs and wake him, she went back to the sitting-room and shut the bedroom door.

Then she brought a small Christmas-tree, already decorated, from her own bedroom, put it on a table near the window, and arranged Hugo's more serious presents round it. Her own gifts were a light, portable easel, which she hoped he would use in the park, or at any rate somewhere in the fresh air, and a pair of lamb's wool gloves. There were three books from Magda, *Treasure Island*, *Dr Jekyll and Mr Hyde* and *The New Arabian Nights*, a silk muffler and three pairs of socks from Miss Tredennick, and from Mr Bray the envelope which he had entrusted to Magda that evening. Mrs Muller hoped that this year it contained a pound instead of ten shillings. She looked at the little heap and wished it could have been bigger. But there was still a Christmas cake in store and a box of lovely fat crackers. Then she knelt down in front of the Christmas-tree and prayed:

'O most merciful Father, I beg Thee to grant my dear, sweet son a happy Christmas, and a happy New Year. Grant him long life and prosperity, I beg Thee, and grant that I shall never see him ill or in pain or suffering in any way, and that when I die, I shall leave him happy. Visit not the sins of the fathers upon the children. O God, bless my darling Hugo, now and for ever. Amen.'

She went into her bedroom and began to undress, and then remembered that she had forgotten to put out her presents for Magda, who was already in bed. With a sense of effort, she took the parcels from a drawer—a hat and a blouse—went back with them to the sitting-room and laid them on Magda's desk.

[2]

Since half-past nine, when she had dismissed the nurse for the night, Miss Tredennick had been wide awake, despite the sedative that Dr Jamieson had prescribed for her. The night was chilly, but both her windows were open eight inches at the top. She had heard the bustle of Christmas Eve die away, and the shrill or raucous performances of the carol-singers become more and more infrequent till they ceased. The only sounds now were the noisy closings of a few front doors, the swish of an occasional car in the street and footfalls on the pavement.

All the bravado which had sustained her so gallantly throughout the day and early evening, and had made her illness seem like a heroic and not unamusing adventure, had suddenly vanished. She felt desperately alone and frightened, and for the first time for many years found herself sobbing. (Could these belated tears bring back her sight?)

She feared that the doctors might be in league with one another to deceive her. Was she going to die? Her father had lived for seven years after his first stroke, and had passed them fairly happily, but he hadn't gone blind till a fortnight before he died. She had started with blindness. They had said it was only a temporary phase, a neurotic spasm, and that in quite a short time she would recover perfect vision. But she wasn't neurotic. She had never been a hypochondriac like Mr Bray or Mrs Fawley. When her arthritis was painful, there was no self-pity or anxiety in her cantankerousness. She had adjusted her life to it—with complaints, it was true, yet without mental anguish.

But could she make that far more terrible adjustment which total blindness would demand of her? Could she bear to be dependent on the eyes of a paid companion? Some pert or cringing creature, like the nurse, perhaps, who would say, 'Now, Miss Tredennick, I've made you some really lovely bread and milk. . . . You know where I've put your tablets—just here, by the bell-push. . . . I think there's rain in the air. I do hope it holds off for the holidays. . . . You'll be feeling ever so much brighter to-morrow. After all, Christmas only comes once a year and it's our duty to make the best of it, and this is such a comfortable room to spend it in. I put those four cards, which came by the last post, on the little table by the window. There isn't any room on the mantelpiece. I don't think I've ever seen so many before—and such handsome ones, too. . . . Now are you quite sure you've everything you want? Remember, you've only got to press the bell and I shall be with you in less than half a minute. . . . Good night,—and sleep well.'

Then she had a still more terrifying thought. If sight could go, without warning, as hers had gone, couldn't touch, taste, smell and hearing also go in the same way? Was it true that there were people with vigorous minds, who had to lie completely motionless except when somebody moved them, tasting nothing even when they were forcibly fed, hearing nothing—not even the silly chatter of a nurse or a doctor's lies—feeling nothing that was tangible, unaware of the scent of freshly made broth or the soap with which they were washed or the flowers left hurriedly by some embarrassed visitor, and in utter darkness except for those wistful or fantastic images which memory or the tormented brain evoked deep behind the eyes? Surely the brain would snap under the strain of such a cruel introspection? Perhaps that was the only hope such people had left,—the hope that the misery of rational thought would some day be spared them, and that their consciousness would become a long dream without an awakening.

As a development of this idea, she tried to relax the tension of her thoughts and to let them flow through her of their own volition, like a languid current which, instead of washing obstacles away, seeps through them imperceptibly and then reforms itself.

She glided back nearly seventy years to Christmas Eve in Warwickshire, the big church on the hill, the glow of the stained-glass windows as she and her mother walked up the snowy path to the midnight service, the drip of wax from tall candles,—then, with a shift of scene, to her father wasting half a box of matches while he tried to light the brandy on the plum-pudding, the little sprig of holly on the top that crackled in the flame and gave out an acrid smell, while Melford held the dish in his tremulous hands. (Of course, one New Year's Eve, he was sacked for being drunk.) Next came the pink-coated hunt streaking the crisp white fields, the children's parties and the Beresford boys almost tearing off Monica Fielding's fancy-dress. What little devils they were! However, her father had told Gwen's father to give them a real old-fashioned horsewhipping the next day. Gwen's father was then a very handsome young groom, though it was easier to remember him as he was thirty years later, with a fringe of straw-coloured hair round his bald pate, and Gwen, a shy, serious, rather stupid girl of ten, not unlike what Magda was destined to be thirty years later still, when the Mullers came back from Germany to Cornwall. Cornwall, stuffed birds, the damp crawling up the walls, the long dreariness of the black-out, the bombing of Falmouth and Truro.

No, it wouldn't work. The retrospect led her back remorselessly to the present. She was alone and blind, on the top floor of Number Ten Pollitt Place, without real friends or any real ties with life except her money and her will to live.

One o'clock struck. The street had been very quiet for a long time,—but was that the sound of a car? Yes, it was,—a car coming nearer, round the Crescent towards the Place. Suppose it should pull up at Number Seven, would she be able to hear the tell-tale tune on the radio? But on Christmas Eve, the most abandoned foreign station would hardly broadcast *Me doodle 'em*. She hoped Hugo was awake and on the watch. His eyes at least would be faithful. But he'd been up very late the night before and ought to be sleeping so soundly that nothing could rouse him. Should she summon the nurse? She could hear a muffled snore, coming through the door between her bedroom and the sitting-room, where Nurse was sleeping on an improvised bed. What a dreadful woman she was, with a subtle, inner commonness about her, such as was altogether lacking in Gwen and Magda.

The car seemed to have stopped at the end of the Crescent. Perhaps it had no connexion with 'Y.V.' What was *she* doing that night? Lurking in alleys or plying for hire at some shady club? Or might this be the one night of the year when she gave her trade a rest? Her name and her swarthy colouring indicated some sort of a Roman Catholic origin. Had she been to confession and to Midnight Mass, washing away with one evening's penitence, the guilt of three hundred and sixty-four evenings? Oh, if only it were possible to see whether or not a light was burning behind the thin curtains of her bedroom window! How beatific and rapturous a vision that well-known glimmer of pale peach would be!

For one moment, Miss Tredennick thought of getting out of bed and groping her way to the window (as she had done only the night before, and many other nights, too,—though they belonged to a different incarnation), and peering across the street with all the strength of her will. But she remembered the oculist's advice, supported by one of the doctors. 'Don't strain your eyes. Don't even make any effort to distinguish between light and darkness. Let things take their course. Otherwise you might impair the optic nerve. You must try to live like a cabbage for a few days.' 'Days' did they say,—or was it 'weeks' or 'months'? A feeling of hysterical impotence came over her and she quivered with fear and anger. The eiderdown slid off the bed on to the floor, but even so, the bedclothes were too heavy. The air of the room seemed stale and stifling. (O to be standing naked on the top of a wind-swept mountain!) How could she hope to sleep, in that heat and encompassed by a darkness which had no end?

If suffering, as some say, atones for sin, Miss Tredennick atoned for a good many sins that night.

XV

CHRISTMAS DAY

'A HAPPY Christmas!' Nurse was the first to say it, and she added, 'It's a bright, lovely day, but a bit on the chilly side. Hadn't I better close one of the windows?' (Oh, go away!) Magda's turn came next. 'May I wish you a very happy Christmas, Madam?' The girl spoke diffidently and self-consciously, as well she might. A happy Christmas indeed! Soon, they'd all be in,—Gwen, Dr Jamieson, Mrs Fawley, on some excuse or other, and perhaps even the reluctant Mr Bray, for the sake of good manners. Hugo alone,—the only one she really wanted to see—to *see*, that was a verb she had better try to forget!—would never come up unless she sent for him.

There was another tap on the bedroom door. Life had become a succession of doors opened and doors shut. 'Come in.' This was Gwen. She had a heavy walk for such a slim woman.

'Good morning, Madam, and a happy Christmas, I'm sure.' Her voice sounded strangely excited,—not at all like a voice modulated to the decencies of a sick-room.

'The same to you, Gwen. Is there anything—anything special— you want to say to me? Nurse isn't here, is she?'

'No, Madam, she's in the bathroom. Oh, I must tell you, there's been a piece of the most startling news—though it's very sad— from Number Seven over the way. The young lady who lives in the top-floor front was found dead half an hour ago.'

'That woman—*dead*?'

Miss Tredennick almost shouted the words and raised her head and looked straight into Mrs Muller's eyes, which were sparkling with pleasure, while her cheeks were red and her fingers fiddled with a button on her house-coat. Miss Tredennick thought, 'She seems quite delighted—and it makes her look so silly, like a young bird that's going to be given a worm.' Then she gasped and felt

138

as if she were going to choke. This was real. She could *see* Mrs Muller. She could see the whole room and everything in it.

She said very quietly, 'Oh, Gwen, I wonder if you'd arrange those cards on the mantelpiece. One's fallen on to the floor near the radiator and that blue one with the daffodils is right on the edge.'

With instinctive obedience, Mrs Muller turned round to do as she was told, then suddenly the truth dawned on her too, and she turned round again.

'Why, Madam, you can—are you—are your eyes——? Oh, Madam, I don't know what to say.'

'Yes, Gwen. I can see as clearly as ever I did. It's a miracle. That's to say, it's as miraculous as my going blind.'

Mrs Muller wiped her own eyes with a handkerchief. 'Oh, Madam, I'm so thankful,—so very thankful.'

'So am I, Gwen—though I suppose I might have been still more thankful if the whole thing had never occurred at all. But that's a tricky question. Now tell me at once, what happened to the poor woman at Number Seven? How did you come to hear of it?'

'Through Mrs Petcham, Madam,—who works at Number Fourteen in return for the basement. Mrs O'Blahoney came over to ask her advice. They've always been friendly. Mrs O'Blahoney said that when Miss Wheeler—she's the elderly party who has the first-floor back at Number Seven—came out of her room—she was going to early service—she noticed a strong smell of gas coming down from the landing above. There's still an old gas-bracket on the top floor, which hasn't been disconnected, though it's never used—and gas-fires in the bedrooms. So Mrs O'Blahoney went up to see what was the matter, and as soon as she turned the corner of the stairs, she saw a sheet of drawer-paper on the young lady's door. It was fixed there with sticking-plaster, and had written on it, "Gas—Beware". She telephoned to the gas people at once and then came across to see Mrs Petcham. Of course, Mrs Petcham asked her if she'd rung up the police, but Mrs O'Blahoney—who, between ourselves, Madam, I don't think is any too fond of the police—said she hadn't. Well, Mrs Petcham said she must ring them immediately and suggest they should send a doctor or bring one with them, and she said she would. They came in a car just before eight o'clock—I didn't see them, but Mrs Petcham told me—and found the young lady lying dead on her bed. She was dressed in her day-clothes. According to Mrs O'Blahoney, she never left her room since she came back yesterday afternoon at half-past five. That's all I know, so far.'

Miss Tredennick said reflectively, but without any trace of mournfulness in her voice, 'Oh dear, oh dear! What a thing to happen in Pollitt Place. I can't pretend—but one mustn't speak evil of the dead. Was there no note? These people usually leave something behind by way of explanation, even if the explanation isn't quite true.'

'I haven't heard of any note being found, Madam.'

'Well, I suppose we shouldn't be too curious. I'm glad to see it doesn't seem to have spoilt your Christmas for you.'

Mrs Muller blushed at the question implied by Miss Tredennick's steady scrutiny. It was quite true she felt an enormous relief. Hugo had said that somebody in the house was going to die before the end of the year. Obviously, when he said, 'in this house', he had meant to say, 'in this street'. And with this small amendment, not only was his gift of prophecy confirmed, but all was well. That worry, at least, was done with. But she couldn't confess all this to Miss Tredennick, who, for twenty-four hours had seemed by far the most likely victim of Hugo's clairvoyance. So she changed the subject and said, 'And now, Madam, what are your plans for the day? Dr Jamieson said he'd be round at ten o'clock.'

Miss Tredennick said quickly, 'I shall see him, of course. Then the first thing I shall do will be to get rid of that nurse. After that I'll ring up all the friends whom you had to put off from coming to tea with me this afternoon, and tell them I'm quite well again and expecting them. Please tell that to Mr Bray, as soon as you see him.'

Mrs Muller breathed still more freely. She had been terrified that Miss Tredennick, in her blind loneliness, would summon Hugo to have tea with her, and though in the ordinary way she had no objection to his having as many meals with Miss Tredennick as he might be invited to share, he had announced with a quiet inflexibility that he would be out to tea that afternoon. Magda was there when he said so, and had given him a very odd look, but he took no notice and turning to his mother he had said, 'I promise you I shan't get into any harm—or mix with bad companions. I'll be back for supper with you at home.' And when he kissed her, he had looked so happy that she hadn't the heart to ask him where he was going.

'Quite so, Madam. It'll make you forget this terrible time you've had. There's the doctor. Magda's downstairs and will let him in. And Nurse is back from the bathroom. I can hear her in the sitting-room. Shall I tell her—or would you rather——?'

Miss Tredennick said simply, 'Ask her to wait till she shows Dr Jamieson in.'

'Good morning, Doctor. You're looking rather hot. You shouldn't scamper up the stairs like that. . . . No, I'm not bluffing. I've recovered my sight. Please God I keep it.'

Dr Jamieson gave her a long and penetrating stare, nodded and said, 'It's very much as I thought—though of course I couldn't be sure. I'm delighted—delighted. I needn't tell you that. Well, now we shall have to think of what we are going to do about things. Your only appointment to-day was with Mr Faring.'

Miss Tredennick said sarcastically, 'I suppose at overtime rates! It would be rather fun to see him and not let him know what has happened. I should love to lead him just a little way up the garden-path.'

Dr Jamieson shook his head. 'These people aren't such fools as they look.'

'Does he look a fool? Remember, I never saw him. But I picture him as a young middle-aged man, with a slightly effeminate face and perhaps the suggestion of a lemon-coloured moustache.'

'Quite right. And does Nurse here look just as you pictured her, too?'

Miss Tredennick turned her gaze towards the nurse, who was standing near the door with an indignant expression. She answered wickedly and mendaciously, 'No, not at all. When I tried to visual-ise her, I saw a tall, rather delicate, slender woman with a sad face and an artist's tapering fingers.'

Nurse spoke for the first time. 'Come, come, Miss Tredennick, it's too bad of you to tease me like that. But I can't say how pleased I am to find my patient so very much better this morning. Well, doctor——?'

Before he could answer, Miss Tredennick said very firmly, 'Let me make it quite clear that there's nothing wrong with me. I'm in just as good health as I was before I had this ghastly attack. If I *should* have another, I'll be most grateful for everybody's assistance, though I hope I shouldn't feel quite so worried about myself another time. But till and when that happens—and I'm not going to let the possibility of it bother me—I intend to live my ordinary life. I should like to start it now, and get up at once!'

Ten minutes later, when the nurse had gone down to the hall with Dr Jamieson, she said, 'Doctor, do you think she was shamming the whole time?', and he replied, 'That isn't at all an easy question to answer. No—I don't think she was shamming in the sense that she was putting on an act to deceive us. I've no doubt Faring could get to the bottom of it, if she'd co-operate with him, but clearly she wouldn't. And why should she? She's past the age when he could do her any real good. Well, Nurse, I'm sorry you're being so bustled about at Christmas-time, but you'll be able to give yourself a rest for the next six days, if you want one. No doubt you realised it was hopeless for me to suggest that you should stay your time out here as a kind of lady-companion.'

Nurse tossed her shoulders, and said, 'No, Doctor, of course I understand that. I've never been one to force myself on a house where I'm not welcome. I may think a good deal, but I can keep my thoughts to myself.'

Dr Jamieson hid his mild dislike of her under a smile, shook hands, said goodbye and walked back to his home in the Crescent.

Miss Tredennick was sitting in her usual chair by the window, gazing into the street. Every detail was visible to her keen eyes. They reviewed in turn every threshold, every door-knob, every knocker, every door, fanlight and window. The two windows on the top floor of Number Seven were open to their widest extent.

Surely, it would have been more decent to draw the curtains, if *she* were lying there, dead on the bed. Or had they taken the body to the mortuary? But, of course, the room had been full of gas, and it would be some time before it was properly aired.

Who would have the room next? Some dull, modest old woman, who'd sit behind the net curtains like a witch and spy through a narrow slit on Number Ten? Even now, no doubt, there were women keeping watch at most of those windows. Those on the north side of the street had heard of the sudden catastrophe at Number Seven, while those on the south side were hardly less agog over the catastrophe at Number Ten (not knowing that the excitement there was over), and were peeping out in the hope of seeing a nurse's uniform or a doctor's top hat—Dr Jamieson always wore a top hat when he visited Miss Tredennick—or better still, an oxygen-cylinder or some fantastic piece of medical apparatus brought to the door by Allen & Hanbury's van.

Like herself, they were waiting and watching. They could see everything that wasn't hidden from them by blinds or curtains. But like herself, they could find nothing worth looking at. And in all probability, there'd never be anything worth looking at again.

With a sigh, she brought out her Journal, read it through and began to tear it into very small pieces.

[2]

Of all those who lived at Number Ten, Magda alone had been really shocked by Miss Varioli's death, the cause of which, though it might be a matter of conjecture to others, was to Magda quite clear. The wretched woman, whose wickedness had been only too openly revealed by her conduct, her face, her voice, and the way she walked, had committed suicide in a fit of remorse for her sins. But she was not the only sinner in Pollitt Place, and when Magda—though her creed set little store by prayers for the dead—said an impulsive prayer for the dead woman's soul, she added a prayer that when her own turn should come, she might be given the leisure and the grace to make a sincere and adequate repentance.

When Dorothy heard the news, she said, 'Oh, how sad! But

these things always happen to women of that sort in the end,'
while Robert said nothing, but thought the world the poorer
for the loss of Miss Varioli's fine body,—not of course that these
days she meant anything to him. Justin said, 'What a tragedy!',
and remembering how only a few weeks before he had compared
himself with the gay hoyden who lived opposite, he found a grim
satisfaction in the thought that his elderly feebleness should have
outlived her youthful vitality.

Mrs Muller was still in a radiant mood. So many good things
seemed to have happened that day. Miss Tredennick was better—
whatever schemes Mrs Muller might have had for the disposition
of Miss Tredennick's money, she was too loyal to wish her anything but good health—they had got rid of the nurse, who in her
short stay had already begun to make a nuisance of herself, and
Hugo, though quiet, was happy and really pleased with his presents. And above all, there was no need to worry any longer about
his terrifying prediction, which quite obviously had referred to
Number Seven and not Number Ten. That's what he had meant,—
that's what he must have meant.

But she couldn't bear not to have his own confirmation, so that
the last of her niggling doubts might be set at rest, and when they
had finished their midday meal in the kitchen—their Christmas
dinner was to be in the evening,—she turned to Magda, who was
starting to clear away, and said, 'How right Hugo was, when he
said that someone round here was going to die before the end of
the year!' As Magda shrugged her shoulders and didn't reply, Mrs
Muller appealed to Hugo, who had been very silent throughout
the meal. 'Did you hear me, dear? Aren't you feeling proud of
yourself?' Hugo shook his head. 'But why not, darling? Why not?
You knew there would be a death in this street before the end of
this year and told us so. Don't you remember?' Hugo almost whispered, 'Did I say in this *street*?' His mother trembled, but did her
best not to show it. 'Not actually, darling, but that's what you must
have meant. You did mean it, didn't you?'

'I only meant what I said.'

Magda looked over her shoulder and said brusquely, 'He said
in this *house*—and he was completely wrong. I do wish, Mother,

you wouldn't encourage him to talk such nonsense.' Mrs Muller sat down with her elbows on the table and covered her face with her hands. Then Hugo, with an unusual look of contrition, went up to her, put his hand on her shoulder and whispered in her ear, 'It's all right, Mutti. Don't worry about it. As Magda says, I was completely wrong.'

Before his mother could look up at him, he walked to his room, so that she didn't see the guilty colour suffusing his cheeks. The lie direct, even told in a good cause, never came easily to him.

[3]

Three hours to get through. He would go for a stroll in the park, but that wouldn't fill the difficult afternoon. Had it been summer, he might have taken his easel and passed the time sketching, but it was far too cold to sit about, despite the burst of bright sunshine that cast its beam a few feet inside his window.

He was now nervously regretting his boldness in accepting Bert's invitation. What kind of figure would he cut at the party? He would be tongue-tied and awkward, all his natural good manners rendered boorish by shyness and the wish to please. And what kind of woman was this wife of Bert's? If she was the sentimental, motherly type, all would be well. He could feel at home with such women. But if she thought of herself as 'pretty and attractive'—a description given by Sunday newspapers to nine out of ten female witnesses at trials for rape—she wouldn't like him at all. Nor would he like her.

And the young people—all those nephews and nieces—would be still more of a peril. They wouldn't be able to talk, but they'd know how to shout and to make amends for their lack of mental ability by crude displays of bodily vigour, rough-and-tumbles and practical jokes that might turn to horse-play. They would either chum up with him or reject him pointedly from their fellowship. In any event, they would be bound to feel that he didn't want any of them to be there, and would have preferred to have tea alone with Bert and his wife—or better still, with Bert but without his wife. Yet, if he'd said to Bert, 'No, I'm afraid my mother wouldn't

hear of my going out on Christmas Day,' he could never have forgiven himself for his cowardice.

In this mood of diffidence, which gained on him as he wasted
the minutes, gazing idly through the area railings into the street,
he had a sudden impulse to see Miss Tredennick, who, he felt,
might in some strange way give him counsel or comfort. How odd
it was that the oldest female and the youngest male at Number
Ten should have such a kinship. Why not put it to the test? At the
worst, she would say, 'You shouldn't come here without my sending for you.'

After making sure that both his mother and Magda had left the
sitting-room, he slipped out into the passage, went quietly up the
three flights of stairs and knocked on the door of Miss Tredennick's bedroom.

'Come in. Why, Hugo, it's you!'

'Oh, Madam, you must excuse me, but I felt I had to come up
and tell you how glad I am to hear your good news,—and to thank
you for the beautiful scarf and socks. Mother says I wear out my
socks terribly quickly. I've such small heels. Are you really well
now, Madam?'

'Yes, thank you, Hugo. As well as I ever shall be. I wonder if you
can understand what a grim thing that is to say.'

'Yes, Madam, I think I do. Sometimes when I'm in a hurry—you
know, when I have to, I can get about far quicker than people think
I can—I say to myself, "Hugo, you'll never be able to walk more
quickly than this."'

She nodded, was about to make a sympathetic reply, then
checked it. 'Tell me, Hugo, what exactly did you hear about my
recovery?'

He looked puzzled and she went on, 'What I mean is, have you
heard it suggested that I'm nothing but a tiresome fraud?'

'No, Madam, I heard nothing like that. The nearest that came
to it was when the nurse was saying goodbye to Mother. She said,
"Old people get all sorts of fancies in their heads, and you just have
to humour them." Mother didn't like it and said that of all the
people she had met, you were the last one to be fanciful.'

'And what do you think?'

He looked down at the carpet before answering, and then said, avoiding her eyes, 'I think you really hated the woman opposite.'

'Well, if I did? She and her friends were noisy and vulgar and I'm sure she led what is called an immoral life. But it isn't hatred, it's love, that's supposed to make people blind. And it's a very long time since love has troubled me. Poor boy, I imagine you're just reaching the age when you'll have to go through it.' Hugo raised his eyes and studied her, sitting very upright in her chair by the window. He remembered his mother saying to somebody, 'She mayn't have a title, but she looks every inch a lady.' Her room was very much his idea of a lady's. It wasn't a museum of beautiful things like Mr Bray's. Hugo's acquaintance with the furniture-shops in Parkwell Road had familiarised him with the difference between the 'antique' and the 'secondhand'. Quite a number of Miss Tredennick's things were obviously the latter. Yet taken collectively, they gave an impression of gentility that was lacking in the slap-up prettiness of Mrs Fawley's drawing-room.

He said, 'I'm going to a tea-party to-day with a lot of people I don't know.'

'Who invited you, Hugo?'

'One of the dustmen who clears away our rubbish. His name is Bert.'

'Oh,—do you mean the big, good-looking, red-headed one?'

'Yes, Madam.'

'Does your mother know where you're going?'

'She knows I'm going out, but she doesn't know where. I somehow didn't like to tell her that.'

Miss Tredennick smiled ironically, then a trace of wistfulness came into her expression.

'Well, Hugo, as we seem to have got on such confidential terms, I'm going to tell you a secret about myself. There was a time when I was madly in love with your grandfather,—I mean your mother's father, of course. I expect you know he used to be our coachman, till we gave up carriages and took to motors. Then he stayed on as our chauffeur. But he was our head-groom when I was in love with him. I must have been about eight. He was very handsome—or I thought he was—and I adored him in a way I've never adored any other human being. I used to spend as much time as I dared in the stables, watching him at his work. Once, even, I gave him some cigarettes which I'd stolen from the silver box in the smoking-room. (In those days, you know, private houses had smoking-rooms.) I'm sure he must have found me a thorough nuisance. I was a very ugly child, strong-minded and much too talkative. This was long before he married your grandmother, but when he did, although I'd quite grown out of my silly passion—or thought I had—I couldn't help feeling jealous. You look pale and worried. Take a walk in the park, but don't over-tire yourself. Arrive just a little late. You may not enjoy this tea-party very much—and it's no use my trying to give you any advice as to how you should behave or what you should say—but I'm sure that when you get home again, you'll be glad you went. Now I'm expecting Magda in a few minutes, so you'd better go. I wish you a very happy afternoon.'

'Thank you, Madam. I wish you the same.'

She shook her head slightly, as if to indicate that such a wish was most unlikely to be fulfilled.

He went downstairs slowly, exaggerating his limp. *I was a very ugly child.* Miss Tredennick's phrase haunted him not only on his way down to the basement, but in Kensington Gardens. And its force came home to him still more keenly when he reached the Round Pond and saw half a dozen children sailing their boats and scampering excitedly along the bank, to intercept them before the new paint got a bump against the stonework. They were all younger than Hugo, but so full of animal spirits that he shrank from approaching too closely, in case one of them should jostle him into the water. Their faces glowed a bright pink in the rising north wind.

He continued his walk and noticed at one of the corners of the pond—for the Round Pond has corners of a sort, despite its name—two very small boys kneeling close to one another and sobbing bitterly into a handkerchief which they shared between them. Hugo judged them to belong to a different class, both socially and physically, from the well-fed, prosperous group whose exuberance had dismayed him a few minutes before.

He soon realised what the two children were crying about. Their streaming eyes kept turning to a small patch of green which bobbed up and down some twenty feet from the shore. It was evidently the keel of their little boat which had turned turtle, and was drifting away with tedious perversity towards the middle of the pond. He went up to them and said shyly, 'Is that your boat?' Hearing his grown-up voice they looked round hopefully, but when they saw it was an under-sized cripple who had addressed them, their spirits sank. One of them said ruefully, 'Yes, that's our boat, that was! And Mum only give it us this morning.' Hugo was at a complete loss for words. He had no practical advice to offer—they had already tried throwing sticks and small stones without effect—and abstract commiseration seemed valueless. There was only one thing to do.

He asked, 'Do you know how much your mother paid for the boat?'

'Yes, Guv'nor, three and sevenpence-'apenny. It was marked on the sail.'

Hugo felt in his trouser-pocket, where he knew he had fourteen shillings and six pence, and took out two half-crowns. 'Here you are,' he said awkwardly, 'you'll be able to buy yourselves another boat—perhaps a better one—when the shops open again.'

The children opened their mouths and stared at him. Then the one who hadn't yet spoken said, 'Cor! But, Mister, you can't spare all that. We've each got a bob. If you give us 'alf a dollar, we'll have enough.'

Hugo said grandly, 'No, you'd better have half a crown each. I've been lucky this Christmas. Here you are.' He bestowed his largess, avoiding contact, so far as he could, with the two grubby hands that accepted it. 'Golly, you're a real gent, you are——' But he was already hurrying away.

The experience both shook him and exalted him. He felt like a nervous god, and hoped that his newly acquired divinity would at least endure throughout the afternoon. There was something consoling about the episode. Talk of ugly children—both the boys were repellent. One had a discharge from his nose, and the other a sore in the middle of his cheek. Their ears were filthy, and despite the keen wind they smelt as if they slept with their clothes on and wetted their bed. Yet it was possible to be sorry for them and be fond of them. Miss Tredennick had said that love was supposed to make people blind. But could it not also bring enlightenment?

He would have liked to sit down and try to think things out, but it was too cold, and he continued to walk, though a good deal more slowly. The sight of the tall, leafless trees, with their upper branches tossed backwards and forwards, gave him a pleasure that was new to him. Their strength and their resilience seemed to be his. Whatever was to happen, this was one of those days selected by fate to be a landmark in the emotional history of a life-time. One may sink back afterwards and say, 'My word, how soppily romantic I was that afternoon!', but one has been changed and enriched, brought nearer maturity—nearer to death, perhaps. These are moments when the soul stands outside the flux of time, if the body cannot, and Hugo's imagination—though less articulate than this epitome of what it brooded upon—almost carried him to a dimension in which the ticking of clocks is an irrelevance.

Then happily—or unhappily—his practical nature reasserted itself. And he thought, 'If I walk right round the Serpentine, as I should like to, I shall be much too tired to enjoy the party. And I shall be late for it,—even later than Miss Tredennick would recommend.' And he went home.

[4]

Exhausted with his climb up eight flights of stone stairs, he leant against the cream-distempered wall, dizzy, breathless and frightened. What had now become of that god-like force which had entered into him while he walked among the trees between the Round Pond and the Serpentine? (O that he could have stayed there and prolonged that moment of vision for ever!) Meanwhile, the longer he waited for his strength to come back, the feebler he felt. His legs began to tremble, and he wondered how soon he would be unable to stand. There was nothing for it,—he must either go back, a crestfallen failure, to Ten Pollitt Place, or ring the bell at once and hope that they'd offer him a chair as soon as he was inside.

He rang the bell—it was one of those clockwork bells that go off alarmingly an inch or two from your hand—and a woman opened the door. She was thin and pale, with high cheek-bones and large greenish eyes which looked as if they might easily break into tears. She reminded Hugo a little of Mrs Fawley, except that she was much taller. She held the door almost shut, while she studied him in the dim light of a bulb hanging over the staircase. Then she opened it fully and said, 'Oh, you must be Mr Muller. Bert doubted if you'd come, with all our stairs, and being away from your mother on Christmas Day. Come in,—you're welcome.' She showed him into a narrow passage, opened a door on the right and called, 'Bert—here's Mr Muller.' The room seemed full of people and their voices made a terrifying hubbub. Then Bert, looking very clean in his smart blue suit, with his red hair smarmed close to the sides of his head, strode out, took hold of Hugo's two hands, shook them vigorously and said, 'A happy Christmas! It's good to see you. Let me take your coat. Come inside.' Introductions began. 'The wife—but you've met already. My sister-in-law, Mrs Rintoul—Mr Rintoul—Alec, Ian, Jennifer—they're all Rintouls too—Mrs Bentley—she's another sister-in-law—and the little ones there are Alice and Pansy Bentley—Billy Bentley—Mrs O'Donovan—Moyra O'Donovan—neighbours of ours—this is Hugo Muller, a friend of mine. Tea will be ready in about ten minutes.'

Bert's wife suggested that Hugo might like to spend the interval with the Rintoul boys, who were playing with a new train. He would far rather have surveyed the company and the room, which was festooned with a criss-cross of paper-chains and chinese lanterns and had a big bunch of mistletoe hanging down from the oxidised chandelier in the middle of the ceiling, but Mrs Rintoul took charge of him and pushed him towards a corner, where her sons squatted over their toy. (Hugo recognised the model at once. Twenty-seven and nine. He had seen it in Garrows, and in the toyshop further down Parkwell Road. There was a cheaper set at nineteen and three and a more expensive one at forty-eight shillings.) The two boys displayed no interest in him at all, but Jennifer Rintoul and Moyra O'Donovan who had joined the group, plucked at his sleeve and kept showing him their dolls. Then Billy Bentley came up with a cardboard box. He was a sturdy little boy of eight, with thick, straight black hair and black eyebrows which met on the bridge of his nose. He said, 'I've been given a pirate's dress. Would you like me to put it on?' Hugo, whose nature was attuned to any latent abnormality, hesitated and then said, 'Yes, I should.' Billy said, 'If we do play pirates, I'll have to take all your money and cut your throat.' Then Hugo suggested, not without malice, that pirates might rob trains as well as ships, and pointed to the self-satisfied Rintoul boys whose little engine was still performing patient figures of eight. 'Gee, that's an idea,' said Billy, with glistening eyes. But at that moment Bert's voice rang out, 'Come on all, tea's ready.' Then Mrs Rintoul, who was the wrong sort of motherly type, and whose body seemed to exude a greasy smell which Hugo found almost nauseating said, 'You sit by me.' But Bert's wife came up and rescued him, and said that the greatest stranger must sit beside her,—'though I shan't have much time to make conversation with you, as I shall be kept busy dishing up.'

In Bert's household, tea meant much more than tea, and Hugo shuddered as he thought of the Christmas dinner he was supposed to eat that night with his mother and Magda in the quiet of Number Ten. But the food was good. There were hot sausages, sardines, shrimps, winkles (and pins, with which to prick them out of their shells), crumpets, paste-sandwiches, jam sandwiches, currant bread-and-butter, fancy cakes of all colours and a big Christmas-cake with a snowman on the top and Hugo, who had been too much on tenterhooks to make a good lunch, found his appetite again and gave way to it, though he couldn't match the capacity of the other young people.

Bert's wife did her best to talk to him, and asked him where he went to school. He told her rather reluctantly that he went to a tutor. And what was he going to be, when he grew up? He wasn't sure, but he rather liked the idea of becoming an artist. At this point, Billy Bentley, who had been following the conversation closely, said, 'Oo! And paint people when they're bare?' His mother, who overheard, declared loudly that he was a rude, dirty-minded boy. Hugo blushed and said, 'No, I meant landscapes.' Then he turned to Bert's wife and added quietly, 'Though I did a sketch of your husband the other day, while he was busy outside our place.' 'No, did you really? You must let us see it.' 'Oh, but I couldn't. I haven't shown it to anyone at all. It wasn't a good likeness.' He blushed still more deeply and continued, 'I might be able to improve it, if you could lend me a photograph of him.' Bert's wife said that her husband had never sat for a photograph since they were married, though of course she'd got some snaps of him. A friend of theirs had taken quite a number only last summer, when they were having their holiday at Westgate. Now, wouldn't he have another slice of cake?

Soon, everybody began to pull the crackers, examine the little novelties and trinkets inside them, read the mottoes and put on paper-hats. There was a call for round games, which Hugo dreaded, but the Rintoul boys said they'd rather play with their train and Billy was eager to show himself off in his pirate's costume. The girls formed a quizzical little group near Hugo, but he kept his distance and waited till he saw Bert coming out of the kitchen. Then he made a dart, and said, 'You promised to show me what our house looks like from your window. Do you think I could see it now?'

Bert answered, 'We'll have a try,' and drew back the curtains. 'There, that's where I make it. The big building on the right is Garrows' warehouse. You see those two tall chimneys to the left of it, in line with that window down there with the red blind? There's a gap in the roofs, just to the left of them. . . .'

But Hugo couldn't follow the indications, and Bert brought down his head to the level of Hugo's and found that the lower line of vision was interrupted by some buildings in the foreground. He said, 'Let me lift you up,' and putting his hands under Hugo's armpits, raised him high in the air, till his head was even higher than Bert's.

'Now can you see it? Garrows' warehouse—the chimneys—the gap. . . .'

It was a clear, bright night, and by good fortune a brilliant light in an uncurtained window in one of the houses lying at right-angles to Pollitt Place, shone across the intervening backyards and gardens and enabled Hugo to recognise Number Ten.

He clapped his hands like an excited child, and said, 'Yes, I can, I can! I can see the window of Miss Tredennick's sitting-room and the haunted room in the roof. Oh, don't put me down yet,—unless I'm too heavy.'

Bert laughed. 'What, *you* too heavy? You forget the kind of things I'm used to lifting,—up and down steep iron or wooden steps—and very rickety some of them are too. I don't suppose you've noticed the steps at Number Seven in your street. They're dangerous, they are. The Council ought to see that they're put right. . . .'

He went on talking, as if to make it clear that the burden of Hugo's body was too slight to be thought of. But Hugo wasn't listening. Letting himself rest limply against Bert's broad, strong chest, he was filled with a rapture, such as Ganymede, nestling in the divine eagle's warm down, must have felt on the skyward journey. Chimneys and spires seemed to bow like reeds, clouds parted and strange aerial vistas revealed themselves to his ecstatic gaze. Then he sighed with such an intensity of joy, that Bert, who thought that the height must have made him dizzy, put him down gently, pinched his cheek and said, 'You quite all right?' Hugo was too full of emotion to speak, and looked up at him so strangely that Bert was uneasy. Then Hugo said huskily, 'Oh, that was lovely. Oh Bert, do promise me you'll let me come here again—when it's quieter—and—and——' Bert said, 'Sure. Now here's Moyra who's saved a cracker to pull with you.' The girl sidled up archly and Bert left them together.

At half-past seven, when Hugo had made his farewells to the general public, and was saying goodbye to Bert, who had come out on to the landing to see him off, he produced a packet containing three handkerchiefs from his coat pocket and said, 'I brought you this little present. I know I ought to have brought one for your wife, as well, but I will, as soon as the shops are open. I'll bring it round.' Bert patted him on the shoulder and said, 'Oh, don't you worry about that, sonny. It's been nice having you here. Now take the stairs gently. They're nasty things to have a tumble on. Bye-bye.' They shook hands. Hugo said, 'Goodbye—and thank you so very much,' and began the long descent from cloud-capped Olympus to the grimy plain.

Half-way through his Christmas dinner at Number Ten, he suddenly had to leave the table and go and be sick. It was more the result of nervous strain and excitement than of over-eating. His mother was filled with sympathetic alarm, but Magda, who was worn out with work and worry, couldn't help saying, 'Well, what can you expect, if you let him go to the kind of house where they have winkles for tea!'

[5]

As the clock in the Fawleys' drawing-room was striking ten, Dorothy said to Robert, 'Very well. For goodness sake go and repair that musical-box, if that's your idea of a happy Christmas-night. But please don't pretend you're doing something useful. Nobody'll want to hear it when it *is* mended. As I've told you before, all this show of using your hands is simply an excuse for not using your brain. But go along. I'm too tired to argue with you.'

This was the climax of a dreadful day. Their expedition to Hack-field had been a more wretched failure than even Dorothy could have anticipated. She had found their self-satisfied hostess and her plump, ineffectual husband so *petits-bourgeois*—she was fond of the adjective—that they hardly seemed real, while the guest of honour, a purse-proud, middle-aged man, who was some sort of a relation of theirs, really appalled her by his vulgarity. He was uncouth in person and loud in voice and made all general conversation impossible. He either delivered himself of dogmatic opinions, for which no one had asked, or paid gross compliments to a dumb but dimpled tennis-playing young woman who had been asked to join the party for his benefit. To Dorothy he was almost pointedly rude, when he didn't ignore her, and said before dinner (as they called the meal) was half over, 'You can keep your central London. It's a well-known fact—and I have it on the authority of two leading doctors in Halifax—that anyone who lives there more than five years suffers from liver-trouble. Why, you've only to look at a Londoner to see that at once. Do you suppose this charming young lady here would look as she does, if she spent her days cooped up in Oxford Street?' Nor was it long before he found the one chink in Robert's somewhat thick-skinned good humour. He named two leading trade unionists and said they ought to be shot as traitors to their country and their Queen,—a remark which Robert, with his Leftish bias, couldn't take lying down. An embarrassing wrangle followed, and Dorothy was dismayed to find her husband behaving almost as badly as the stranger. 'Any man who doesn't see that the whole capitalist system is on the verge of collapse, is a blithering idiot.' In vain their hostess said soothingly, 'Well, well, it takes all sorts to make a world.' The two men became more and more abusive to one another, and Dorothy, whose bread had always been buttered on the Right side, began to give a grudging sympathy to the North-countryman. But she soon withdrew it, after Robert had gone with their host (as she knew they would) to the garage, and she was forced to sit and listen to the stranger's elephantine gallantries, not one shaft of which came her way, or the stream of practical advice poured out by her hostess. 'I always say that if there's a pipe-smoker in the house, net curtains ought to be washed every fortnight.' (If Dorothy had heard this observation in Garrows, it would have delighted her, whereas, heard at 92, Nettlebed Grove,—with herself as its target—it made her want to scream.) As the dreary minutes dragged on, the room became chilly. Her hostess was a believer in lots of fresh air and stingy fires. And when at last the two men came back from the garage—she noticed a big smear of oil on Robert's trousers—she had to wait while they went and washed themselves and her hostess made them a cup of tea. She was almost hysterical when she had to say 'thank you for a thoroughly delightful afternoon'.

But her troubles were not yet over. She and Robert had barely walked a hundred yards in the direction of the station, when she ricked her ankle stepping off a kerb. Although the injury wasn't crippling, her progress was painful and she suggested to Robert that he should go back and ask if he could borrow the car. He shook his head and said the car was still out of action. 'What, after all that time you spent fussing over it?' Robert said gloomily, 'I'm afraid so. I knew it was the coil right from the start, but Tom was so sure it was the carburettor that I gave way. Here, let me take your arm. Put as much weight on me as you can.' But the close physical contact, though it made walking easier for Dorothy, gave neither husband nor wife any kind of pleasure.

When at last they were in the train,—after hanging about for a quarter of an hour on the draughty platform—Dorothy said, 'So those are the sort of people you'd like us still to have for our friends. Thank goodness we don't live in the suburbs any longer.' 'I must say,' Robert agreed, 'that Bessie's cousin was a blot on the landscape. In fact, he's a living argument for the immediate raising of death-duties to ninety-nine per cent,—not to mention a——' Dorothy interrupted him petulantly. 'For goodness sake don't start all that again. We heard plenty of it at luncheon. I felt quite ashamed of some of the very silly things you said. I wasn't only thinking of Bessie's cousin, I was thinking of that insipid young woman, and Bessie and Tom,—the whole frightful set-up of Nettlebed Grove and all those other roads round it and the third-rate people who live there. That's where, if you had your way, I'd be spending my life. Thank God I got you to cut adrift from all that. The reminder of it that we've had to-day still makes me shudder.'

For a few minutes, Robert was too angry to speak. Then he made up for his silence by saying, 'There's nothing wrong with Bessie and Tom, who are old friends of mine, even if you don't think them good enough for you. If it comes to that, what friends have *you* made, since we came to the Pollitts? You haven't a single one in Pollitt Place, or the Square or the Crescent or within a mile of us. Do you suppose that if you were in trouble, any of our neighbours would stir a finger to help you? Of course, they'll talk about you behind your back and spy on you. Do you remember that night when you broke a pane of glass in the sitting-room window, and all the curtains twitched across the street and fifty faces peeped out between the chinks? That's all *our* neighbours are good for. So far as I can see, all you get out of living where we do, is being within easy walking distance of Garrows. What do you know of the social life of London—if there is such a thing any longer? Why, you were hard put to it to make up the numbers for to-morrow's party. You talk as if you'd refused a dozen classy invitations for lunch to-day. Be honest. What would you have done, if Bessie and Tom hadn't invited us? Sat indoors, I suppose, and waited in the hopes that some Duchess would ring you up and ask you to join her at Claridges!'

Dorothy murmured affectedly, 'What eloquence!' and gave him a look intended to convey a tolerant contempt. Neither of them spoke during the rest of the journey.

When they reached home, she lay down and rested her foot. Robert brought her some tea and set about preparing for their evening meal. When they came to eat it, they were not unlike two strangers who have been asked to share a table in a crowded restaurant. None the less, when Robert had made the coffee and washed up, he came and sat with her in the drawing-room, reading a technical magazine. Dorothy was looking through a volume of Oscar Wilde's plays, which Susan had sent her for Christmas, and couldn't refrain from reading aloud a provocative titbit every few minutes.

'MRS CHEVELEY: *Science can never grapple with the irrational. That is why it has no future before it, in this world.* SIR ROBERT CHILTERN: *And women represent the irrational.* MRS CHEVELEY: *Well-dressed women do.*'

She laughed to herself and turned over some of the pages, while Robert remained glumly silent.

'*Really, if the lower orders don't set us a good example, what on earth is the use of them? They seem, as a class, to have absolutely no sense of responsibility.*'

Robert looked up and asked, 'Is that supposed to be clever or funny?' She said drily, 'Yes, very clever *and* very funny,' and read on to herself, though it wasn't long before she gave him another sample.

Robert kept up a show of indifference as long as he could, but when she read out somewhat pointedly, '*Never speak disrespectfully of Society, Algernon. Only people who can't get into it do that*', he was goaded into retaliation, and quoted the specification of a new electronic device. Dorothy put down her book, looked at him and asked, 'Why exactly do you suppose that rigmarole should interest me?' Robert blushed angrily and said, 'Don't you think I might ask *you* the same question about all that stuff you've been boring me with?' She replied dogmatically, 'No, I don't. The two things are quite different. What you've just read to me is meaningless except to people who have had a narrow, specialised form of training. What I gave you was something which ought to appeal to anyone who has any taste or general intelligence. I wish I could get you to realise that literature is a part of every gentleman's equipment. It's not just a thing which you may or may not take up, like biology or metallurgy. It's universal. It's no use saying you didn't do it at school. I happened to at mine, but at really good boys' schools the clever boys read classics, not English. They get their knowledge of English literature spontaneously. Can't you understand that science doesn't educate the mind? It may equip people for menial jobs, but it doesn't begin to touch their higher faculties. You might at least give yourself the chance of becoming more of a——'

He got up and, deliberately turning his back on her, threw his magazine on to a chair and walked towards the door of his workshop. It was then that she said, 'Very well. For goodness sake go and repair that musical-box, if that's your idea of a happy Christmas-night. But please don't pretend you're doing something *useful*. Nobody'll want to hear it when it *is* mended. As I've told you before, all this show of using your hands is simply an excuse for not using your brain. But go along. I'm too tired to argue with you.'

As she heard his furious slamming of the door, the full hate-fulness of her own behaviour throughout the day as well as the evening came home to her. She had picked a quarrel, in spite of all the good resolutions she had made on her return from Brighton. What was the matter with her? Could it be because, the previous evening, when they'd got back from their tour of the West End, she had been unusually affectionate to him, making it clear that, if he wanted it—— Oh, the thought was hateful! *She* didn't want it, of course. There was nothing she wanted less. But his complete lack of response had hurt her pride and upset her nerves.

Still, that was no excuse for her. Ever since they had set out for Hackfield that morning, she had been nothing but a nuisance to him. If their Christmas Day had been spoilt—and it had been, for both of them,—the fault was hers. She had made the worst, not the best, of the luncheon-party and made the most of her trifling mishap. She had been insulting about Robert's old friends and had been deliberately offensive to him when he was kind enough to sit with her after a meal which he had cooked for her. If she went on in this way, she would wear through the last shreds of his patience.

She looked round the room, and thought how pretty it was with its ingenious Christmas decorations. The ideas might have been hers—not without some indebtedness to the shop-fronts in Parkwell Road,—but the skill had been Robert's. She hadn't stuck in a pin or cut a ribbon or applied a single dab of gum or silver paint. The Christmas-tree, that twinkled at that moment on the balcony with a splendour unique in the Pollitts, had been set in position, decked and illuminated by Robert alone. She had merely done the shopping, paid the bills and given him orders. What would she do, if when next Christmas came, she had to fend for herself?

How could she bear to get up in the morning alone, spend the day alone and go to bed alone? Some people, like Miss Tredennick and Mr Bray, passed their lives like that,—but though they'd never known anything else, you could see they weren't really happy. It wasn't a question of sex—it was that intimate companionship which marriage, of all social relationships, brings the most easily—if not necessarily the most fully. For those who have tasted that nectar, no other drinks, however brightly they bubble with romance, can slake the thirst of the soul. 'O Robert, Robert,—my husband—with all your faults—and still more, with all mine,—I want you, I want you!' Hysterical tears suddenly streamed down her face, and forgetting about her ankle, she ran to the door of his workshop, paused, wiped her eyes and knocked gently.

She was only just in time. Since Robert had left her, he had been too angry to mend the musical-box or anything else. He walked up and down the little room—three strides at the most, either way,—telling himself that this was the moment he'd been waiting for, and rehearsing the words with which he would take his final leave of her. 'You've made it clear to me several times to-day that I and my friends aren't good enough for you. You've told me I'm not educated and not a gentleman. You knew that when we married,—though then you said these things didn't matter. I can't alter myself—even if I wanted to, which I don't. You're sick of me and you'll probably get much sicker. Very well, I can take it. I'm clearing out here and now, and I shan't come back. I'll give you all the evidence you want for a divorce. I can only hope we shall both be happier without one another than we've been together.'

He was almost shouting the last words, but Dorothy was so intent on what she had to say that she didn't hear. She knocked again, timidly. When he opened the door and she saw his furious face, she put her hand to her head, as if she feared he were going to hit her. Then, looking at the floor, she said, 'Robert—forgive me. I've behaved like a—like a cad. I can't expect you to love me—because I'm not a lovable person—but I do ask you to bear with me and to be kind to me, if you can. You're naturally kind and I'm not. A sort of devil gets into me and makes me say awful things—things I don't mean. O Robert, I love you and I can't do without you.'

In spite of himself, he opened his arms mechanically, let her body rest against his, and putting his hands behind her head, drew her face towards his lips. Then, after giving her a light kiss on the cheek, he held her by the shoulders at arms' length and said, 'Go to bed, old woman. You're far too strung up, to-night. Sleep it off. We've somehow rubbed through this Christmas Day, and I've no doubt we shall rub through a good many others together, before we've done.'

She kissed him on the forehead and went to the bedroom. As he watched her go, and realised what he had said to her, his expression changed to one of hopeless dismay, and he thought, 'This has been my great chance. I shan't ever have another. O Magda, darling, what would you say, if you knew!'

XVI

THE TWENTY-SEVENTH OF DECEMBER

'ROUTINE inquiries—a distasteful task. . . .'

The Inspector was like a large, well-groomed tabby cat,—a 'doctored' cat, Miss Tredennick thought to herself, and thus immune to the temptations inherent in his peculiar calling. It was half-past eleven, and they were sitting together by her bedroom window, Miss Tredennick in her favourite arm-chair, and the Inspector on an upright Sheraton chair, the seat of which was a little too narrow for him. A small round table, bearing a decanter of pale sherry, two glasses, a seed-cake and a box of cigarettes, stood between them. Although it was cold in the street outside, the sun seemed to strike the glass panes with tropical force, and the Inspector, who sweated readily, mopped his brow more than once during the interview.

'Those, of course, were her windows,' he said, as if to himself. 'What a splendid observation-post this would have made, if we'd been keeping watch.' Then with a glance at his hostess, he added, 'I suppose, if she had the light on and forgot, or didn't bother, to draw the curtains, one might almost see right into her room?'

Miss Tredennick thought for a moment, and then said, with an assumption of nervousness which she was far from feeling, 'I don't want to lose your good opinion, Inspector—and still less to shock you——'

'Shock *me*, Madam? If you knew the type of case I've had to handle for the last twenty-five years, that wouldn't worry you!'

Miss Tredennick said airily, 'Oh, I didn't mean that kind of shock at all. The shock I was thinking of is aesthetic, rather than moral. So as to save your time, I may as well be frank with you. I know you've come to find out what I've seen, during all the many hours I've spent sitting up here alone. My fear is that when you find out that I've seen quite a lot, you may put me down as a dirty-minded old woman. But I don't think I am. They say there's a streak of obscenity in all of us. I'm told that the language of nuns on the operating-table is quite appalling. I make no pretence to being a saint and I've never slobbered over virginal purity like a Victorian poet or novelist. On the other hand, I don't think I get the vicarious satisfaction out of sex-crimes and nameless orgies that apparently titillate the readers of some of the cheaper newspapers. Till this unfortunate woman came to live here, I ignored such things. It was only in self-defence that I—took the notice I did.'

'In self-defence, Madam?'

'Yes. I have an old-fashioned, perhaps snobbish, regard for this house, this street and this neighbourhood. It grieves me to think that almost all the houses opposite are lodging-houses. However, that's the so-called march of progress and I can't stand in its way, much as I should like to. But the thought that some of these houses were becoming mere *brothels*, and this once highly-respected, residential district was sinking to the level of Paddington or Bayswater, was too much to bear, and I determined to do everything in my power to root out this new evil that was creeping amongst us. Did I use the word *evil*? That's describing it far too sanctimoniously. This *nuisance*, I should have said,—this *disgusting* nuisance. I'm not intolerant. I shouldn't mind in the least if some minor royalty, or even some captain of industry took the house next door and kept his mistress there in a gilded cage. But the sight of these shameless harlots at their trade—— Yes, Inspector?'

'I must say, Madam, I find what you're telling me of the greatest interest. It sheds quite a new light on my investigations.'

His sentence amazed her—or was it ironical? 'A new light?' she said. 'But surely—tell me this. Some weeks ago, Mrs Muller, my housekeeper, informed me that the police had raided a house in Pollitt Rise for the very reason we are now discussing. You must know that?'

'Yes, Madam, indeed I do. In fact, I was in charge of the operation.'

'Well then?'

'But, Madam, we're talking of Seven Pollitt Place, which is quite another matter. We know a certain amount about the residents,— Mrs O'Blahoney, who's the lessee of the house, Miss Wheeler, who has the post of secretary to a charitable organisation, Mrs Casey, an elderly Irishwoman and Miss Proudfoot, who is also somewhat advanced in years and not unlike yourself,—with certain obvious differences, of course. That only leaves us with Miss Varioli, whose death, as I told you, we are investigating.'

Miss Tredennick said smartly, 'Quite so, Inspector. But I can't help wondering why, if the authorities are merely concerned to ascertain the cause of her death, they didn't entrust the task to a member of the Homicide Bureau—or is that purely an American-ism?—instead of the Vice-Squad, to which I gather you belong.'

He gave her a look of such frank admiration and such an agree-able smile, that he won her heart.

'You're too shrewd, Miss Tredennick. I must admit that the Homicide Bureau, to give it your title, has done most of the spade-work, and that I was simply called in as an extra,—just in case there should happen to be some other angle to consider. By the way, I understand that about two months ago, or rather less, perhaps, someone defaced the front door of Number Seven with a most offensive inscription. Did you hear about it?'

'I not only heard about it, I saw the inscription. And, I may say, I was highly amused.'

'Had you any kind of idea who might have been responsible?'

Miss Tredennick looked him calmly in the eyes and said, 'Abso-lutely none! But I'd like to give the woman who did it—it must have been a woman, don't you think?—a pound for her trouble.'

The Inspector said thoughtfully, 'Is that so? Well, yes, I see your point of view.' He paused, as if to encourage Miss Tredennick to say something more, but as she maintained an imperturbable silence, he went on, with a very slight shrug of his shoulders, 'As I was going to tell you before this little digression, there seems, on the face of things, little doubt that this poor young woman killed herself in the old-fashioned way, by stopping up the cracks in the windows and under the door and turning on the gas. But why did she do it? She was perfectly healthy. She had about a hundred pounds in the bank and some savings-certificates. She had a good job as secretary to a business-man who was often called out of London, so that she had a good deal of free time. What's your idea, Miss Tredennick? Did she strike you as the suicidal type? Was she morbid or worried?'

'Far from it. She seemed full of life and much too pleased with herself,—until, perhaps, the last week or two.'

'Yes? Do you think you could tell me when you first began to notice her existence, and how she came to arouse your—what shall I say?—I don't mean curiosity, of course——'

'Yes, you do, Inspector, but never mind. I think it was about the end of last July when it first struck me that she was a resident at Number Seven. There was something about her that demanded attention, an air of "sexiness", shall I say? In fact, after I'd seen her with one or two men, I put her down as a bad lot.'

'You mean, a professional? Not merely a woman who leads an immoral life for her own personal gratification, but to speak plainly——'

He paused, as though he found it difficult to speak quite as plainly as he had intended. But Miss Tredennick helped him out.

'I couldn't believe that any decent girl, whatever illicit intrigue she might be conducting, would behave in public like Miss Varioli. There was such a brazen, come-hither look about her. At first I suspended judgment, but the more I saw of her, the surer I felt that she was "in the racket". Is that the phrase?'

He nodded and she went on, 'Then one night in the middle of September, she came home in the small hours of the morning with a man who had a very noisy car. It woke me up. They turned on the radio and danced in the street. After that, I felt quite certain.'

The Inspector repressed a smile. 'But, Miss Tredennick, professional prostitutes—you see, you've taught me at last to say what I mean,—aren't in the habit of dancing on the pavement.'

'Are you sure?'

'Yes, quite sure. It would be a waste of time. I can understand your being furious at having your night's rest so rudely disturbed, but you jumped to a wrong conclusion. If she'd been what you took her for, there'd have been a stream of clients during working hours. Tell me, how many different men did you see her with, altogether?'

Miss Tredennick pondered. Of course, it had all been recorded

in her Journal, but she had destroyed it on Christmas Day. What
a pity! Though, in its unexpurgated form, enriched as it had been
with her own poetic embellishments, it would hardly have been
a suitable exhibit to parade before this pleasant, neuter tabby-cat.
She said, 'I think eight.'

'In how many days,—or weeks?'

'In these last four months.'

'Really, Miss Tredennick! If the woman had been what you took
her for, she'd have been broke.'

'But it wasn't only eight times in all. I've seen her with the same
man more than once. Don't these people ever have *regulars*?'

'They may, sometimes,—but not so exclusively, if you know
what I mean.' He rose, and drawing himself up to his great height,
he looked down at her with a humorous pity and said, 'No, no,
Miss Tredennick. I've no doubt whatever that you hoped you could
collect sufficient evidence against her to turn her out of this street
and hand Number Seven over to the National Trust. But I'm afraid
your diagnosis was wrong. She was nothing more than a rather
vulgar young woman with a strong fondness for the opposite sex.
It's common enough nowadays. Just one more question. I'm told
that the last night but one before her death, a man drove her home
in his car. Had you seen it before?'

'As you know, Inspector, that was the night I had my attack. I
don't like thinking of it. Yes, it was the car that drove her home in
September, when they danced on the pavement. What happened
this time, I can't tell you exactly. But I've good reason to think she
shook her fist at it, when it drove away.'

For a moment only, the Inspector looked a trifle grim. He said,
'I've already seen your housekeeper's son. Would you regard him
as a reliable witness?'

'Yes, most reliable. I've always found him a very truthful boy.'

'Then, Madam, I don't think I'm justified in taking up any more
of your time.'

'Oh, please, Inspector. Do have one more glass of sherry—or
some cake—you haven't tasted it yet. And *please*, before you go,
tell me the answer. *Why* did she kill herself? You've already asked
me that question; now you must let me put it to you.'

'Incredible as it may seem, I really think she killed herself for love.'

'For *love*? Is it possible?'

'Yes, even in these days. Goodbye and thank you for a delightful morning.'

He gave her a smile and a bow, and walked almost casually out of the room, as if he lived in the house. Miss Tredennick sat back in her chair and looked out of the window. Yes, that had been *her* house, and those had been her windows. She'd stopped up the chinks with newspaper and turned on the gas and died—for love! Where was she now—in Heaven or in Hell—or was she nowhere at all? How sad it all was! What a pitiful, humdrum ending to what might have been an enthralling *cause célèbre*! As it was still the holidays, Pollitt Place was deserted, except for a few cars parked by their owners' front doors. How dull it looked!

The front door of Number Ten opened, and Magda's head appeared as she showed the Inspector out. He turned to the right and walked towards Lampstone Lane. Magda closed the front door slowly and quietly. To Miss Tredennick, it symbolised the closing of a delightful book which she was destined never to open again.

[2]

Magda had finished the washing-up,—not this time in Miss Tredennick's kitchen, nor in the basement of Ten Pollitt Place, but in the kitchenette of 25, Underbourne Mansions, Twickenham. It had only taken her about seven minutes, but it seemed an age since the front door of the flat had clicked to, and Robert's footsteps had died away on the stairs, leading down to the entrance.

He had warned her that he might have to leave her soon after nine, so as to join his wife and her friends at their supper-party, and almost his first words that evening had been, 'I did my best,—but I couldn't get out of it.' And a little later he had added, as if by way of explanation, 'The wife and I had a bit of a row on Christmas-night.' *The wife!* There was something possessive and binding about the phrase which made Magda unhappy. (Hitherto she had never been really unhappy while he was with her.)

Nor had he fixed any date for their next meeting. She had hoped he would say, 'On New Year's Eve, you and I must be together.' Instead, when he realised that part of her mind was prowling into the future, he said, 'My dear, don't let's waste precious time looking ahead. Let's live for the present like two happy animals, and make the very most of it while we can.' His love-making had been as eager as ever before, but it had a greedy and brutal quality that was new. It was as if he too were pricked by a twinge of conscience, and were trying to stifle it by whipping up his passions to fever-heat.

She had read somewhere that lust may turn to love, thereby finding its justification. But was the opposite process possible? Her own feeling for Robert, after the ecstatic bewilderment of her initiation, had tended steadily towards a more and more romantic idealism. She would have been almost willing to exchange her lot for Dorothy's,—to be the wife in the background, to whom, after whatever infidelities, he would always return. And had he not promised her that some day she should be?

Her longing for that day implied no change in her beliefs. She was still firmly convinced that the stealing of another woman's husband was not absolved by any subsequent marriage. It was merely that her desires had veered towards a more domestic kind of bliss than she had envisaged in the earlier days. The flat had now really become her home,—a sinful home, to be sure, but of all temptations the most seductive.

She went into the sitting-room, sat down and looked at the little clock which Robert had given her as a Christmas present. She could stay where she was for another hour at least, before turning out to face the quizzical smirk of the night-porter, and, far harder to bear, the moment of her arrival at Number Ten.

Her life in that house was now becoming a nightmare. There were times when she thought Miss Tredennick had guessed her secret, though she found the old woman's shrewdness nothing like so embarrassing as Dorothy's lack of perceptiveness, and Magda hated her for it. On the night of Christmas Eve, when she had been so affable in the hall,—'My husband insists I shall go out with him and see the decorations,'—Magda had longed to strike her in the face and say, 'You fool, don't you understand that he wants me, not you? Go back and talk to your budgies. Nobody else here wants to talk to you or ever to see you again!' Yes, one of these days, if the strain were too prolonged, she would break out and ruin everything.

Ruin everything? The words gave her a jolt. Weren't they waiting—hadn't Robert said he was waiting—for some crisis, which would enable him to do in hot blood what he couldn't do in cold?

There had been moments during the past three days, when her common sense had suddenly reared its ugly head and plagued her with painful questions. If Robert was really as eager as he said to get rid of his wife, why did he still take so many precautions to prevent the truth getting about? Why must they always start the outward journey separately? Why had he gone out of his way to introduce her as his niece to the hall-porter? When she had protested against the lie, he had said, 'But darling, when Dorothy divorces me, *you're* not going to be named as the co-respondent. That's all I'm worried about.' At the time she had been quite satisfied by the explanation, but now it suggested all manner of doubts.

Making an effort of will, she transferred her thoughts to her mother and Hugo, who were also sources of uneasiness. (Of all those who lived at Ten Pollitt Place, Justin alone brought her no kind of worry.) Between herself and her mother, an armed neutrality had developed. All might have been well, if only Magda had been able to leave Hugo alone. But there lay the trouble. She had written to the secretarial college for their prospectus in an access of spite which she couldn't control, though she knew no possible good would come of it. She knew equally well that her repeated criticisms of him to her mother were sheer folly, yet she found herself impelled to make them almost every time he was mentioned. When she spoke to him, she could hardly keep the acidity out of her voice. It was something very much deeper than jealousy. Apart from what he might in his sly way suspect, he had become the symbol of all her frustrations, and as such, the arch-enemy.

She looked at the clock again, then round the room at all the little things which were hers and Robert's. Was it conceivable that some day she and he would be there in their own right? The room had been very cold that evening when first they came in, and Robert had lit the gas-fire and turned it up to full strength. But now, as Magda sat directly in front of it, the heat was unbearable. She got up, turned it down and then out, trying the tap three or four times (as people do, who aren't used to gas-fires), to make sure that the gas was completely cut off. Her precautions suddenly reminded her of what had happened only three nights before on the top floor of Number Seven Pollitt Place, and of the Police Inspector's call that morning at Number Ten. He had questioned all three Mullers for a few minutes. Hugo had put on his inno-cent baby-face and done his best to appear like a child of eight. But evidently he wasn't quite successful; for the Inspector, after dismissing him from the interview, had turned to Mrs Muller and said, 'By the way, I forgot to ask your son how old he was?' And when he heard that Hugo was fifteen and a half, he said, 'Really— as old as that!' with a slight lift of the eyebrows, and Magda had felt a malicious satisfaction. The Inspector had gone on to ask both her and her mother if they had any theory as to what had induced the young woman to kill herself. Mrs Muller had answered, 'No, no theory at all,' and Magda had said the same thing, though some-thing in her tone prompted him to say, 'I feel, Miss Muller, you have at least thought of some possible reason. Please tell me, how-ever strange it may seem.' And she had replied, 'The only possible reason I can think of, is that she had something on her conscience she couldn't bear.' And she had added, with an attempt at a smile, 'I know that may sound rather silly.' But he had answered quite seriously, 'No,—it is a possible motive. But you hadn't formed the idea that she might have been—to use an old-fashioned phrase— crossed in love?' 'She—in love? Was she capable of it?' Magda's voice was indignant as she put the question. The Inspector had looked at her searchingly and said, 'That's something I think none of us can answer.'

Remorse or love—whichever it might have been—the impulse had been strong enough to drive a full-blooded young woman to desperation. If a creature like that, with her hard-bitten worldli-ness, her common sense, her appetite for pleasure, had given way under the strain, how could Magda hope to survive an ordeal that was ten times as harassing to her pernickety conscience,—especially now that the rapturous moods which had hitherto sustained her were troubled by introspective forebodings?

The clock on the mantelpiece struck half-past nine. Magda looked at it and then again at the fire below it, which now showed no kind of glow, and seemed as inert and harmless as the waste-paper basket by the writing-desk. Yet the sight of it both repelled and fascinated her. The door of the flat was flush with the wall, of which it seemed a part, and the windows, unlike the old wooden windows in Pollitt Place, were metal and sealed the room completely when they were shut. One turn of the gas-tap would be quite enough. People said it was an easy form of death. But what happened afterwards? Was suicide, too, an unforgivable sin?

[3]

Robert was glum and awkward when he arrived at the supper-party after the theatre, but Dorothy was so grateful to him for coming at all, that she pretended not to notice his sulkiness. Besides, he thawed during the meal and even seemed to enjoy being lionised by his hostess, a jolly, middle-aged woman who said silly things quite entertainingly. When Dorothy was alone with him in the taxi, on their way home, she longed to ask him if he hadn't found the meal more stimulating than their Christmas-dinner at Hackfield. It would have been a triumph, had he agreed, but she prudently avoided the comparison, and surprised him by saying, 'Do you know, I'm really glad you went to your film first, instead of coming to the theatre with us.'

'Why?' he asked. 'Was the play so bad, or was it too highbrow for me?'

'Neither. But the wife was such an appallingly selfish woman, I'm afraid it might have given you ideas about me.'

'What did she do?'

'Oh, she just nagged and nagged and had nerve-storms and always got her own way,—till the end.'

'What happened then? Did he kill her?'

'Oh no. He simply went off with another woman.'

'That sounds rather immoral.'

'Immoral or not, I sympathised with him.'

'And what became of the wife?'

'She got drunk and turned on the gas. Then the husband, who was really rather conventional, came home and found her dead.'

Robert said thoughtfully, 'I wonder if that poor woman at Number Seven had seen the play. I suppose it is possible for someone with overstrung nerves to be influenced like that. It would be interesting to see the statistics for that particular form of suicide and to find out if there's been any rise in the rate, since this play has been on.'

'If there was, would you ban the play?'

'No, I don't think so. After all, the type of person who gives way to these impulses isn't as a rule much loss to society. I think murder-plays are much more dangerous. For example, if the husband had killed his wife, there might be a good deal to be said for banning the play.'

Dorothy said bravely, 'Well, if he had, I don't think anyone could have blamed him.' Robert didn't answer, and she wondered what he was thinking about, and if he realised how abjectly she had been apologising to him. Probably not. She changed the conversation, but when they reached home and he switched on the electric fire in the bedroom, she couldn't refrain from saying, 'Anyhow, I'm glad there aren't any gas-fires here.'

Robert who had forgotten the reference said, 'Are you? I've often wished we had them. They warm up a room so quickly.' He was thinking of the snug room in Underbourne Mansions and Magda sitting cosily in front of the fire by his side on the sofa. He blushed, but Dorothy didn't notice it and went on, 'When Father and I had that flat in Queen's Gate, there was a gas-fire in my bedroom. I used to be afraid I might get up in my sleep and turn it on without lighting it,—and sometimes, when I was very unhappy, the idea did come to me—not very seriously—that it would be an easy way of getting out of my troubles.' But there was no sympathy in Robert's reply. 'You might just as well have been afraid of getting up in your sleep and jumping out of the window. I seem to remember your flat was on the fifth floor. A drop of sixty feet on to the pavement would be quite effective.' Then seeing that she looked hurt and miserable, he added, 'But what a silly subject. Anyway, you don't have troubles now, do you?' She smiled and said, 'No, not really, I suppose—thanks to you.'

Robert felt it was the moment to give her a kiss. He did so, and was almost embarrassed by the glance of affection she gave him in return. She said, 'Well, Christmas is really over now. You know, next year Christmas Day is on a Tuesday, owing to Leap-year. I suppose instead of having two Boxing Days we shall have two Christmas Eves,—the Saturday and the Monday. We shall have to plan it all quite differently, shan't we?'

'Yes, quite. Do you want me to take the Christmas-tree in from the balcony to-night?'

'Oh no. It must stay there till over the New Year.'

'Well,—good night, ducks.'

'Good night, my darling husband.'

XVII

NEW YEAR'S EVE

WHEN Hugo left Mr Middleton that morning, instead of going straight home, he went to the block of Council flats where Bert lived. It wasn't that he expected to find Bert in—for he would have been embarrassed if he had; it was Bert's wife whom he was calling on.

The cold weather of Christmas had given way to a mild spell; indeed, barring the incidence of dawn and dusk, it was the type of day with which English people are familiar throughout the year,— a mingling of sunshine and grey skies and a luke-warm breeze with a threat of rain from the west. Hugo, who was wearing his thick overcoat, was flushed and hot when he reached the top of the stairs, and a little nervous, though not nearly so nervous as he had been when he arrived for Bert's party on Christmas Day.

Bert's wife, who was in the middle of doing her washing, was as hot and flushed as Hugo, and rather more flustered. When she answered the bell, she stood and gazed at him in perplexity and he thought she wasn't going to recognise him. But she said, 'Why,— it's Mr Muller—Bert's friend from Pollitt Place! I'm sorry you find me like this,—but do come in.'

She threw the door open, but Hugo hesitated and said, 'You must excuse me. I ought to have known the morning would be a bad time to call.' Bert's wife recovered some of her composure and said, 'But why should you know? I expect your mother does her washing on a Monday or a Tuesday, but I have to fit mine in when I can. But if you don't mind——' She paused and Hugo said, 'Of course not. My sister does our washing as a rule, and she hasn't a regular day either. I really won't keep you. I came round to thank you for the lovely party and to bring you a little present for the New Year. It's nothing at all.'

He took out of his pocket a small package wrapped in tissue-paper and handed it to her. She said, 'Oh, isn't that nice of you! You shouldn't have troubled. You really shouldn't, you know. Now you must come in and see me open it. Just put your coat anywhere.'

He followed her into the sitting-room, which looked much smaller now that the furniture had been put back into place, though the Christmas decorations were still there to remind him of the party. Bert's wife undid the parcel, which contained a very small plastic work-box, and while Hugo was thinking how amazing it was that he should have secured this foothold in Bert's home and was wondering how often he would go there, she began to thank him. 'Oh, how sweet! What a clever boy—I beg pardon, I mean young man—you were to find it! So useful too! Do sit down. Won't you let me make you a cup of tea? I could do with one.'

Hugo answered, 'No thank you. We shall be having our dinner quite soon. I suppose your husband never gets home at midday except on Sundays.'

'Well, he does sometimes get Saturdays off, like to-day. But he didn't ask me to get anything ready, so I expect he'll get a bite at a pub and go on to the Dogs. Bert's fond of pubs. He likes playing darts and talking to the people,—which I don't. Besides, the doctor says I mustn't drink. But if you marry a man who's younger than you are, you mustn't complain if he likes a bit of fun and goes out with the boys. He's a good husband to me.'

Hugo said gravely, 'I'm sure he is.' Then he added, as if by an afterthought, 'Do you remember, I told you at your party that I'd tried to do a drawing of him, but it wasn't any good, and you said perhaps you could find me a snapshot of him which might help me? Do you think you could give it me now, or am I being a nuisance?'

'Oh no, Mr Muller. It's no trouble at all. I think they're all in here.' She went to a chest of drawers, took out a box full of photographs and laid them out on a table.

'Here you are. Don't look at that awful one—it was taken when we were just married. My word, I was a fright! That's Bert before I knew him. He's filled out a good bit since then, hasn't he? That's my sister Mary. That's Mr Rintoul you met at the party, though you mightn't think so. That's . . . Ah, here we are. This is the lot that was taken at Westgate. That's Bert and me. That's me—tear it up. I look so dreadfully ill. The doctor said the air was too strong for me. It affected my liver. That's Bert and some girls,—three sisters we got to know. That's Bert and their brother,—the one who took the snaps as a rule, though one of his sisters must have taken this one. That's Bert coming back from his bathe. That's him again, but on Sunday. That's where we stayed. That's the steamer at Margate starting for Southend. Take which one you fancy. I don't often look at them.'

Hugo affected to delay his choice, but said, in the end, 'I think this one is the best likeness. It seems to have caught him off his guard, if you know what I mean. Please, may I borrow it?'

'Of course, Mr Muller. Keep it, if you like.'

It was Bert wearing bathing-trunks, with his arms akimbo, like a bear.

Hugo looked at his watch. 'My word, what a long time I've kept you. I shall get such a scolding at home for being late. Do you really mean I can keep that photograph? I'll give you my drawing in exchange, if it's good enough, though I'm afraid it won't be. Now I really must go.'

He got up and looked out of the window. Somewhere over

there, if he were tall enough, or had someone to lift him up, he could see the upper windows at the back of Ten Pollitt Place. His heart fluttered. How easy everything was, if one had the will and the courage to exercise it,—the will and the courage. The courage would be put to the test that very afternoon.

[2]

Justin was walking with a slow, philosophical stride through the Park. He had been lunching with a friend, who was both a literary critic and an author, and whose opinion he greatly valued.

In the kindest possible way, this friend had urged him to give up writing novels. The advice was sweetened with sufficient praise to turn any author's head, but in spite of this, it was quite definite.

'Your trouble—*our* trouble—is that we're hopelessly out of touch with the present age. However painstakingly we try to adapt ourselves to it—however carefully we vulgarise our style and purge it of its youthful classicism,—doing our best to forget we've ever read Caesar, Cicero, Dr Johnson or Gibbon—whatever slick phrases we borrow from the other side of the Atlantic, we can't really keep up. . . .

'Our whole attitude to life is retrospective. We can't disguise the fact that we think it a pity the world isn't what it was in nineteen-ten, and when we remember that most of our readers don't think so at all, we become cross with them, and tend to point out what very poor creatures they are, in their hey-day, compared with what we used to be in ours. Not unnaturally, they don't like it.

'Nor do they like any subtle analysis of character. The luxury of a complex personality—like the luxury of having a dozen servants—is unknown to the "little man". He's far too busy making a living or lapping up mass-produced entertainment to enlarge his own ego. . . .

'You brought all this out very well in *Seven Silent Sinners*, and it may have been perhaps for that very reason that the book had only a limited appeal. I suppose it's a question of overtones. I mean—take that scene—which I found most moving and beautiful—when you described the old man longing wistfully to be at Cambridge again, sauntering through the Backs on a summer day and communing with the ghosts of Horace Walpole and Gray, just before he gets the telephone-message telling him that the *Amphisbaenic Review* is ceasing publication through lack of funds and can't take his next article. The contrast between his day-dreaming, with its reminiscences of Frances Cornford and Rupert Brooke, and the brutal reality into which he wakes, is—for most people—simply meaningless. They're not tuned in to that wavelength. They can no more receive it than you could be thrilled by an account of a boxing-match or a cup final. . . .

'Besides, it holds up the action too much for their taste. The test of a book nowadays isn't "How does it *read?*", but, "How does it *look?*" It's almost impossible for us to realise how enormously the popularity of the cinema and television have changed the process by which most people now absorb the written word. They translate it instinctively—provided of course they can understand it at all—into something *visual*. They want to *see* rather than *understand*, because understanding demands a mental effort they don't care to make. . . .

'If you want to keep yourself occupied, why not take up some form of biography? I know that research is a nightmare to the imaginative writer, but I think you could get by with very little. A revival of Lytton Stracheyism might be an excellent thing. Or how about some more "Dialogues of the Dead"? Or a reshaping of some classical myth, giving it one of those wry, slightly immoral, twists, that you're so good at? Try anything—but if I were you, I shouldn't try to write another novel!'

It was impossible to be offended or even annoyed, but it was only too easy to be sad,—and Justin was very sad.

Without his writing,—without that faint hope that some day he would produce a masterpiece universally acclaimed as such—the whole of his future seemed an aimless blank. Why go on, why face the gradual gathering of infirmities, if one's existence was to have no other aim than length of years and the avoidance of pain? But his friend was right, there must be no more novels.

As soon as he got back to Ten Pollitt Place, he opened a drawer

in his desk and took out some sixty sheets of manuscript. The first
one bore nothing but attempts at a title,—*The Righteous Heart, Old
People have Voices, Old Faust was no Fool, Three Elderly Oracles* and
many others. Their varying ineptitudes made him blush, and he
turned to Chapter One and began to read:

*It was an afternoon in early May of 1922,—a drowsy damp hour of
cuckoo-calls and the scent of lilac-blossom exhaled in a rainy sunshine.
The stone Tritons, waist-deep in the ornamental water, hydraulically
stimulated in their hinderparts, blew gay jets against a background of
green, and filled the air with a thousand little rainbows.*

He thought, 'It's not so bad. It isn't bad at all. I should rather
like to pick up a book with that kind of beginning.' Yes, but pay
fifteen shillings for it? Would he do that? And if not, who would?
Besides, any fool can write an opening chapter. Could he sustain
that note of airy moisture, which was meant to pervade the whole
work as an ironical symbol of wasted effort, frustrated ideals and
fate's indifference? No,—he had to confess it—he couldn't keep it
up. The story would intervene. He would analyse, hint at crises
then play them down, and the *motif*—or *theme-song,* if that was
the name the present generation preferred—would vanish as the
plot took its humdrum shape. And even if, by some miracle, he
succeeded in doing what he had set himself to do, who, nowadays,
would set store by such an achievement?

He tore the page into small pieces, and then with a quick glance
at each successive page, did the same. By the time he had finished,
the waste-paper basket was half full and his fingers ached. He
sighed very deeply and looked out of the window. A youngish
woman, not unlike the unfortunate creature who used to live on
the top floor of Number Seven, minced down the street with a
dachshund on a lead. As they neared Number Ten, the dog made a
dart for the doorstep, and cocked its leg, while its owner stood by
with a complete lack of concern. Justin's fury flared up, but when
he was about to rush into the hall, he remembered what had happened to him the last time he had had a row with a woman whose
dog had offended in a similar way. The old pain came back into his
heart at the thought of it, and he sat down in an arm-chair by the

window and watched the thick, stinking, yellowish liquid trickle slowly to the edge of the step, where it first made a pool, then splashed, drop by drop, down into the area.

He yawned with disgust and weariness. Once more, he had walked too far. Half a mile was quite as much as he could manage without over-tiring himself. By the end of next year, a few hundred yards might be more than enough for him—while the year after that, he might hardly be able to get to the bus-stop in Parkwell Road. What a New Year's Eve meditation! With an effort, he rose from his chair, and went into his bedroom, where he took off his shoes, coat, tie and collar, and lay down on the bed.

He woke at a quarter to four and his first thought was, 'I'm no longer a novelist!' Then he remembered that he had promised Miss Tredennick to have tea with her and help her to entertain two elderly spinsters who had been her neighbours in Cornwall. It was not a thrilling prospect, and he dreaded climbing up the two flights of stairs, but it was better than having tea alone, regretting the past and brooding over the future. Meanwhile more than half an hour lay between him and tea-time, and he decided to fill it by writing a letter which he ought to have written and posted before luncheon.

[3]

At half-past five, Hugo crept furtively to the top of the house. Pausing a moment on Miss Tredennick's landing, he could hear voices from her sitting-room,—her own, keen-edged and incisive— 'Cornish weather is distressingly like English cooking',—Justin Bray's, a dull, hesitant boom, and two twittering flutes, which completed the quartet at the tea-party. They were hard at it. Let them keep at it and hear no sounds but those they made themselves!

The box-room, or haunted room, as Hugo called it, from which he had been allowed to watch the fireworks, was not directly over the sitting-room, though too loud a footfall might be heard down there. His hope was that the skylight wouldn't squeak when he opened it; for he planned to get out on to the roof and wave from there to Bert's window. He had brought a strong torch, an old

white tablecloth of his mother's, and a white scarf, so as to make
himself so conspicuous that Bert couldn't miss him.

It was his first experience of any sort of mountaineering, and
when he had climbed the eight rungs of the emergency-ladder,
pushed up the skylight (which was counterweighted, and moved
easily and silently enough), put his head through the gap and peered
sideways into the dark, his courage was strained to its uttermost,
and had he not had a superstitious fear that if he failed in his purpose he would lose Bert's friendship for ever, he would have come
down ignominiously and made his signals from the box-room
window. But his mind was made up, and murmuring a prayer to
whatever god may look with favour on romantic exploits, he sat on
the sill, dragged his right leg through the skylight and then the left,
so that they rested against the slates sloping down to the lead-cov-
ered gulley. His toes soon touched an iron rung let into the slates,
which helped him in his descent. The gulley, which lay between a
pair of gables,—additions since the days of William Pollitt—was
two feet broad and ran the whole length of the house from Pollitt
Place to the back. In the front, there was a parapet so high that
it almost hid the gables from the street, and Hugo couldn't have
looked over it. But at the back—and it was only from this direction
that he could hope to have a view of Bert's window—there were
two iron bars, fixed so low down that they seemed designed to trip
you up rather than save you from falling. Hugo went cautiously
to within a yard of the precipice, then paused and scanned the
horizon of houses that towered round him. Lights from a thousand windows, some near, some distant, stabbed the blackness and
made it impossible for him to see the gap through which Bert's
torch should answer his. But Bert was high up,—enthroned like
a god on Mount Olympus—at an altitude from which the lower
world could hide no secrets. Though the human eye might not see
him, the eye of faith was assured of his watchfulness.

Slowly and solemnly, Hugo draped himself in the white table-
cloth and walked up and down in the shadow of the gables, for fear
he should display himself too soon. He felt as if he were robed as
an acolyte, and wondered if it would be a thrill to serve at Mass
in Brompton Oratory, the dome of which rose dimly in the dis-

tance,—or was that, perhaps, the Victoria and Albert Museum? All outlines were strange, and the city seemed transfigured as if expectant of some revelation, after which nothing would be as it had been before.

He flashed the torch on his watch. Three minutes to go. Like Ganymede awaiting the eagle's swoop, he advanced towards the extreme edge of the gulley. Another six inches and his knees would have touched the bars at the end, and the shock might have made him lose balance and plunge down, head foremost, into the maze of little backyards and gardens that filled the shapeless area below him. But he stood erect and motionless as a statue, while the breeze from the west blew damply against his cheek and fluttered his draperies.

Then the clock on St Ethelred's church, behind the Square, slowly struck six. Hugo flicked on the torch, and holding it in his left hand waved it round in a circle which had as its diameter almost twice the length of his arm, while with his right hand he twirled the long scarf in high, fantastic curves, and his eager eyes, directed to a point slightly north of due west, sought an answering flash of light, or at least the dim waving of a handkerchief,—perhaps one of the handkerchiefs which he had given Bert on Christmas Day— somewhere on a level with the lower stars.

But nothing happened. Innumerable pinpoints of light twinkled round him, but showed no change in their position. Perhaps Bert couldn't hear St Ethelred's clock? His watch might be wrong, or he might be preparing their evening meal just at that moment. A few minutes passed, while Hugo sought excuses for his friend's remissness, and when he had found half a dozen, he repeated his performance, though with rather less gusto than before. But what was that? Something whitish appeared in a window, then two thin arms that shook it, then a woman's dark head that for an instant caught the light from within. No, it was much too near. Bert's window must be three or four hundred yards further away, and very much higher.

Bewildered and miserable, Hugo lowered his eyes and looked almost perpendicularly downwards, till he could see a shaft of light falling from Magda's window into the yard. And there was Magda herself, removing some washing from the clothes-line. There was something grotesque and terrifying about her movements, as seen in this odd, vertical perspective. She looked like a puppet, jerkily put through its paces by a showman who wished to raise a laugh from the spectators. As Hugo watched her head bobbing up and down, he had an impulse to fling his torch at it. Then it occurred to him that if she moved to the far side of the yard and looked up at the roof, she would think she was seeing a ghost and might really believe that the box-room was haunted, as he had declared it was. She had always scoffed at his gift of second-sight and said his parade of it was a cheap way of drawing attention to himself. What a chance this was of really frightening her! For a moment he almost forgot his disappointment, and what his real purpose had been that evening.

But she went indoors, and then the full bitterness of Bert's betrayal came home to him. He straightened himself up, and with tears in his eyes waved the scarf and the torch a third time with frantic vigour, till his arms grew tired and his head reeled, and suddenly he seemed to hear his own voice prophesying that before the year was out, someone at Number Ten was doomed to die. Never once, since he had made that prophecy, had he dreamt that he might be foretelling his own death. But now, in that spasm of despair and giddiness, when a false step would send him crashing down on to the flagstones fifty feet below, he felt as if he were caught in his own trap.

As he tried to turn round and seek safety in the middle of the roof, a strange and intimate pain shot up his left leg from the ankle to the hip, and he was forced to put the whole of his weight on his right foot, which quivered under the strain. If only he had something to hold on to,—but the slope of the slates either side of him was so gradual that he couldn't touch them with his finger-tips. Even the uppermost bar at the end of the gulley was six inches too low unless he stooped down towards it. The cramp in his left leg was by now so acute, that he couldn't bend it at all, but he bent the right one slowly, inclining his body perilously forward till the fingers of his right hand found the bar. The feel of it gave him a moment's hope, but as he grasped it more firmly and began to shift his body sideways, so that he could fall backwards against the slates and somehow shuffle along towards the skylight, there was a sound of rusted metal being torn from its socket, the bar came away free in his hand, and he screamed and fell.

[4]

The two old ladies from Cornwall were sipping their cherry-brandy and chattering with a shrill vivacity. Miss Tredennick and Justin, both of whom preferred a dry sherry, encouraged them with appropriate nods and smiles and the stimulus of an occasional word. But the sitting-room window, which was almost directly below the gulley on the roof, was open several inches at the top, and Hugo's cry was loud and clear enough to shock the little party into silence.

Miss Tredennick's quick wits were the first to approach the truth. She said, 'That must be someone on the roof, and he's had an accident.' The old ladies were thrilled. 'What, a burglar—a cat-burglar, do you think?' But while Justin was suggesting they should ring up the police, Miss Tredennick said, 'No,—I'm pretty sure it's Hugo. He's fond of the box-room, for some reason or other, and I think I've heard him creeping up there before. He must have climbed out on to the roof by the fire-escape. Oh, Mr Bray, do please go and have a look. There's no danger to you. The little stair-case on the left of the landing leads straight to the box-room door. There are some easy steps inside the box-room that run up to the skylight. If you'd just put your head out and see what's happened? The poor boy may have broken his leg.'

For a moment Justin was inclined to protest that it was a job for a policeman or a fireman, but reminding himself that he was no longer a novelist and that his life was henceforward valueless to posterity, he put his glass down, got up heavily from his comfortable chair and without saying a word, went out on to the landing.

He thought even the little staircase bad enough. There were only six steps, but they were both narrow and steep and there was no kind of threshold by the door at the top, which opened awkwardly outwards and nearly knocked him down. Inside the room, he was still more disconcerted by the eight-runged ladder set against the wall at an angle that was formidably acute. Besides, the ladder was extremely dusty, except where Hugo's hands and feet had touched it, and Justin was wearing his newest suit that afternoon.

The skylight was open, as far as it would go. Very gingerly he climbed the three lowest rungs, put his head out and called, 'Is anyone there?' Somewhere in the darkness a voice answered, 'Help! Come quickly.' Justin gritted his teeth, completed the ascent and somehow wriggled himself on to the sill, where he found that to turn himself round and get his legs through was a tricky and most exhausting manœuvre. When this feat, too, was accomplished, he had to rest for two minutes till his breathing became more normal.

In front of him rose reassuringly the western gable, but to the right, at the end of the gulley, there was a sickening void. He remembered how, when many years before he had read in Thomas Hardy's *A Pair of Blue Eyes* the scene that took place on the 'Cliff without a name', he had almost fainted, and the thought of the distress into which that literary peril had plunged him, made his position seem doubly vertiginous.

'Help! Hurry, or I shall fall!' Justin's eyes were now accustomed to the darkness. He looked in the direction of the sound, which came from the open end of the gulley, and saw a white heap in the space between the gables. Forcing himself forward from the sill, he stretched out his long legs till they found a footing on the lead of the gulley, stood upright and walked towards the gap. When he was about two yards away, he trod on Hugo's torch, lost his balance and fell heavily on to Hugo's legs. Hugo gave another cry, but the physical contact seemed in some way to revive him; for he stirred, raised himself on his elbow and sat up, bumping Justin's nose with his head. 'Oh, it's Mr Bray! I had cramp in my leg and got dizzy and fell down and daren't move in case I fell over the edge. Are you all right, Mr Bray?' Justin said vaguely, 'I suppose I am,' then disentangling himself from the folds of Mrs Muller's table-cloth, he struggled to his feet and put a hand on the slates to steady himself. Then he added, 'I don't think I can get you in by myself. I must go for help. Perhaps Mr Fawley is in. He'd find it quite easy. Can you move at all? I don't like leaving you so near the edge.'

By way of answer, Hugo flexed his leg and got up without any apparent difficulty. 'The pain's quite gone. Shall I see what it's like getting in?' Without waiting for an answer, he brushed past Justin and hurried to the skylight. He was so short that he couldn't get his foot on the rung below the sill, till Justin gave him a shove from behind, but from there he climbed quite easily through the sky-light and down the ladder inside. A moment later, he saw Justin's head and shoulders silhouetted against the sky.

Justin found getting in even more laborious than it had been to get out. His muscles trembled and didn't respond to the instruc-tions given them by the brain. However, as if by a happy accident, he did at last put himself in such a position that he could use the ladder, while Hugo looked on, half anxious and half impatient. As soon as Justin touched the floor with his feet, he made straight for an old-fashioned trunk in a corner of the room, sat down on it and rested the top of his back against the match-boarded wall. Hugo said suddenly, 'Oh, my torch! I've left it behind. I'll go and get it. I shall be quite all right.' But Justin said wearily, 'Don't be a silly boy. You can go and look for it in daylight to-morrow, if you must, but don't expect me to come and rescue you, if you get cramp. I don't think I've ever been on a roof before, and I'm certainly never going on one again.'

The effort of speaking seemed to cost him something. Hugo looked with alarm at his greyish face and asked, 'Shall I get you some water?', but Justin replied ungraciously, 'No, go away. Don't look at me like that. I shall be all right after I've had a short rest. Tell Miss Tredennick everything's all right, and that I'll be down in a moment.'

Hugo nodded gravely, murmured, 'Yes, Sir,—and thank you very much for your kindness to me,' and went down the short stairway. When he reached the landing, he met Magda who was coming up from below. She gave him her automatic glance of fear and dislike, and then, noticing the dust and dirt on his hands, face and clothes, she said, 'What on earth have you been doing? In any case what are you doing up here?' He said sullenly, 'I've a

message for you to give to Miss Tredennick. Tell her Mr Bray will
be down in a moment and that everything's all right.' Before she
could make further inquiries or protest, he hurried past her down
the next flight of stairs. By the time he had reached the basement,
all he thought of was Bert's broken promise.

Justin sat on the trunk in the corner of the box-room, swaying
slightly, with his left hand on his chest. He said to himself, 'I shall
be all right very soon. It isn't as bad as when I chased that woman
with the dog. It's nerves,—only nerves. Dr Jamieson said it was
nerves. Too much adrenalin getting into the blood,—or something
like that.'

But the pain increased, and he began to realise that he was passing through an experience unlike any other he had had in his whole
life. It was terrifying; yet such a rift had developed in his consciousness, that while one half of it struggled with pain and fear, the
other half dreamt irrelevantly of being at Cambridge again, as a
young man, communing with Frances Cornford, Rupert Brooke,
Gray and Horace Walpole in one of the college gardens leading
down to the river. The air was warm and moist, and all the birds of
early summer were singing in the trees. Why not? Why shouldn't
he go there again as an undergraduate, and read some leisurely
subject for a pass degree? How much happier he would be—and
how much less lonely—than in Ten Pollitt Place! If only the new
novel he was going to write turned out a success,—if only he could
make one supreme effort——

His cry, like Hugo's reached the room below, and this time there
was no chatter to drown it. Miss Tredennick and her two friends
were talking in apprehensive whispers, while Magda was uneasily
clearing away the tea. Miss Tredennick called her as she was carrying a tray into the kitchen, and said softly, 'Magda, I can't help
fearing Mr Bray has been taken unwell. Will you go to the box-
room and see?'

[5]

They found this half-finished letter on Justin's desk:

New Year's Eve   *10, Pollitt Place, S.W.*

I am so grieved and distressed, my dear Lady Victoria, to learn of your abominable accident. I know how brave and uncomplaining you will be, but the pain must be dreadful, and the prospect of three months' captivity in a room with two unchosen companions is more than I can bear to think of for you. This at least it is in my power to remedy, if only you will let me. I do beg you—if not for your own sake and not for mine—for the sake of my mother, whose memory I know is still precious to you after all these years, to accept the cheque which I enclose. She would never forgive me if I didn't send it nor should I forgive myself,—despite the rebuffs with which, as you must confess, any little attempts of mine to make life easier for you have met hitherto.

My wants are now very few and will soon be fewer. I have more than enough to see me out, unless some government, resolved on the utter destruction of the *rentier*, introduces a punitive form of capital levy. And in that case, it will give me great satisfaction to think that before I was ruined, I did at least try to do something for someone else.

I have done so very little for other people in the course of my pampered and self-indulgent life. I used to think that 'my art'—this sounds as if I were a *diseuse* or a film-star—justified all my selfishness. I had to enjoy every comfort and be surrounded by beautiful things, if I was to give of my best. In a lazy way, so far as I could, I kept my side of the bargain. I gave of my best,—but it wasn't good enough.

I had luncheon to-day with George de Lacey. As you know, he has long been both one of my dearest friends and one of my kindest and most encouraging critics. I talked to him of a new book I have been writing for the last few weeks, and asked him for his advice on one or two points. Alas, his advice,—when it came—(I had to drag it out of him, to begin with)—was that I should give up any idea of ever writing another novel. He tried to soften the blow as much as he could. He instanced George Moore (both in his opinion and mine a greater writer than any now living), who is in almost total eclipse, perhaps because he regards his characters

not as units in the social organism, but as ends in themselves. I
admit, de Lacey suggested other aspects of literature with which I
might occupy my declining years. But novels, no! He said, 'Nowadays, a readable novel has to be an intellectualised strip-cartoon,
and that's a technique which, however hard you try, you will never
master.'

I had to agree with everything he said. So, instead of being
Justin Bray the novelist, I am now Justin Bray, the elderly man-
about-town,—a period-piece, a quaint, pathetic survival.

But how very much too seriously we take ourselves, we would-
be 'serious writers'. Our egotism may not be as gross, uncritical
and full-blooded as that of the successful tennis-player or boxer,
but in its insidious, introspective way, it is no less poisonous. I read
a passage in Hawthorne the other night,—it comes from the intro-
ductory chapter to *The Scarlet Letter*—which impressed me very
deeply.

*'It is a good lesson—though it may often be a hard one—for a man
who has dreamed of literary fame, and of making for himself a rank
among the world's dignitaries by such means, to step aside out of the
narrow circle in which his claims are recognised, and to find how utterly
devoid of significance, beyond that circle, is all that he achieves, and all
he aims at.'*

The letter broke off at this point, and the cheque, which was to
accompany it, was still unwritten.

XVIII

TWELFTH NIGHT

'Magda,—just one moment. We can talk in here.'

Robert, who was setting out for his work, had met her in the
hall. The door of Justin's sitting-room was wide open, and he
went in while Magda followed nervously. The room was already
half stripped. The more precious ornaments had been stowed in
packing-cases, and the furniture was stacked ready for removal.

The rugs had been rolled up and the floor was covered by dust-sheets littered with paper and straw. The pelmets, the thick curtains and the net curtains had all been taken down, and inquisitive passers-by had a clear view of the half empty room. To Magda, who had kept it clean for so long, with all the pride of an old-fashioned servant, its bleakness and disarray seemed strange and inexpressibly sad. But Robert who had only once had the privilege of seeing the room in its glory, noticed no change. Besides, he was far too preoccupied with other matters to feel any sentimental regrets for the breaking-up of a gentleman's establishment.

He shut the door and said almost peremptorily, 'Magda, I've got to see you this afternoon. I can get off a bit early. Can you be at South Kensington station at half-past five?'

She answered, 'Yes, I could go there as soon as I've cleared away Miss Tredennick's tea. But I could only be with you till a quarter past six—unless I can arrange with Mother to——'

He shook his head and said, 'Oh no, I'm afraid Twickenham is out of the question to-night. I'll try not to keep you more than half an hour.'

Something odd in his voice and odder still in his manner alarmed her, and she longed to ask him for some hint of what he wanted to talk to her about. But he said, 'Well, I suppose I must be off. Goodbye, my dear.' He gave her a pat on the arm and she looked apprehensively at the uncurtained window, as if to warn him that anyone outside could see them embracing. But he went straight out. As she watched him walking briskly towards the Crescent, it occurred to her that he might have taken her into Justin's bedroom at the back, where they could have kissed one another in safety. But perhaps, being unfamiliar with the ground-floor flat, he didn't know that the bedroom windows faced a blank wall.

Then the front-door bell rang, recalling her to her duties, and she admitted two swarthy black-coated gentlemen who said they had come to appraise Justin's pictures, which were still hanging in their usual positions. As she hadn't been told to expect these visitors, she decided she ought to stay and watch them at their task, though there were now very few small objects about such as they could have made away with. Their professional talk jarred on her nerves. 'My word, the old man wasn't a fool. . . . It's funny what a nose these literary blokes have for buying the right stuff. . . . Pity though, he didn't invest in Klee or Picasso, but I suppose he was too much of a back-number for that. . . . Can't say I feel very happy about this one. Look at that bright yellow. . . . I should say twelve hundred. I'd give nine, myself. . . .'

At last they put away their lenses, shut their note-books and nodded a curt goodbye. When they had gone, Magda found to her surprise that her eyes were wet, and she realised for the first time how much she had become attached to Justin, in a dull, unadventurous way. His solicitors had told her that by his Will he had left her and her mother a hundred pounds each and twenty-five to Hugo—towards whom her feelings had now grown so bitter that she would have been quite willing to forfeit her own legacy if by so doing she could have deprived him of his.

Since Justin's death, Mrs Muller, whose superstitious terrors were now finally routed, had never ceased to sing Hugo's praises and to vaunt his uncanny gift. 'He sees into a world that is hidden from us. How right my darling boy was! He said—I remember it now—he said *in this house*—those were the words he used—someone would die *in this house* before the end of the year. When that woman killed herself on Christmas Eve, I thought he had been just a little mistaken. I hoped and prayed so. It was too terrible to think that it might be one of us. But he was quite right. *In this house* it was. I'm very sorry, of course, about poor Mr Bray, but the relief—oh, Magda, the relief!'

This theme had become so wearisome that Magda found it intolerable. To hear Hugo, whom she both despised and feared, thus elevated above the common run of humanity, extolled as a saint, a prophet divinely inspired, made her long to speak her mind about him and tell her mother what a little monster she was cherishing. So far she had kept glumly, if prudently, silent. But when the three of them were having their midday meal in the kitchen that day, and her mother turned yet again to the nauseating subject, Magda's pent up exasperation broke out at last.

She stood up suddenly, with blazing cheeks, and said, 'For

goodness sake, stop it, Mother. Has it never occurred to you, that if Hugo hadn't disobeyed you and gone upstairs without being sent for by Miss Tredennick, Mr Bray wouldn't have died? No, I'm going to speak. It's quite time you knew the truth. *Hugo* killed Mr Bray—I don't mean on purpose, of course—but have you ever asked him *why* he went on the roof?'

Mrs Muller was so dazed by the unexpected attack, that she could hardly answer, but under the compulsion of her daughter's eyes, she gasped, 'To look at the view—and see the lights. That was it—wasn't it, Hugo? You told me that.'

Hugo who had gone very white, said, 'Yes, I went there to look at the view and see the lights.'

'That wasn't all!' Magda spat out the words, and went on, 'I'm going to tell you the whole story, whether you like it or not. You didn't know, I suppose, that he's got a morbid mania for the dustman—the red-headed one. He can't leave him alone. He pesters him whenever he comes to the house. He even asked Mr Bray for some cigarettes so that he could pass them on to his precious friend. Or so Mr Bray said. I think myself Hugo stole them.'

'Magda, how dare you!'

Magda made an angry gesture with her hand and continued, 'I think Mr Bray was simply trying to shield him. It would have been far better if he hadn't. If only he'd sent for the police and charged Hugo with theft and had him imprisoned or put in a reformatory, poor Mr Bray would have been alive to-day—and there wouldn't have been all this talk of Hugo's wonderful powers. No, Mother, I'm going on, and you can't stop me. As for why he went on the roof, it wasn't to see the lights or the view,—it was to signal to his dustman-friend.'

She paused for a moment, breathless, and her mother said feebly, 'Magda, what do you mean? I think you must have gone mad.' But Magda shouted, 'No, I'm not mad. If anyone's mad in the family, it's Hugo. Would you like to know what I happened to hear yesterday, when I was taking down the curtains in Mr Bray's room? Hugo was waiting in the area, pretending to look at those bulbs he keeps in a box near the coal-cellar door. (He only keeps them there as an excuse for hanging about there. I told him they'd do better in the backyard, but of course he didn't take any notice of me.) Well, the dustman said, "What's up with you to-day? Anything wrong?" Hugo didn't speak and turned away, but the dustman put his hand on the back of Hugo's head and turned his face round, so that Hugo had to look at him. Hugo said, "I went up to our roof on New Year's Eve, and waved my torch at you for a long time, but you didn't take any notice. Then I got cramp and nearly fell over the edge and killed myself." The dustman said he was a silly boy, and that he'd told him to wave from the box-room window, and not to go on the roof. Hugo said, "Anyway, you wouldn't have cared if I had killed myself. You didn't bother to wave back at me. I suppose you were out somewhere enjoying yourself and had forgotten all about your promise." The dustman said he hadn't forgotten at all, and waited for Hugo for a quarter of an hour, from eight to a quarter-past. Then Hugo said, "But we said six, not eight," and began to cry and went indoors to his room. Then I saw the dustman go to Hugo's window and look in through the bars. I think he was talking to Hugo inside, but I couldn't hear what he said. But I'd heard quite enough to make me feel sick and disgusted,—just as I feel sick and disgusted when I hear you saying how wonderful Hugo is to have known Mr Bray was going to die. Poor old man! I'd far rather Hugo had fallen off the roof—he's *abnormal*, I tell you, *abnormal*——'

She stopped suddenly, realising what an awful disclosure she had made of her innermost thoughts. Her mother and Hugo both got up very slowly from the table, as if their movement was con-certed, while Magda covered her face with her hands, broke into hysterical sobs and ran to her room.

[2]

Dorothy was standing in a queue of a dozen people, all waiting for a place at one of the tables in the Pâtisserie Mouton, just off Parkwell Road. Mouton's light luncheons were famous for savoury omelettes, *vol-au-vents*, fancy cakes and coffee. The prices were on the high side, but Monsieur Mouton could have had twice the number of customers, if his premises and his staff had been twice the size, and it was a tribute to his cooking that so many regulars came day after day, knowing that they would have to stand a quarter of an hour, and sometimes longer, before they could sit down.

They were nearly all women, but immediately in front of Dorothy there were two young men with bright peach-coloured complexions and fair hair set in elaborate waves. Their voices were high-pitched and penetrating, and she couldn't help overhearing their conversation—which, however, was not at all like the conversation she was apt to overhear at Garrows.

One of them said, 'Oh, my dear, the corner-table's on the move at last. Yes, the brown-tweed muffin is getting out her bag and scratching about in it for her money. Why *do* they have to take so long over it?'

The other one answered, 'No, I'm afraid she's only looking for her lipstick,—as if anyone could care what she looks like! There! She's dropped her bag and knocked over all those cheap looking parcels the creature in pillar-box red put on that shelf. *Aren't* they clumsy!'

His friend agreed readily. 'Yes, I've noticed that on the top of a bus the slimmest woman is clumsier with her bottom than the fattest old man. They bang it against your shoulder or into your face and simply never, never apologise. Move up, Paul. Only three in front of us now. This really is a test of endurance.'

Paul moved up and hissed, 'Beware of that harpy in the puce brocatelle! She's pretending to look at the cakes on the counter, but she's really trying to jump the queue. They're not only clumsy, inconsiderate and selfish,—they're so dishonest. And the awful thought is, they've nearly all got a husband or are going to get one. Imagine yourself coming home every night and finding a brown-tweed muffin or a pillar-box red or a puce brocatelle sitting waiting for you! We have a good many things to bear, my dear, but at least we're spared that horror. . . . Come along. Those two little drabs at the side-table are getting up. . . . No, Madam, *that* is the end of the queue,—just by the door. You'll find it rather draughty.'

They scuttled to their table with an arch avoidance of obstacles, and Dorothy was left at the head of the queue. Luckily another exodus soon gave her a seat.

What she had heard, instead of rousing her (as well it might have done) to a feminist fury, only increased her own forebodings. The two young men—why did they hate women so much?—had talked of husbands coming home every night to tedious and uncongenial wives. Of course, she had seen the subject discussed in evening newspapers, though it had always struck her as cheaply exaggerated. But now she wondered in all seriousness if that was how Robert really felt about her. Did he dread the moment when he opened the sitting-room door and found the same woman waiting night after night, with, more often than not, a grievance on her lips? 'Why are you so late? . . . I've got another sore throat. . . . I shan't go to Garrows' fish-department any more. I told the man he'd given me haddock instead of halibut, and you wouldn't believe how insolent he was.' These little pinpricks, when a man has just got home, tired with his work and standing in the Tube, were quite enough to make him long for a change—even a change for the worse. There must come a moment when he'd break out and say, 'This is the end.'

She still thought of her behaviour on Christmas Day with great contrition and doubted very much if Robert had forgiven her. It was true that the miserable evening had ended in a kind of reconciliation—for which she may have had her tears to thank—but she was sure Robert had by no means forgotten what had happened earlier on. It wasn't that he had been any less attentive to her than usual. Indeed, he had gone out of his way to do one or two things which gave her pleasure.

On the Tuesday after Christmas he had turned up at the supper-party given by her friends, in spite of the loop-hole he had left himself for getting out of it, and a week later, on the third of January, when the undertakers had called to collect poor Mr Bray's body, he had made the sad event an excuse to take her to a theatre and give her supper afterwards at a restaurant. Only the previous night, instead of going to his work-room after washing up, he had sat in the drawing-room with her and said he'd like to read one of Oscar Wilde's plays. Yet there was a formality, almost an excessive politeness in his manner which made her uneasy. He behaved with her, as one might behave in the presence of someone whom one detested, but who, one knew, was very soon going to die. He had fits of abstraction, too, as if his mind was busy with a problem he hadn't quite solved. She had asked him once if his work was worrying him, and he had simply said, 'No,' without asking her what could have put such an idea into her head. She had nearly gone on to say, 'Well, then, what is it?', but feared to irritate him. It was easy to see that he wasn't happy, and still easier to blame herself for being the cause of it. Since her childhood she had been used to long periods of unhappiness and feeling out of sorts, but it seemed unnatural that Robert, on whose equanimity and vigour she so much relied, should suffer as she had suffered.

She finished her meal, and bearing in mind the strictures that the two unpleasant youths (who were still eating cake after cake), might pass on her, if she loitered too long at the table, she called for her bill, paid it and went out. The weather had changed again. It was now very cold—far colder than it had been at Christmas. The sun was shining, but between such menacing clouds that it only gave the sky an angrier look. Hail, thunder, snow—perhaps the end of the world—seemed to hang over her head.

This was no day for gazing into the windows of the shops in Parkwell Road. Besides, the sales were on, and the displays had sacrificed their usual elegance for a catch-penny utility. Even Garrows was full of alien goods, an alien staff and alien customers. For Dorothy, who liked shopping luxuriously, it had temporarily ceased to be a magnet. Still, she needed some new dusters and—if one had to spend money on such dreary things—perhaps this was the moment to buy them. And it would pass an unwanted half-hour.

She fought her way in, feeling very frail among the Amazonian bargain-hunters from the obscurer suburbs. How different they were from the smart and prosperous buyers of Christmas gifts. Those eager and acquisitive days seemed far away, but their memory was still precious. How happy she had been almost all November, and December too, right up to Christmas Day, when things went wrong. She had a feeling that the New Year, now six days old, was fated to bring her some calamity.

The counter at which the household linen was sold was one of the most popular in the sale, and it was nearly half-past three when she left the shop. As she was going out into the street, she saw Magda coming in by the same entrance. The girl was red-eyed and looked blue with cold. Or was she ill? With a mingling of concern and curiosity, Dorothy intercepted her and said, 'Why, Magda, what a surprise seeing you here! I've just been buying some dusters, but I really don't think the ones I chose were reduced at all. I might just as well have left it till next week, when these awful crowds will be gone.'

Magda seemed too listless to look at her, and with her eyes fixed on the mosaic of the threshold, she said weakly, 'Miss Tredennick sent me in to buy some dusters—and a dozen tea-cloths—and——' She broke off, as if it was a strain to finish the sentence. Making an attempt to rally her, Dorothy said, 'If you take my advice, you won't buy anything that's much reduced. All those things you see marked down in the window, aren't their regular lines, and I'm sure they wouldn't be good enough for Miss Tredennick. If it weren't so cold, I'd show you the dusters I bought. Magda, are you quite well?'

Instead of answering, Magda gulped down a sob, went through the door and vanished in the crowd. For a moment, Dorothy thought of pursuing her, but feared to seem officious. Magda was neither a friend nor a servant of hers. If the girl was in trouble, it was Mrs Muller's place, not Dorothy's, to get her out of it. But it was all very odd.

She made her way along the bustling pavement, and wondered again if Magda were in love and wretched on that account. It was rumoured that the woman at Number Seven had killed herself in a fit of jealousy,—which is presumably a form of *Liebestod*. What tragedies seemed to have centred themselves round Pollitt Place,—Miss Varioli, Mr Bray and now Magda. The thought of these three persons' unhappiness—though it might be a mistake to think of Mr Bray as unhappy—relieved her own, by distracting her from herself.

When she reached Number Ten, and saw the uncurtained windows of Mr Bray's sitting-room, she realised for the first time that there was now a flat in the house to let, and began to speculate about the new tenants. On the whole, she favoured two middle-aged spinsters, who would be available for tea or gossip when she was at a loose end. Failing them, she would choose an elderly married couple. The husband might be keen on photography, and although few things were more tedious than having to look through other people's albums of snapshots, the hobby might provide an interest for Robert, who could help the old man to do his developing in the bathroom, while she sat and talked with the wife about plays and books and what they had seen in the shops. They might even be fond of a game of three-handed bridge—Robert hated cards—which would help to pass the time when he was kept late at his work or went to one of his scientific films. At all events, she hoped very much that if they were 'nice people', they would be neighbourly—without, of course, that intrusive suburban matiness which she had found so distasteful at Hackfield—and unlike Mr Bray, who, for all his gentility, had made it clear that he regarded himself as belonging to a different world and didn't want any truck with his fellow-lodgers.

Upstairs, in the sitting-room, she switched on the fire, tapped the barometer, which showed a sensational fall since the morning, tapped the glass of the aquarium and threw a pinch of ants' eggs on to the water, watching the fish flash upwards with mouths agape to devour the titbits. Then she went across to the budgerigars, said, 'Tweet, tweet,' to which they obligingly replied, and poked her finger through the bars of the cage to be pecked,—and they obliged again. It was a pity that they couldn't talk, but she had been told that if you had two of them, they talked to one another in their own language and wouldn't bother to learn yours. But to keep one poor little bird shut up all alone seemed too cruel, and she had decided that if she lost one of her pair, she would at once buy a mate for the survivor. Lucky creatures indeed, for whom a devoted companionship could be provided so easily!

It was twenty to four. In less than two hours and a half, she should be hearing Robert at the front door, and his quick, springy step on the stairs. There might have been times—though it shamed her now to think of them—when his presence had bored her, but it had never failed to give her a feeling of safety, such as she craved for

more than ever that afternoon. At all costs, she must keep herself
from imagining catastrophes,—street accidents, railway accidents, or even an accident in the laboratory at the works. (There
had been one, two years before, and a colleague of Robert's had
been blinded and nearly killed.) She knew from experience that
her bouts of panic—however silly they might seem afterwards—
could be agonisingly painful at the time. One of them seemed to
be taking shape within her at that very moment, and she longed to
be set some strenuous manual task which should keep it at bay.

What was there she could do? Three years before, she had learnt
petit-point, but had given it up with the excuse that it strained her
eyes. However, she had had new spectacles since then, and it might
please Robert to find her, just for once, doing something with her
hands.

She went to the cupboard in which she thought she had put the
tapestry and the silks, but they weren't there, and it was some time
before she came across them. (Four o'clock. Only another two
hours to go.) The silks were in a tangle and the shades all mixed
up. She sorted them and arranged them in the compartments of
her work-bag, methodically, like Robert replacing his tools in the
tool-box. The half-hour struck before she was ready to make a
stitch. Should she have some tea first? But at that moment, there
was a knock on the door.

[3]

'Come in. Oh, it's Hugo! What is it?'

She felt confused and full of apprehensions. He seemed to have
changed from a pathetic under-sized child into a tragic and digni-
fied young man. She went on, 'Do you want to speak to me? Mr
Fawley isn't back yet.'

'No, Madam. It's you I should like to speak to, if you're not too
busy.'

'Of course I'm not. Do shut that door and come in. There's a
bitter draught. I was just going to make myself some tea. Can I
give you a cup?'

Three minutes before, it would have seemed impossible that

she should ever offer Hugo—the house-keeper's son—a cup of tea in her drawing-room, but now the invitation came out quite naturally. He shut the door gently, but stood by it, while he said, 'No thank you, Madam. I couldn't say what I've got to say to you, over the tea-table.'

His slow delivery of this ominous sentence filled Dorothy with alarm. 'Don't say——' she gasped, 'don't say they've sent *you* to break some bad news to me!'

He looked at her gravely, as if he were choosing words with which to soften the blow. Reading a hint of compassion in his expression, she could bear the suspense no longer and cried, 'Is it bad news of my husband? Has there been some message from the place where he works? Tell me outright, and don't try to disguise it.'

Hugo shook his head and said, 'No, Madam, there's been no message. So far as I know, Mr Fawley is quite well. Though what I have to tell you, does concern him.'

Dorothy's relief took the form of indignation. '*You* have to tell me something that concerns my husband? What can you mean?'

Hugo ignored her outburst and went on, 'It's about Magda too. Oh, Madam, if you could guess, it would help me so much. It's about your husband and Magda. Think, for a moment!'

He watched her while she thought, and saw her face contorted by a suspicion of the truth. Her first impulse was to break out into defensive abuse and order him out of the room, but remembering her chance meeting with Magda at Garrows' main entrance that very afternoon, and how ill and woe-begone Magda had looked, she said, with all the calmness she could muster, 'Hugo, before you speak, be very sure you're speaking the truth. You're old enough to know what slander means. It's a serious thing and you can be sued for it in a court of law. If you've heard some silly gossip from one of the local tradesmen or errand boys',—at this point her voice became more conciliatory—'I shall be glad to hear it, of course, so that Mr Fawley and I can take steps to deal with it. If on the other hand'—her voice hardened—'if it's something you've imagined or invented, or something you've been put up to by your sister——'

She paused in the middle of whatever threat she was going to make. Could it be that Magda was expecting a baby and was accusing Robert of being the father? Had she sent Hugo to blackmail them? How did one deal with such a situation? That little flaxen-haired boy with his angel-face, on which the bitter experience of a thousand years seemed suddenly to have left an imprint—what an envoy to choose!

Hugo read her thoughts as easily as if she had uttered them; for he said, 'It isn't Magda who asked me to tell you this. *She* doesn't blame your husband. She's in love with him. I think she'd really like you to divorce him, so that they could marry. But she's very religious in her way, and I don't think even if Mr Fawley did marry her, her conscience would ever be easy. She'll be unhappy all right—you needn't worry about that—but you can't stop your husband from going out with her. All you can do is to threaten to divorce him.'

As he ended his speech, he put his head on one side and looked at her interrogatively, as if he expected her to collaborate with him. But the full implications of what he had been telling her, hadn't come home to her yet. Playing for time in which to collect her wits, she said coldly, 'I can only think you're suffering from delusions, or that you're an evil-minded little boy and have invented all this to upset us—and perhaps your sister as well. What evidence have you got? What do you know?'

He answered calmly, 'I've only got one piece of real evidence, but that's strong enough. Do you know a block of flats in Twickenham called Underbourne Mansions?'

'No. Wait a minute,—yes, I do. A colleague of my husband's lives there. What about it?'

'About ten days before Christmas I followed Magda there. She went by bus and walked the last bit of the way. I took a taxi. I saw her going in—so did the taxi-driver. I've got his number.'

'What was the number of the flat she went to?'

'I don't know that; we stayed outside near the entrance.'

'Then what makes you think your sister's visit there has any connexion with my husband—or his colleague? It's a large block, so far as I remember.'

'Just as we were driving away, your husband went in. I saw him clearly by the light of a lamp in the road.' He paused for a second, and then, as if her incredulity annoyed him, went on more ruth-lessly, 'Of course, it might only be a coincidence. Magda may not have gone there to meet Mr Fawley and Mr Fawley may not have gone there to meet Magda. He may have been going to see a gen-tleman-friend—that colleague of his you spoke of.' He looked at her closely, saw her shake her head slightly, and continued, 'All the same, I think Mr Fawley and Magda did go there to be with one another. You see, when you were away in November, she used to go and sit with him up here. At least, I think so. I've no proof of it, but unless she spent a very long time indeed with Miss Tredennick, or by herself in the box-room, I don't know anywhere else she could have been. She wasn't downstairs; and I should have heard her if she'd been in Mr Bray's rooms. But why not ask her? She won't lie to you. If she says she's not in love with Mr Fawley and has never been with him up here or in Twickenham, I shall believe her. But she won't say that.'

Dorothy tottered feebly to a chair, sat down and rubbed her forehead with her hand. Then she asked weakly, 'Why have you told me all this? Did you want to make me miserable?'

For a moment he didn't reply. Then the colour suddenly came into his cheeks, and raising his voice for the first time since he had begun to speak to her, he said, 'I've told you this because I want to hurt Magda. Not you. I'm sorry if I've hurt you. I wasn't sure you cared for Mr Fawley. But Magda is really wicked. She said things about me to my mother to-day—nothing I'm ashamed of—but things that upset my mother very much. And she said she wished I'd fallen off the roof and died instead of Mr Bray. She's a hypo-crite. That's what I hate about her. Listen——'

He opened the door a couple of inches, put his ear to the gap and whispered, 'She's given Miss Tredennick her tea. You can catch her as she comes down, and ask her if what I've told you is the truth. Come——'

As if hypnotised, Dorothy got up slowly and joined him by the door, which he opened to its full extent. Then, leaving Dorothy trembling in the doorway, he went out on to the landing and stood by the head of the lower flight of stairs.

Magda was so busy with her own thoughts that she reached
the landing before she saw Dorothy. But when she did, she stood
quite still against the wall, knowing at once that something serious
had happened, and waiting warily for Dorothy to speak. Dorothy's
throat had gone so dry that she had to swallow several times, as
if she were choking, before she could gasp out—'Is it true—that
you—that you and my husband—have—are——'

Her abject feebleness suddenly put Magda on her mettle. This
was the moment she and Robert had been waiting for. Very well.
She would make the most of it. Raising her eyes and looking at
Dorothy with contempt, she said, almost brazenly, 'Yes, Robert
and I are lovers.' Then, turning her head a little to the right, she
caught sight of Hugo, who was barring her way down the stairs.
Something about him,—complacency, or an expression of malicious triumph,—roused a devil within her. Losing all self-control,
she shouted, 'So it's you,—you loathsome sneak!', and ignoring
Dorothy, who staggered back into the sitting-room, she darted at
him with her hand raised to strike him in the face. But Hugo, who
had seen the glint of murder in her eyes, was already on the half-
landing, below, and before she could overtake him in the hall, he
dived into Justin's room and slammed the door, intending to lock
it. But the key was missing, and though he gripped the handle,
Magda's wrists were stronger than his. He released his hold, and
ran across to the grate to find a poker with which to defend himself. However, even before he realised that all the fire-irons had
been packed away, Magda's hands were on his shoulders. He
shouted, 'Mother! Help! Help! Mrs Fawley!' But Dorothy, who
was half fainting in a chair, heard nothing and Mrs Muller was at
that very moment searching in the Men's Department at Garrows,
for a present which should make it clear to Hugo that she had forgiven him and would always forgive him.

There was no escape. Though he struck at Magda's face and his
nails drew blood, she forced him on to his knees and then flat on
the floor. He screamed again and again, but disregarding his blows
she took his head in both her hands and banged it hard against the
green marble of the empty hearth. She thought she heard a click
and he lay very still. She drew her hands away, and then, quite

deliberately and without any trace of passion, took his head again and banged it down four times more, as if with each blow she were driving another nail into the coffin of her happiness.

Five minutes later, after a fit of sobbing so violent that she thought her heart was going to burst, she picked up the receiver of Justin's telephone, which was still on the top of his desk, and dialled Dr Jamieson's number. When he answered, she said, 'This is Magda Muller speaking. Will you come at once? Hugo's had an accident. He's dead—or dying. He—his head hit the marble hearth in Mr Bray's room. Please come at once. Please——' She dropped the receiver, hurried over to Hugo and tried to feel his heart, though an obscure instinct prevented her from opening his shirt. She detected no sign of a heart-beat, but thought she noticed a slight rise and fall of his chest. Then she knelt down beside the body, till the front-door bell rang.

When she answered it, she let in not only Dr Jamieson, but her mother who had met him at the corner of the Crescent on her way home.

[4]

As to what happened during the next quarter of an hour, even Dr Jamieson wasn't very clear. He admitted, when he was questioned afterwards, that he was confused and thrown off his balance. 'A younger man might have coped with things more efficiently,— though after all . . .' They couldn't really blame him for anything, except perhaps for not ringing up the police as soon as Magda began to accuse herself of having murdered her brother. But she and her mother were both so clearly hysterical that he didn't bother very much with them, as long as he had his patient to consider.

He found Hugo bleeding at the nostrils, and diagnosed a case of concussion and possible fracture. Magda's first story was that Hugo had slipped and hit his head on the marble. It was true that her face was bleeding, and that there was blood on her hands and on her white apron, but he assumed, to begin with, that all the blood was Hugo's.

Mrs Muller was much harder to manage. When he was ringing

up for an ambulance to take Hugo to hospital, he had to break off
and stop her by force from taking Hugo's body in her arms and
carrying it downstairs, so that she could put him to bed. He had
to slap her on the face several times and warn her that if she inter-
fered, Hugo would most unquestionably die. 'As it is,' he told her,
'no one knows what will happen when he recovers consciousness.
He may be deaf and dumb, or paralysed, or blind,—or an idiot. For
God's sake, do as I say!'

It was then that Magda began to scream, 'I killed him. It's all
my fault. I knocked him down and banged his head on the marble.
I wanted to kill him.' And when the doctor had tried to calm her
down, she rushed from the room, and before he knew what she
intended to do, she was running down the street. He couldn't leave
his patient and chase after her, and Mrs Muller was in no condition to give him any help. As others could testify, she was almost
uncontrollable at the hospital.

[5]

'I simply haven't the guts to leave Dorothy.'

While Robert sat in the Tube, he repeated the sentence to
himself, time after time. It was only fair to Magda that he should
bring it out almost as soon as he saw her. He knew it was bound to
wound her grievously, but he hoped she had too much sense and
self-command to make a scene in public. Scenes in private seemed,
for the time being, quite outside the picture.

Unfortunately, he would have to say a good deal more to her
than just that one key-sentence. Putting it crudely, he would have
to give her the option of continuing to be his mistress, though with
little hope of ever becoming his wife. 'Don't think for a moment, I
love Dorothy, or that I don't want *you*.' Yes, he could say that with
full sincerity. He did still want Magda—or rather he knew there'd
be times when he would want her.

Meanwhile, however, he didn't know what he wanted. Since the
nightmare of Christmas Day, when Dorothy had given him in such
full measure the opportunity for which he had been waiting, and
which, when it came, he had been too feeble to seize, he had lost

all confidence in the strength of his will. He felt only half alive,—as it were, emasculated,—incapable of either loving or making love to anyone.

'I simply haven't the guts to leave Dorothy.' That summed up the whole position only too well. He hadn't the guts, when Dorothy was behaving like a schoolmistress in a temper to say, 'That's enough. I'm quitting, here and now. Divorce me, sue me, do whatever you like, scream, go on your knees, or find a convenient gas-fire and turn it on,—you've lost me for good and all.' One couldn't say things like that in cold blood, of course, but his blood hadn't been cold. It had been seething so feverishly, that he had nearly stormed out of his workshop into the drawing-room to deliver his ultimatum. But he hadn't done so, and when Dorothy came tapping at the workshop door, he had crumpled up completely in thirty seconds, simply because he couldn't face a scene,—even the very scene that he had longed for.

The thought of scenes carried his mind forward once more to his meeting with Magda, now only ten minutes ahead. Suppose, after all, she did become hysterical. How would he deal with her? Simply walk away—or give her in charge for molesting him? What had happened to him that he could now think of her so callously? Had his whole passion died even more suddenly than it had come to life? His feelings, so far as they existed beneath his numbness, were in the melting-pot. A tilt of the crucible to this side or that would pour them into a permanent mould. If Magda made a scene of sufficient violence, he would give way to her no less abjectly than he had given way to Dorothy. If only Magda could have a show-down with Dorothy and spare him the unpleasantness,—insensitive though he was to verbal niceties, the pansy phrase made him smile for the first time that day—he was quite likely to take Magda to Twickenham and spend the night with her there, not now for the sake of a few more romantic hours, but so that she could burn his boats for him, and make his return to Dorothy impossible. But if she didn't do the dirty work for him,—if she simply pouted and sulked and piped her eye——Oh Hell! Two women were tugging at his destiny. Let the one who tugged hardest, win. At the time he hardly cared.

Magda was standing by the door of the lift, when he got out, but he didn't recognise her till she touched his arm. Her cheek still oozed a little blood, and she was still wearing the blood-stained apron. She looked like an old hag who had been having a rough-and-tumble in a slaughter-house.

He stared at her in horror and said, 'Magda,—what on earth—what's happened?', and then shrank back as she drew so close to him that her body was almost rubbing against his. She gripped his arm fiercely in her strong fingers and whispered, 'This is goodbye. Hugo has told your wife everything about us. They're taking him to hospital in an ambulance. I tried to kill him. I think I *have* killed him. I'm going to give myself up. Somehow I——' She broke off, looked at him wildly, shook her head and then pushed her way through the ring of spectators which had already begun to form round them, and ran out of the lift-hall into Pelham Street.

Robert had been so painfully aware of the odd looks which were coming his way, that his embarrassment quite outweighed the awfulness of what Magda was saying to him. He wished the earth would open and swallow him up. Any fate seemed preferable to standing by her in the middle of that inquisitive crowd. When she left him, he stood where he was for a few seconds and then, realising that people were still watching him suspiciously, he walked with as much bravado as he could into the station-arcade and out into Thurloe Street, where snow was now falling heavily.

He was too dazed to try to think out the implications of what must have happened. One thing alone was clear. Since Magda would henceforth play no part in his life, he might as well go straight home.

When he reached Ten Pollitt Place, he found the front door wide open and Dorothy on the threshold, gazing vacantly up and down the street. She was wearing her Persian lamb coat and a black felt hat, which he had always thought one of her silliest. It was shaped like the roof of a house, with a gable at either side and a gulley between them. He noticed that there was snow in the gulley and that some flakes were melting among the curls of her coat.

She was very pale. When she saw him, she said, as if she were talking to herself, 'I can't get a taxi—what am I to do?' He asked, 'Do you want one?' and she said, 'Yes, I—I did,' and looked round at two suit-cases just inside the doorway. Robert said, 'If you like, I'll try to find one for you, though I don't suppose there are many about in this weather.' She didn't reply, and at that moment they heard the imperious ringing of a bell in the basement. Robert said, 'That must be Miss Tredennick. Do you know, I've an idea that she's alone in the house. Don't you think we ought to see what she wants and get her some dinner?' Dorothy said, 'Yes, I suppose we ought to.' Robert shook the snow off his mackintosh, shut the door, picked up the two suit-cases and carried them upstairs, while Dorothy followed him.

[6]

At half-past ten Dr Jamieson knocked on the door of Miss Tredennick's bedroom and walked straight in. The light was on, and she was sitting up in bed with a book. She looked worried but resolute. As soon as she saw him, she tossed the book aside and said, 'Thank God you've come. What's the news? Is he going to die?'

'You mean Hugo?'

'Of course.'

'No, he'll be all right. He began to come round as soon as we got him to the hospital. We had him X-rayed and there was no sign of a fracture. The blood was evidently a nose-bleed. That boy must have a very tough little skull.'

'And there won't be any after-effects?'

'A few headaches perhaps, for the next week or two, but nothing more. No, he'll get perfectly well and lead his mother—and others too, I dare say,—many a dance. I'm a good deal more concerned about his sister.'

Miss Tredennick gave a big sigh of relief and said, 'At the moment, Doctor, I'm concerned about you. You look at the end of your tether. You'll find all the usual drinks and some glasses in the corner-cupboard in my sitting-room. Please do help yourself and come and sit down, before you tell me the rest of the story.'

He obeyed, and when she saw him settled in the arm-chair

near the window with a brandy and soda, she went on, 'I've got a touch of cold—nothing much, no temperature—and have spent the whole day in bed—so I didn't see the ambulance arrive. But I heard something of a commotion down below, and when Magda didn't come up to clear away my tea, as she usually does at about quarter past five, I rang and rang, but nobody answered the bell. In the end,—it must have been well after six o'clock—both the Fawleys came up and told me Hugo had had an accident and had been taken with his mother to hospital. They were rather like two timid conspirators and I felt they were keeping something from me. But I was so distressed about poor little Hugo, that I didn't press them. Besides, they were so kind. Mr Fawley made me a delicious omelette for dinner,—much better than Magda's. Well—what's happened to her? Mr Fawley said he'd seen her in a state of hysteria at South Kensington station.'

Dr Jamieson said wearily, 'She went to a police-station and accused herself of having murdered her brother. Of course, they hardly believed her, but she mentioned my name and they got in touch with me and came round to question me, and I had to admit she'd told me the same thing. So she's in custody, poor girl, and they'll have to bring some sort of a charge against her. But if she gets a sentence of imprisonment, I don't suppose it'll be a very long one. The Superintendent told me she kept talking about expiating some dreadful sin on her conscience, but he gathered it had nothing to do with her attack on Hugo. Perhaps prison will get that trouble out of her system.'

Miss Tredennick said sharply, 'Do you think she may have been having an affair with a married man?'

Dr Jamieson shook his head doubtfully, half shutting his eyes, and answered, 'I really don't know. It could be. In any case, I don't suppose you'll see her again, unless you send for her. Mrs Muller won't have her living here,—which brings me to *your* problems. I've managed to get my housekeeper's niece to come here for the night. She'll sleep in Magda's room and look after you to-morrow morning. But I hope by that time Mrs Muller will have pulled herself together. I think I set her mind at rest about Hugo, but I sent her to bed and gave her a sedative. I'm afraid she won't find it too easy to get an efficient substitute for her daughter. What a good thing poor Bray isn't here. He would only have been an extra complication. Oh dear——'

He yawned uncontrollably, covered his tired face with his hand and continued, 'I do apologise. I really think I shall retire tomorrow. I'm too old now to be much use to anyone.'

Miss Tredennick made no comment, and at length, wondering if she had fallen asleep, he looked up and saw her gazing at the fireplace, deep in her thoughts. As he stood up and walked towards the bed, she turned her head to him and said, 'I beg your pardon. I was trying to think something out. Tell me, did you have a word with the Fawleys on your way upstairs?'

'Yes, I thought I'd better let them know what arrangements I'd made.'

'How did they strike you?'

'Well, I thought the husband was looking rather shaken.'

'And his wife?'

'She must be one of those women who thrive on excitement. I don't remember seeing her look so happy.'

Miss Tredennick smiled and wished Dr Jamieson good night.

ALSO AVAILABLE FROM VALANCOURT BOOKS

MICHAEL ARLEN	Hell! said the Duchess
R. C. ASHBY (RUBY FERGUSON)	He Arrived at Dusk
FRANK BAKER	The Birds
CHARLES BEAUMONT	The Hunger and Other Stories
DAVID BENEDICTUS	The Fourth of June
CHARLES BIRKIN	The Smell of Evil
JOHN BLACKBURN	A Scent of New-Mown Hay
	Broken Boy
	Blue Octavo
	The Flame and the Wind
	Nothing but the Night
	Bury Him Darkly
	The Face of the Lion
THOMAS BLACKBURN	The Feast of the Wolf
JOHN BRAINE	Room at the Top
	The Vodi
R. CHETWYND-HAYES	The Monster Club
BASIL COPPER	The Great White Space
	Necropolis
HUNTER DAVIES	Body Charge
JENNIFER DAWSON	The Ha-Ha
BARRY ENGLAND	Figures in a Landscape
RONALD FRASER	Flower Phantoms
GILLIAN FREEMAN	The Liberty Man
	The Leather Boys
	The Leader
STEPHEN GILBERT	The Landslide
	Monkeyface
	The Burnaby Experiments
	Ratman's Notebooks
MARTYN GOFF	The Youngest Director
STEPHEN GREGORY	The Cormorant
THOMAS HINDE	Mr. Nicholas
	The Day the Call Came
CLAUDE HOUGHTON	I Am Jonathan Scrivener
	This Was Ivor Trent
CYRIL KERSH	The Aggravations of Minnie Ashe
GERALD KERSH	Nightshade and Damnations
	Fowlers End
FRANCIS KING	To the Dark Tower
	Never Again
	An Air That Kills
	The Dividing Stream
	The Dark Glasses
	The Man on the Rock

CPSIA information can be obtained
at www.ICGtesting.com
Printed in the USA
FSHW012044210320
68336FS